Love You Like a Sister
By Susan L. Gilbert

Love You Like A Sister (LYLAS)

Susan L. Gilbert

Published by Tell Me Your Story Books, 2020.

While every precaution has been taken in the preparation of this book, the publisher assumes no responsibility for errors or omissions, or for damages resulting from the use of the information contained herein.

LOVE YOU LIKE A SISTER (LYLAS)

First edition. October 9, 2020.

Copyright © 2020 Susan L. Gilbert.

ISBN: 978-1393110347

Written by Susan L. Gilbert.

For Adam—my rock, my support, and the love of my life. Thank you. With deep appreciation to my children Craig, Lizzie and Jake, who give me the love and confidence I cherish.

And a big thank you to Arielle Pearl whose cover design is as beautiful as she is--inside and out.

And finally, this novel is in memory of Spencer, Shaina, and all the teens who suffered and lost the battle with drug abuse.

Published by Tell Me Your Story Books
October 2020

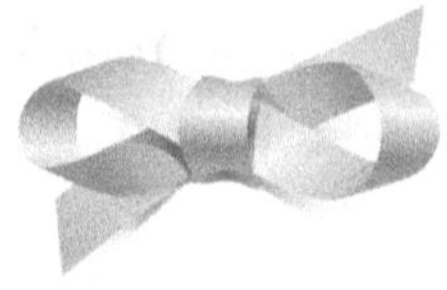

Chapter One—911

"I give up. I can't fit all of my furniture into my new room." I shoved the dresser across the room, facing my bed. I could hear my mom's music from her bedroom. Fleetwood Mac's "Rhiannon" blasted from her Echo speaker. Kelly Green rested quietly on the silky down comforter at the end of my bed. She opened her beady poodle eyes and rolled over, looking for a tummy rub.

I heard my mom say, "Alexa, off," and Fleetwood Mac went quiet. She yelled down the short hallway, "Ivy, have you heard from Carly? It's eleven thirty and I'm beginning to worry."

"No, but I'm sure she's fine. She always is." I checked my iPhone. Nothing. My older sister didn't usually ghost me like this.

"Ow!" I'd banged my toe against the weathered antique dresser. No matter how many times I tried, the dresser just didn't look good in this room. There were indelible scratches on the newly varnished floors from dragging it all around the room. In desperation, I moved the area rug to cover the damage.

"What happened?" Mom yelled. We were both unpacking and trying to settle into the new home. It had been only two days since the movers carted all of our belongings from our house across town into this much smaller duplex.

"It looks beautiful, honey." Mom walked into my disorganized, freshly painted bedroom. I had picked a calming light-gray color for the walls and a light blue for the trim.

Sweaty and tired, Mom resembled a willowy yoga instructor or a graceful dancer, just like Carly. Instead of their long and lean limbs, I inherited the more compact Eastern European Jewish body, short and broad with muscles like an athlete. Carly also got the better hair, blond and straight compared to my curly mess.

Mom pointed to the two glass vanity trays on my dresser. "Nice. Your perfume bottles are back where they belong." I had collected over twenty-five unique bottles since I was ten and had rearranged them in my new room.

"This is a nightmare." I looked up, noticing for the first time how pale and drawn her face looked. I didn't want her to feel worse about moving than she already did, so I perked up.

"Actually, I think the room looks pretty good. I'll put my Paris poster over here." I pointed to a narrow wall between two windows. I was dying to go back to Paris. We went seven years ago for Carly's bat-mitzvah when I was ten. From the more popular sights like the Louvre and the Eiffel Tower to off-the-beaten-track flea markets and food halls, we traipsed around the city for a week, enjoying the sites. We ate croissants every morning at little round bistro tables facing the Seine, and at night we chose dark, quiet restaurants near the small hotel we stayed in. The magical feeling of being in a foreign country had seeped into my blood and I wanted to go back to Europe as soon as I could.

"That'll look nice." Mom ran her fingers through her hair and looked at her watch. I knew she was thinking about Carly. This morning, Carly had promised that we'd go to the mall in the afternoon to shop for a back-to-school outfit for me and get frozen yogurt for dinner. When I hadn't heard from her by four, I figured she was blowing me off like she had all summer. I was used to it but still never stopped hoping that we would find some time together before she went back to school for her junior year.

When she first started at Vassar, she made me feel welcome in her circle of artsy girlfriends. I visited her and went to parties even though I was younger. I thought maybe I'd apply early decision, just to stay close. I wasn't as creative or musical as Carly, so it wasn't an ideal match, but Vassar had a great reputation, it was nearby, and the people seemed really cool and real, so I figured why not? Now I was having second thoughts about being at the same school.

Knowing Carly, she was pregaming at someone's house and then partying with people whose names I didn't know. She had been out all summer long. Tonight wouldn't be any different.

"I know I'm being silly. It's still early," Mom said. "I'm going to go back to finish unpacking. Don't stay up much later, honey. We need your help tomorrow at work."

"No worries. I'm good." I thought about all that had happened in the past few months. We moved to save money after Mom and her sister Allie opened a catering business. It'd better succeed, I continuously thought, since I seemed to be the one who was sacrificing the most. Switching schools as a senior was the worst.

At twelve thirty, my phone woke me up with a butt dial from Carly's number. I could hear loud voices and music in the background. I tried calling back, but she didn't answer. A lightning bolt of anxiety shot through my gut. I rolled back onto my stomach. I tried to ignore the sharp pain across my ribs from the underwire bra I hadn't taken off.

I must have dozed off at some point. Before I knew it, I woke up to the sound of a long blast from a car horn. I sat up, blinked, and looked at my phone. Two a.m. I heard Mom's feet hit the floor in the living room. She must have fallen asleep on the sofa. The front door creaked as she swung it open.

Throwing off the covers, I pulled on denim cutoffs, grabbed my flip-flops, and ran downstairs. Kelly Green followed, barking loudly. She was a bit of a yapper, but I didn't have time to put her back in the bedroom.

The front door was wide open when I got downstairs. My mother was kneeling on the foyer tile floor next to Carly who was lying on her side, knees pushed up against her chest in a fetal position. Carly's normally shiny blond hair was matted and her faded jeans and silky sleeveless blouse were filthy. She looked like she had gone swimming in a mud puddle. This bedraggled girl looked nothing like Carly, who always strived to look her best.

"Carly! Carly!" Mom screamed. "Where the hell have you been?" Mom jumped to her feet and tried to pull Carly up and back by the shoulders, but Carly was too heavy from that angle. I looked at my sister. Her purple lace bra poked through the armholes of her shirt.

"Go to bed, Mom," Carly said, slurring her words. She glanced at me. "You too, Ivy." Her eyes were unfocused. I couldn't be sure she was even registering where she was. Carly had always been the one I modeled all of my behavior and values on. But this was not the first time over the summer that I questioned where the real Carly had gone and who this messed-up girl was on the floor.

Carly turned her head toward Mom then looked again at me. I couldn't tell what she was high on, drugs or alcohol or a dangerous mix.

"Snap out of it," Mom shouted in her ear. "Your sister and I cannot sit home night after night waiting for the phone to ring or for the police to show up."

"Really?" It sounded more like "wheelie." Her eyes rolled toward the back of her head for a second but then she snapped to attention. "Why are you both just sitting there? I'm fine."

Carly smelled like beer and a mild mildew scent I couldn't identify, nor did I want to. I had no idea if she was going to be OK or not, but her stupidity pissed me off. I held back what I really wanted to say to her, which was "Fuck you, Carly. Stop being so self-centered." She wouldn't remember anyway.

As gently as I could possibly muster, since really, I wanted to scream, I said, "Your lip gloss is smeared on your face. Mascara is running down your cheeks. And your clothes are a mess. Where were you?"

My mom pursed her lips. "Shh, Ivy." She gripped Carly's arm. "Carly, you can't even hold up your head or keep your eyes open. Come on, I'll help you." My mom tried again to pull my sister up by her upper arm, but Carly's floppy body slumped over onto the floor. My sister looked at me again, this time with a sad, defeated face.

"I don't feel well."

"You don't look so good either. What did you do tonight?" I said.

"Ivy, help me get Carly up." Together, we unraveled her and tried to raise her up by her shoulders. She felt like dead weight in our arms. When I let go, she slumped to the ground.

"Oh my God!" I screamed. Carly's face was white and motionless. Spittle oozed out from the sides of her mouth.

"Call 911. Call 911!" Mom ordered. She crouched next to Carly and firmly slapped her face, but Carly didn't react. Mom put her face right next to Carly's mouth. "Oh God, I don't know if she's breathing."

Time slowed and I leaned in close to see if Carly's chest was going up and down. It was. I felt paralyzed.

"Ivy, hurry. Call 911." I could hear my mom's voice in a far-away spot of my consciousness, but I didn't move. I stared at my sister—her dirty outfit, her mussed up face—and I willed her to open her eyes.

"Ivy, what's wrong with you? Go get your phone." Mom pressed her sleeve onto a bleeding cut on Carly's arm. She kicked Carly's purse toward me so I could use Carly's phone, but I didn't move for another second. I felt stuck, just staring.

Mom took the phone. I heard the beeps of the phone as she touched the numbers. I looked on, vaguely aware of Kelly Green's annoying yaps while she ran in circles around us.

"Hello. This is Samantha Green at 111 Highland Avenue. I need an ambulance immediately. I think my daughter has taken too many drugs of some sort. I'm not sure what's happening."

"OD'd?" I said softly. I bent down and put my palm on Carly's shoulder. Then I held her hand. She looked dead, but I knew she wasn't. This couldn't be happening. Partying, yes. Maybe some weed and maybe some X or even coke, but she would never do enough to kill herself. Oh God, what if what she took was laced with something that could kill her? I felt sick to my stomach.

"OK, thank you. Please hurry," my mom said into the phone.

"Ivy, I need your help. Go get a wet washcloth to cover these cuts."

I tossed my head back and tried to shake myself alert. This was real. And it was bad.

I ran to the sink in the kitchen, wet some paper towels, and brought them to my mom. She placed one on Carly's forehead and the other on her bleeding cut.

Within seconds, I could hear sirens wailing through the night. It was a small town. When someone dialed 911, the EMTs, firefighters, and ambulance corps descended at once. My mom gave Carly a tight bear hug on the floor. I took Carly's hand and again stared at my mom. Neither of us could say a word. We listened to Carly's low breathing. Even Kelly Green remained quiet for a few moments.

The sirens grew louder and louder until the place swarmed with red and blue swirling lights. People in uniforms jumped out of cars and ambulances and ran toward the house.

I recognized a hairdresser from town in an EMT outfit, running up our front steps. She and another EMT with bright-pink hair got to Carly first and checked her breathing and pulse. They clamped on an oxygen mask.

Two police officers tried to gently push us back into the living room while the EMTs worked on Carly. One officer had horrible breath like he had just eaten a ton of garlic knots. They covered her with a thin gray blanket and then began to secure her with thick white mesh straps onto a gurney. Mom wouldn't budge from Carly's side. Kelly Green was barking again and spinning in circles. I picked her up and held her tightly, shushing her and begging her to be quiet amidst all the commotion.

Officer Garlic Knot breathed rapid-fire questions at Mom: "Is she a known drug user? Alcohol abuser? Does she do crack, cocaine, heroin? Where was she tonight? Do you know her friends?"

Mom pushed back a loose chunk of hair off her forehead. "I have no idea. She didn't tell us where she was going or who she was with. And no, I don't think she's a regular drug user, but I obviously don't know anything about anything anymore." Tears rolled down her red face.

The police officer stared hard at me. His lips were chapped and his wide nose had tiny little hairs sticking out on top. "What about you? Do you know anything about your sister's recreational drug use?"

I was huddled against the stair railing, trying to stay close to Mom and Carly, but all the emergency people were blocking me. Kelly Green continued yapping. I held her in my arm like a football, maybe too tightly, and thought about locking her in my room.

Staring down at Carly, now surrounded by medical people, I saw her eyes blink and she looked at Mom for a nanosecond. "I don't know. It's possible," I said.

I wasn't sure of the extent of Carly's drug use and I didn't want to get her into more trouble, but I also didn't want her to die. I knew she had been smoking a lot of weed. She had also intimated doing some cocaine once in a while and drinking, but as far as I knew, that was at college parties, not at home. We hadn't gone out together all summer, since even further back if I thought about it. She had avoided me most of last semester, always giving me some stupid excuse when I suggested I'd drive to Vassar for a night. This was the opposite of freshman year, when she begged me to visit every weekend. I loved her cool friends and sleeping in the dorms. Now I questioned what she had been hiding.

I grabbed the metal railing above the landing. I felt dizzy and nauseous.

"Ivy, what do you know? Tell us!" my mom screamed. She covered her mouth and grasped my arm.

In a hesitant whisper I said, "I think she just smoked weed, that's all. I found a small baggie in her purse last week. And I saw a few pills I didn't recognize. I'm not sure though. She didn't confide in me about her drug use."

The bright lights from the ambulance, fire engines, and police cars lit up the tiny front hall. Blue. Red. White. Blue. I couldn't get Kelly Green to stop whining. I didn't dare put her down for fear she'd nip someone's ankle, or worse, someone would mistakenly step on her in the chaos. I squeezed her tightly, holding her soft fur against my cheek.

The hairdresser EMT spoke loudly into her phone. One of the firefighters, a guy with a handlebar mustache and a bald head, nodded while she spoke.

"We have a possible OD. Probable cause is narcotics."

"What?" I said, but no one answered me. Mom held onto Carly's hand and winced, closing her eyes for just a second.

The tall policeman standing over Carly stood up and looked at me in the eye. He popped a mint into his mouth. "Does your sister use opiates?"

"No, of course not." I said.

"You sure? Heroin, oxy?"

"Heroin? Seriously? I don't think so," I said and squeezed my mother's other hand. "She'll be OK, Mom." She kept crying, tears streaming down her face. When the two women EMTs and two firefighters carted Carly down the steps, Mom quickly grabbed her purse from the coat rack and followed.

"I want to go with you." I took Mom's arm as we trailed next to the stretcher. I didn't want to leave my sister's side. No way. What if she died?

"Only one person can go in the ambulance with the patient," the pink-haired EMT said. "You'll have to stay back." She looked at me.

I stayed close to Mom, who stayed close to Carly on the stretcher. They raised the stretcher higher as we bumped our way toward the open ambulance door. Carly's little head peeked out from the top of the blanket. I thought I saw her blink again, but I couldn't be sure. They backed her into the ambulance. Mom wrenched her arm from my grip and scrambled in behind the stretcher. She looked gravely at me one more time and whispered, "Follow us," before the ambulance doors slammed shut.

The siren blared and the ambulance sped away. I stared at all the other emergency vehicles in the driveway and on the street, while Kelly Green, still in my arms, had finally quieted. I glanced quickly around to see if any neighbors had come outside. I saw a few front doors hanging ajar with foyer lights on but didn't see any people standing outside. Then I turned back and ran inside. I dropped Kelly Green in my bedroom and grabbed a hoodie and my phone.

On the way out, I stopped at the entry to Carly's room. She had nearly finished unpacking. Her old collectible dolls and memorabilia from concerts and trips sat on her shelves, just recently reassembled from the old house.

I drove to the hospital on autopilot, barely registering the street signs or landmarks. I looked up into the dark sky. There were hardly any stars. I whispered a prayer I knew in Hebrew. We weren't religious at all and barely ever went to temple anymore, but if there was ever a time to be grateful and pray to God, it was now. And then I said loudly in English, into the air, into the universe, to my dead grandma if she was listening, to anyone who was out there, "Please make her be OK."

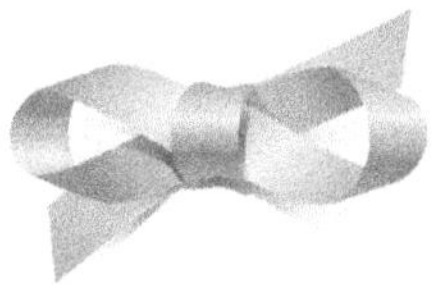

Chapter Two—ER

I was hit by the acrid smells of ammonia and disinfectant soap the second I ran through the glass doors of the emergency room. The receptionist, a frizzy-haired lady with broken fingernails, spoke loudly into her cell phone. She held up a finger in a "one sec" gesture. It sounded like a personal call to me.

In the nearly empty waiting room, groupings of metal chairs were set around two large TV screens that showed TV Land reruns and CNN. A couple of young women slumped across several chairs and a few men were clustered in front of the vending machines.

Suddenly, our EMTs raced out of two large double doors. I ran up to the big one with pink hair.

"Where is she? Is she OK? Did she OD?" I stammered, renewed tears wetting my cheeks.

"Check in with the desk. Your mom is back there now," Pink Hair said. "Your sister woke up for a bit and started yelling and kicking. That's a good sign."

"Thank God," I said. "Can I go in there? I want to go in."

"Ask her," Pink Hair said. "And good luck to your sister. Take care of yourself."

"Thanks for your help," I said, then made a mad face, scrunching up my mouth and wrinkling my eyes at the receptionist who was ignoring me. I knocked hard several times on the desk in front of her.

"Hello, hello. I need to go inside to see my sister," I said rudely.

She didn't hang up but held out her palm. "ID please."

I gave over my license and she took a picture of it with a scanner and then she buzzed me through the two large double doors. She was still on her phone.

I ran down the back corridor of the emergency room. Clusters of gurneys with patients and their companions flanked the hallway. Lots of people were crying and pacing. I found Carly and Mom in one of the small glass bays toward the back corner of the unit. Carly lay asleep in a hospital bed with tubes in her arms and tubes up her nose.

"Hi," I whispered. I gave my mom a kiss and a hug. I sat down on a hard plastic chair with metal legs, shoved to the corner of the small room.

"She's stable," my mother said.

"Thank God," I said for the millionth time that night.

My mom repeated it. "Thank God is right."

"They found oxycodone and alcohol in her bloodstream but no heroin. And they didn't have to use naloxone because she was awake."

I didn't blink. No heroin. That's a slight relief. Still not great, but not quite as terrible.

We sat by Carly's bed. The monitor above zigzagged giant upside-down Vs and beeped over and over while she slept. Her hair was greasy and her cheekbones stuck out. Dark circles bruised the skin around her closed eyes. How weird that I hadn't noticed how gaunt she had become.

This was not the first time Carly had been to the ER for partying. During her freshman year, she drank so much that they had to pump her stomach. Her school friends took care of her and the whole episode was over within hours. Mom and I, and even Carly when we spoke about it, chalked it up to inexperience. Another time, when she was younger, she had accidentally (or so she said) taken too much ibuprofen, supposedly for her period cramps. Back then, we really didn't think twice about the accidental overuse. We even joked about it with Carly. Now, it would seem to me, she had a real problem. Obviously, she needed help.

I leaned down and whispered in her ear, "I'm here, Carly."

. . ⌘ . .

AT WHAT SEEMED LIKE the exact moment I dozed off in the hard plastic bucket chair, Carly woke from her stupor. She immediately began shouting.

"Why am I here? I'm fine. I'm fine," she said loudly.

I jerked back. Where did all this energy come from?

"Shush up," Mom said. "You're going to be OK. You got lucky."

A nurse in blue scrubs and a ponytail appeared. "Let's quiet down now. Everything is under control. We're taking care of you."

Carly wriggled her hands under the blanket. It was then that I realized thick Velcro straps restrained her wrists.

"Do you see this?" Carly ranted. "They are treating me like a psychopath! I can't move! I can't use my hands!"

"Let me talk to the psychiatrist," the nurse said. "They were ordered because when you woke earlier, you were thrashing around violently, and we were afraid for your safety and the safety of the staff around you."

"What could I do to the staff? This is ridiculous," Carly argued.

"Thank you," my mom said to the nurse who had turned to face the sink and counter, busying herself with the supplies in the cabinet. "If you can have the straps removed, that would be great. Carly is calm now."

But was she really? Didn't seem so, but I got it, those straps sucked.

Mom gently touched Carly's shoulder, willing her to be still. She straightened the blanket over Carly's chest. Carly took a deep breath and seemed to mellow out, accepting the situation.

"Carly, try to relax," Mom said. "When the ambulance arrived here and you came to, you swung your arms around and nearly whacked a few people in the process. They needed to get you into a bed and take your vitals. You fell back asleep right away."

The nurse turned toward the bed. "We're waiting for the medical team to discuss a discharge plan. A social worker will be in shortly. I'm sorry, but for now, you're stuck with me. You're on a one-on-one watch, just in case. Would you like some water?" I noticed that her fingernails were perfectly polished in Sugar, the color I liked best. She poured water from a green plastic pitcher into a Styrofoam cup and set it down on the table next to Carly.

"But I can't hold the cup, duh!" Carly tried to sit up, but fell back onto the pillow. "I'm not going to kill myself. Oh my God, all I did was party a little too hard, a little too long."

"Take it easy, Carly. You have to chill." Mom patted Carly's forehead and held the cup of water to her lips. Carly took a few sips. I smacked my own dry lips. I hadn't had anything to drink or eat since dinner. I thought about going back out to the waiting room for a Snapple, but I didn't want to leave Carly and my mom.

"Don't mind me," the petite nurse spoke firmly, directly to Carly. "I have to stay here, but I'll try to give you some privacy with your family." She turned away again.

"I need a shower and some food and then I'll be fine." Carly twisted her head back and forth. Her hair was matted to the back of the pillow and she was still wearing her jeans and top. I pulled my hoodie tighter around me and rubbed down the goose bumps on my thighs.

"Do you want me to wash your face?" I offered. "Mom, maybe we can undo the restraints ourselves." I hated that Carly was pinned down. She wasn't crazy. I didn't think so, anyway.

"You can't do that," the nurse said. "Please be patient and I'll get them removed as fast as I can. It's standard procedure to use them when a patient is excessively agitated or aggressive. As your mom said, when you were brought in and woke up, you were yelling and thrashing around."

"Jeez, I wasn't trying to kill myself with pills, honest. I was partying with those guys from Summit. I just took too much. I let myself go. I didn't mean to. I'm sorry." Carly started crying. Her nose began to run. I wiped it with a soft tissue.

"Oxy? You could have died!" Summit was just the next town over, but it was more of a city with some bad neighborhoods. If she was hanging out there, she was most likely hanging with a dangerous crowd.

"It could have been laced with fentanyl," my mother said. "Like that beautiful girl from our old neighborhood. Remember, you used to dance with her. She OD'd last year. She wasn't even twenty years old."

"I know, Mom. I'm sorry," Carly said. My mom was thinking about our neighbor's daughter who had died of a heroin overdose last summer.

"She always had a smile for everyone. And Kristine's son, Jared. He was only eighteen when he overdosed on oxy while living in a halfway house. What if that had been you?" Tears streamed down Mom's face.

When the small box of tissues ran out, my mom and I wiped our noses with the rough paper towels from the dispenser.

"I know Mom, I know," was all Carly could say at first.

"You scared us," I said quietly.

"It's been such a weird summer." Carly jumbled her words and she spoke softly. I could barely hear her. "The oxy felt good. I didn't realize how much I was taking."

"How long has this been going on?" my mom asked.

Before Carly could answer, a middle-aged woman wearing Birkenstock clogs and a long brown faux-suede skirt came in. She looked around the room at the three of us crying, Carly strapped to the bed, and she shook her head.

"I'm Melanie Shadlow, the overnight hospital social worker."

"Hi there, um, Melanie?" my mom asked tentatively. "I'm Samantha Green, Carly's mother. And this is Ivy, her sister."

Melanie nodded. "Carly, since you're an adult, I need your permission to speak in front of your family."

"Carly, you don't mind us here, do you?" I said.

"They can stay. And I guess her, too," Carly nodded in the direction of the nurse in the corner. "You can ask me anything in front of them." She gave my mom a wan smile. Carly mouthed, "I'm so sorry." Her eyes were alert.

Mom kissed Carly on the forehead again. I shook my head. Yeah, easy to be sorry now after we watched EMTs revive you on the foyer floor. This lame apology seemed too little too late.

"How are you feeling now?" Melanie asked.

"I'm pissed. I want these wrist ties removed like yesterday." Carly spoke in a low tone but with assurance. In a softer tone, she admitted, "But I'm OK."

Melanie came around the bed and stood close to Carly. "We need to talk next steps. Would you consider a short, inpatient stay in a behavioral health unit to stabilize you?"

"Huh? What's that?" Carly asked.

"Behavioral health is what they call psychiatric units these days," Mom explained, carefully enunciating her words. "What exactly are we talking about? I mean, why can't she just come home? She already has a therapist."

"Because Carly nearly OD'd and because she was so distraught, a short stay in a rehab unit might be beneficial," Melanie said. "Carly, if you agree, I can look for either a hospital nearby that has a floor unit, such as City Hospital, or I can try and find a bed in a private facility."

My mother shook her head no. "This was her first time experimenting with opiates, right, Carly?"

Carly closed her eyes. We were all silent. Melanie gave my mom a sympathetic look. I stared at the floor. Part of me felt badly for Carly and another part was angry that she hadn't confided in me.

Mom lightly touched Carly's arm. "What do you want to do? It's your choice. Do you think you would be OK coming home for a few days and then going to school? We'd get you counseling. Or do you think you might need inpatient help? It's up to you." She looked first at Carly and then at Melanie.

I couldn't tell which way Mom was leaning. Did she want Carly to go to rehab or did she think it would be easier for Carly to get on with her life? That would certainly be simpler, I thought.

"Maybe a short stay somewhere would be good," Carly said, opening her eyes and looking at me, then Mom. "It wasn't the first time. I am a regular user. And I haven't been able to stop."

Again, we were all quiet. I had no idea she was taking oxy. "Where did you get it?" I asked.

The room began to spin. I was tired, too. We hadn't slept at all. I rubbed my eyes and looked at Melanie, who was listening closely.

"Where, Carly?" I repeated. I was trying to keep the anger out of my voice. I wanted Carly to know I was there for her because I knew that's what she needed from me right now, but inside I was really mad. She had shut me out when I could have helped. When we were little, we were inseparable, sharing friends and play dates. I used to snuggle with her in her bed all night even though we had our own rooms. I struggled to remember when she had pulled away.

Clearly, Carly had been into all kinds of drugs and had been hiding it from us. All summer long while I was helping Mom pack up the old house, moving to the new place, helping with the start-up of her catering company, and trying to keep smiling, she had been out doing drugs.

"Remember when I twisted my ankle last winter and they weren't sure if it was a tiny fracture or a break worthy of a cast? They gave me oxy for the pain. I took it while my ankle healed, and then I kept taking it. I liked how I felt. Then I realized that other people I knew also took oxy just for fun. People sell it on the street, in the dorm. It's easy to get.

One thing led to the next and I was doing it a lot." She yawned and I could smell her foul liquor breath.

"Ewww," I said. "Before you go anywhere, you need to brush your teeth."

"Thanks Ivy, that should be my biggest problem. But for the record, you need to brush your unruly hair."

I was glad we could still argue; that had to be a positive sign.

"I understand." Melanie looked through Carly's file and scrolled over her iPad, her finger moving swiftly across the screen. "Let's see what your options are. You have good insurance. I think I can find you a bed somewhere nearby."

"That would be really helpful, Melanie. Thank you." Mom spoke quietly, her eyes flickering.

"Please don't send me to a scary place," Carly said. "I don't have a serious problem with drugs, just a little one."

"I'm sure you must understand that there's no such thing as a small drug problem," Melanie said. She squinted at the screen and then looked up, a hesitant smile growing across her face. "Hmm, I thought so. I'll have to doublecheck with admissions, but online it looks like there might be an available bed at Blue Hills in Connecticut. It's got both drug and alcohol rehab and an excellent psychiatric unit, not that we're talking about that at the moment."

"How far away?" Mom asked.

"It's about forty minutes away, located on a renovated private girls-school property. You may have heard of it because sometimes celebrities go there, and sadly the tabloids exploit their personal tragedies."

"That one sounds good." Carly cracked a little smile. "Me and the stars. Good deal."

"Let me get the paperwork started," Melanie said.

My mouth tightened up. I shook my head at her, but she didn't even notice. How dare she poke fun at this process or her diagnosis?

She could have died and she's treating the whole awful evening like it was a chance to go to a spa with celebrities.

"Yeah, maybe I'll get a facial while I'm there." She continued to laugh, but the giggles sounded hollow.

"You're going to a hospital, not the Ritz Carlton," I growled, looking between my cold knees at the floor.

"Ivy, calm down," Mom said. "Carly isn't serious. She's just nervous, right honey?"

Carly nodded. My mom always backed Carly. But this time, maybe she was right, I inwardly conceded. The idea of going to a psych hospital or a rehab place definitely sounded scary to me.

"I'm so embarrassed," Carly said, looking right at me. "It's humiliating to admit, but I do need help. I haven't been able to stop taking oxy every day, but what am I going to do about college? How long would I have to stay there?" Carly asked Melanie.

"It could be a thirty-six-hour observation and referral to outpatient programs, or longer. It's whatever you need. The purpose is to get you clean and educated." Melanie kept her head down, skimming her iPad info.

"If you go to rehab, you'll do what needs to be done." Mom spoke harshly. All summer she had been so lenient with Carly. It was a relief to see her coming down hard for a change. "You could've died last night."

Melanie looked at Carly. "You got lucky. They can take you tonight. Blue Hills is one of the best facilities in the Hudson Valley. And they are giving you a discount in the fee. They offer what they call scholarships through their development department. You only have to pay a small portion of the fee."

"I guess I could ask my mother for another loan," Mom said.

"What about Dad? Couldn't he contribute for a change?" I said. My dad left when were little and now lived in Florida with a new wife and two new little kids. We hardly ever saw him and he hardly ever sent my mom money anymore, but maybe he'd cough up some money for Carly's rehab. This was too serious to ignore.

"I can try," Mom said. "But either way, we'll come up with whatever money we need for Carly."

"So, I should move forward with Blue Hills?" Melanie asked.

I couldn't look at Carly. Her world had just turned upside down. I scratched the dry skin on my arms. The hospital air made me nauseous and I wanted to get the heck out of here.

"I'll go, at least for thirty-six hours," Carly said. "I'll pay you back, Mom. It's been a rough summer. I'm so sorry."

"I want you to get well before, God forbid, you get worse," Mom said. "All I could think about in the ambulance were those other kids who didn't make it."

Carly started to cry again. I took another paper towel from the roll by the sink and wiped away her tears and mine, too. I couldn't stop.

"It's going to be alright, Carly. It will." I said it to her, but I wasn't sure I believed it. Carly used to be so confident and in charge. She walked me to school and directed me to my classes. Is this the same person who played make-believe with me using our dolls and colored wooden blocks to create entire neighborhoods? Now who was going to help me figure out how to navigate in my new school and make friends? Give me advice? Pick out the best outfits? I'm in trouble if it's the Carly sitting in this hospital bed.

Melanie studied my face for a moment. "Maybe you want to go home now? You can probably see Carly tomorrow night at Blue Hills."

"Really, that soon?" Mom asked.

"As long as they finish up with assessment and orientation."

"Are you kicking me out?" I said, but it'd been a long night and I really needed to get back to Kelly Green, so I secretly wanted her to say yes. "Mom? What do you think? Should I go home?"

"Probably best. You can take an Uber and leave me the car. Feed the dog and get some sleep. I'll drive Carly to Blue Hills and come home later."

"Yeah, after these wrist restraints are removed," Carly said.

"I can do that now," the nurse said. She had been hanging by the door, waiting and watching our conversation all this time. "I just got word from the nursing supervisor. One-on-one watch has been removed as well. You're nearly set to go to Blue Hills." The nurse seemed pleased with her own efficiency.

Melanie said, "I think you're making a good decision to go to Blue Hills. You'll get the support and therapy you need."

"Thanks," Carly said, as the nurse undid the Velcro. Carly shook her hands around in front of her chest. "Wow, that feels good. I definitely don't want those again."

"Hopefully never again," my mom said. "I'm going to walk Ivy out. Nurse, will you be here when I get back?" The nurse nodded.

"Get well. I'll see you soon," I said, kissing her cheek. Mom and I walked to the front entrance and I called an Uber.

Mom's face looked sallow and her clothes were wrinkled. "It's been an endless night and tomorrow you start school."

"Oh my God, I totally forgot! It's so soon."

"At least you've got a day to recoup," she said.

"Yeah, after this we both need a lot longer than a day. I know it's not about me, but this has really been a nightmare."

"Ivy." Mom covered her face.

I turned to stare out the hospital lobby window toward the Hudson River, holding back more tears. I had so much to do today to get ready for my new school. I needed to figure out my outfit and try to connect with a few people I knew at Marble Springs. Maybe talk to my cousin Ethan and get some ideas. Regardless of where Carly was or what she was going through, I still had to start a new school my senior year with no help from her.

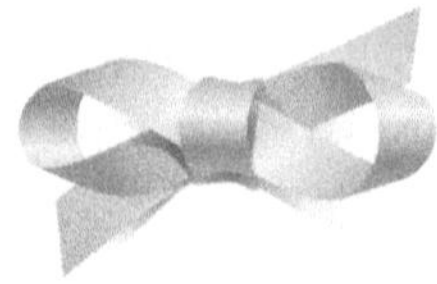

Chapter Three—New Girl

I dabbed on some heavier cover-up under my eyes and used eye drops for the redness. I was not looking or feeling my best on a day I really needed to. Mom and I had been up late talking about Carly, her drug use and now the rehab. Neither of us had any time to prepare for our own days—my first day at Marble Springs High School, and my mom's busy-as-always day preparing catered dinners for the commuter crowd. Tinted moisturizer wasn't going to cover my blotchy face, I realized.

I knew I'd make friends. I was outgoing, but it was a question of who would want to make a new friend in our senior year of high school. I could deal with not being friends with the cool girls. Been there, done that. The cliques had been formed years ago and it would be hard to break in. Well, I could deal with a quiet year on the fringe. Maybe I'd hang with the studious kids or the theater people. It would be weird, but I could do it for one year. I could always see my old friends on the weekends.

I walked over to my closet and stared at the line of clothes on hangers, silently rebuffing me like strangers, daring me to come up with some winning combination of top and bottom. Carly was the fashionista. She usually told me exactly what to wear wherever I was going. I felt like throwing myself back into bed.

"Ivy, hurry up," Mom yelled from the kitchen.

"Ten minutes!" I called back, reaching to pat Kelly Green on the butt. She turned her head and look up languidly, then moved to a different spot on the bed. Kelly Green was not the most affectionate dog in the world, but petting her always made me feel better.

I ducked into Carly's bedroom and headed for her closet. I reached down to grab her brown suede open-toe booties. I put them on, grateful we both wore a size six-and-a-half. There's got to be an upside to her absence, I thought. Then I noticed that she had shoved blue tissue paper into some of her shoes. Was she hiding drugs in there? I picked out some of the paper, but found nothing out of the ordinary. I nudged a few pairs of sandals, looked in the back of the closet, and even pushed aside some of her sweaters folded neatly on the top shelf. Everything appeared pretty normal. It felt a teeny-weeny bit creepy, literally walking in my sister's shoes, but I got over myself.

Last night, the doctor from Blue Hills had called. "He said Carly had settled in and that we'd be able to visit as early as tonight," Mom told me after she hung up the phone. I worried about Carly, but at the moment, the prospect of getting through my first day of school was all that I could concentrate on.

Needing to calm my head, I sat on my bed and opened the meditation app that I liked. I had been trying to do at least five minutes a day since summer. The topic of the day's meditation was "Invincible." How apt, I thought, inhaling deeply. I tried to focus on my breath for five minutes straight, but I couldn't stay in the moment. I kept wondering what it was going to feel like to face hundreds of new kids when I walked through the front door of school.

I questioned if my white top was too bright and decided to switch it out for a black one. Carly always told me, "You can't go wrong in black or Chanel." I think she was quoting Carrie Bradshaw from the *Sex in the City* reruns. And then thoughts of Carly in a hospital seeped into my brain. The lady on the meditation app said to push aside the "monkey brain," but I failed to stop the worry buzz in my head.

Because I didn't have a school parking permit yet, Mom dropped me off in front of the ancient-looking red brick building in the center of town. She waved and headed around the corner to the church where she and her sister Allie rented commercial kitchen space for their new catering business. It was called Dinner, Dear, and so far, people really seemed to like their food.

"Bye, good luck. See you later. Love you." She sounded like a bird, all high-pitched and chirpy. Her forced positivity was annoying. I knew she was covering up her worry about Carly. How could we stop thinking about her for even a second?

Suddenly I doubted my choice of wardrobe. Damn, why didn't I keep the white? It's still summer after all. Too late now. I hiked up the front steps to the large glass doors. A cluster of football players in blue and white uniforms stood in front of some lockers by the front office. I noticed lots of girls wearing skirts and high heels. They obviously were part of the cool group, just like my old friends, but now I was on the outside looking in. I applied another coat of blush-pink lip gloss and tried to inconspicuously tug on the butt of my jeans.

I held open the door for two kids who looked to be freshman age and were holding hands. Everyone seemed to have a friend or a group except me. I knew a few people from growing up in town and I had texted with one or two over the summer but hadn't made an effort to really reconnect. I hoped I'd bump into someone I knew. I texted my cousin Ethan, but he didn't answer right away.

The uniformed security guard by the front office looked at me like I was a felon. It took him a long time to process my temporary ID and check my name against a list he had in front of him.

Finally, past the guard desk, I imagined that people were staring at me, looking at my clothes and my shabby brown suede bucket bag, which was also Carly's. It looked like a worn-out horse feeder but matched the booties I had borrowed, and it was great as a book bag. I was also using an old notebook of hers that I grabbed from her desk. I hoped she would let me keep it all once she came home.

There were at least five minutes before the first bell, and I didn't know what to do with myself. I hung by my locker, opening and shutting it a few times and staring at my phone, trying to look like I had a purpose. I wondered what my old friends were doing at Preston. If only I could have finished my senior year. Mom had tried to hang on financially, but she eventually had to sell our house and pull me out of private school. Dinner, Dear was doing well, but it barely paid the rent at this point. I got it, but right now I could only think about how all alone and awkward I felt. I decided to escape by a side door near the auditorium, wedged open by a small cement brick. It led to a small courtyard.

I leaned against a tree and dug around in my bag, pretending I was looking for something. Nearby, clusters of kids talked together and tried to hide their e-cigarettes.

"Really?" a loud, familiar voice boomed by the auditorium door. Ethan rushed over, nearly knocking down a girl wearing an outrageous black cape and silver-sequined high-top sneakers. "I know it sucks being you, but sneaking around with the stoners won't up your game."

"Guilty as charged." I checked my reflection in my phone, fluffed up my hair with one hand and smacked my lips together, smearing any remaining lip gloss across my mouth. "But let's be honest. I don't have a game. I just didn't want to stand in the hall like a lost soul. Last week during orientation, the only person who talked to me was the girl whose locker is below mine. She didn't even say hello, just, "Move over, please.""

"Rude. At least she said please."

"'Hello' would have been greatly appreciated."

"I'll bet. Hey, how's Carly doing?" Obviously, my Aunt Allie had filled him in.

"I guess she's OK. We're supposed to go there tonight. Crazy stuff, huh?"

"You had no idea?" he asked, wide eyed.

"I mean, now it seems so obvious that she was high all the time, but until the other night, I had no idea it was this bad. She was good at hiding."

"Sorry. I don't know what else to say." Ethan glared at the girl vaping and wrinkled up his nose and lips in the direction of the smokers. "Ewww, there's a funky odor out here and it's going to stick to us if we don't go inside."

A slight breeze blew my unruly hair forward and I immediately pulled it back and wrapped it in a knot. "How come nobody busts these guys?"

"Who knows? You really need to air out," he said, holding his nose.

"Way to make me feel even more like an outcast." I dug into the side pocket of my bucket bag and yanked out a small travel-size vial of perfume, also stolen from Carly's room. I spritzed and walked through the mist. "How do I look?" I straightened out my shirt and pulled my jeans down.

"Gorgeous as ever. I like the black. Et moi?" He used his best French accent.

"Oh, you're always perfect." Ethan was fashionable from head to toe. From his trendy haircut to his tight jeans, lavender linen button-down, and loafers without socks, he was styled. He liked his "stuff," but he wasn't a brat about it.

"Thank you very much. Let's go. We've got two minutes before the bell." He grabbed my sleeve and pulled me forward. "You have French first period?"

"Yeah. Thanks for finding me. I'll make sure to tell your mom you had my back."

"Hey, that's not fair. I'm not doing this for my mom. I've always had your back. When we were little kids in the park, who told the mean girl to get lost? Me, that's who."

"I know, that's true, but I don't want you to feel like you have to babysit me. I'll be fine once I get over the fact that I left all my best friends at Preston."

We rounded the corner past some classrooms and I breathed heavily. "I literally could not have switched schools at a worse time, right?"

"Just let me know when you're done with your pity party."

"Oh, I know, just ignore me. I have no choice but to move on."

"You'll be fine, Ivy. This school is going to love you."

"I'd settle for like at this point." We walked back to the main hall. Five cheerleaders in uniform huddled together. To their left, with eyes glued on the girls, were the football players I saw earlier. My stomach clenched and I suppressed a sigh. No pity party, I reminded myself.

"You got this, girlfriend," Ethan winked. "Those girls got nothing on you."

"Thanks. When I was five, Mom sent Carly and me to cheer camp. Can you imagine anything more ridiculous than cheerleading camp for five- and seven-year-olds?"

"Lame. See that pretty girl over there?" He cocked his head toward a wall of glass cabinets. "That's Phoebe Li. She's in charge. Mostly, she's OK."

I looked in the direction Ethan indicated. The girl was beautiful, with classic straight jet-black hair down her back. She stood next to a really handsome boy. He caught me looking at him and flashed a megawatt smile. I thought I saw him wink one of his electric-blue eyes. I turned away.

"Hey, who's the guy she's with?" I asked.

"Bryce Houston. He's a bit of a jerk."

"Really? He's hot." I looked back as Ethan moved us through the crowded hallway. Kids were lounging against their lockers and slamming the metal doors as they grabbed books and bags and other important school supplies.

"Are they a thing?" I was jealous of her before I even knew the answer.

"Who? Phoebe and Bryce? Nah, they're just friends. They're both really rich and act entitled. It's bullshit. She dates one of the football players, obviously."

"Of course she does. Probably the quarterback," I said ruefully. "You know, I just broke up with Charlie. He was the quarterback at Preston."

"Too bad, so sad. I thought you didn't really like him anyway. Don't worry. You'll be one of them soon enough." Ethan looked back, eying the group of cheerleaders. "Just don't forget about all the little people who helped you along the way."

"Shut up, you goofball." I yanked his arm in an effort to move quicker.

"Hey, what are you doing, don't pull on my sleeve. You'll wrinkle it," Ethan said, shaking my hand loose from his shirt. We kept walking toward the second-floor stairwell.

"I'm sorry, I panicked," I said. "I didn't want them to think we were staring at them," even though I was. We continued speed-walking toward a classroom wing.

"See you later," I said, rushing to my class as the last bell rang, thinking about that guy. Ever the boy-crazy one, my mom always said. I was already looking around. That's a good sign, I thought.

Most of the seats in the classroom were filled already. Up front, there was an identical poster of the Eiffel Tower to the one I had up in my room and another poster of people eating a baguette taped to a side wall. A small French flag hung by the larger American one next to the teacher's desk. I wriggled up one of the aisles and took an open seat in one of the metal chairs with a side-arm desk. Immediately, I noticed a friend of a friend, Zoey Marks, sitting one row over. I remembered her red hair and funky John Lennon round wire glasses from past meetings.

I smiled in her direction. She waved and then looked down and wrote something on a piece of paper and passed it to me via the girl between us. The note said, "Hi, wait for me after class." Over the years, I had bumped into Zoey Marks at birthday parties, during the whole bar- and bat-mitzvah scene, and at CVS or the food store once in a while.

The teacher looked like she was ready to retire. Her gray hair was pulled back in a bun and she wore a brown pantsuit and sensible shoes, but her French accent was impeccable and she was extremely enthusiastic about teaching French. Even so, the class dragged a little and I started to daydream. Out the window, the leaves were turning from greens to yellows and reds. If I strained my eyes, I could make out the steeple on the chapel at my old school that sat on a hill just down the river. I pushed the thought away, not wanting to feel sorry for myself again.

I got of whiff of Carly's cinnamon-scented perfume on my wrist. I was glad we were going to see her today. For the zillionth time, I wondered how she was and what she was doing.

When French was over, Zoey came right over. "Hey, you're Juliet's friend, right?" She had freckles on her nose that wrinkled up when she smiled. Around her neck, she wore a delicate silver necklace with a wishbone charm. Carly had one of those too, in her jewelry box.

"Yes, and you're Zoey. Hi." I tried my best to sound upbeat without sounding desperate, but honestly, I was feeling very self-conscious.

"That's right. Juliet told me to look for you."

I followed Zoey out of the classroom and down the hall toward the cafeteria. It was only second period, but we both had a free class so we decided to grab a cup of hot chocolate. We headed to a corner table.

"So why did you transfer senior year? Seems like a bit of a drag," she said, crinkling her nose again. She had deep-set eyes, the kind that looked somber all the time.

"The short version is that my mom needed to downsize."

Zoey nodded. "Sucks, huh?"

"Yup. I can't imagine a worse scenario for a high school senior, can you?" I said, keeping my voice chipper. The only way it could be worse was if I was the one in the hospital and not Carly.

"Oh, I don't know. You could be sitting here alone instead of with me."

"Perspective. I like that," I said, glancing around the room. "I don't mean to sound sorry for myself. I'm not, really."

Zoey waved at a table full of cheerleaders and nodded her head at another bunch of girls who all looked alike with straightened glossy hair and short skirts. They dressed much like my old friends at Preston. A cute guy at another table smiled at me. I smiled back, trying to appear friendly.

"See those girls?" Zoey said, raising her eyes in the direction of both tables. I nodded. "I'm friends with most of them. I'll give you the rundown on each one if you want. Did you bring anything to eat? I'm starving."

"Aren't they going to wonder why you're not sitting with them?" I asked.

"We can go sit with them if you want. I already texted my friend Kat, the girl in the red dress and flats, that I was giving you the 411 on school. She said to tell you to avoid our group. We suck."

"Ha. Which group are you talking about, the cheerleaders or the pretty girls drinking ice tea?" I furtively glanced over toward the two tables in question.

"Both. Some of them also play volleyball or swim. I act and sing. Kat dances. Lots of those girls also run track, but really just for college applications' sake, and we all see the finish line there, so, yeah, we suck."

"Do they know I'm new?"

"Duh! Everyone knows everyone in this town, and people talk. Word about you got out quickly. The girls wanted to know who their new competition was, and the guys wanted to know what the new girl looked like, so yeah, people talk."

Oh God, I thought. I really am not up for such scrutiny. I had gone to nursery school with some of these kids and been in gymnastics class when we were little, but now I felt like an alien in a strange land.

I swiveled to the left and noticed the long tables of science nerds, stoners, and athletes. It was just like any other high school in America. I decided I'd rather fit in than not, so I plastered on a fake smile and looked at Zoey.

"Well, when do I get to meet everyone?"

"You ready? Here comes Phoebe Li, the Queen Bee."

"So I heard." Sure enough, the gorgeous Phoebe Li was walking right toward our table.

Unfortunately, she wasn't with the hot guy I saw her with this morning. Flanking her on either side were two girls dressed in cheerleading uniforms.

"Hey, Zoey." Phoebe's voice was lilting and smooth. There wasn't a wrinkle on her crisp white tank top or her red silk skirt.

"This is Ivy Green. She just transferred from Preston," Zoey said. "Ivy, meet Phoebe, Dani, and Erin."

"Nice to meet you," Phoebe said, and the other two sort of mumbled, "Same." "Good luck here." Phoebe said, "See you around." The three girls walked off as quickly as they had arrived.

"That was weird," I said.

"Not really. They just wanted to say hi. They're all right," Zoey said as they walked off. "Full of themselves for sure, but harmless." She pushed some hair behind her ears and nudged her glasses higher on her nose.

"Thanks for making this a little easier," I said, patting down my own fly-away hair.

"I know what it's like to be the center of attention, both good and bad," Zoey said, bending down to fix her shoe, or maybe she was hiding her feelings from me. I thought about asking her what she meant, but honestly, I didn't have the emotional strength right now.

"Question," I said instead. "This morning I noticed Phoebe standing with a really cute guy, but he wasn't wearing a football uniform. Dark curly hair, kinda tallish. I think his name is Bryce."

Zoey began to gather up her books. Other people around us were also beginning to move about. I guessed the bell for next period was gonna ring soon.

"I'm guessing it was Bryce Houston. They're BFFs." I followed her toward the exit. I was anxious to continue the conversation about Bryce, learn if he had a girlfriend, figure out his place here.

"Just wondering," I said, feigning nonchalance. I was pretty sure he winked at me this morning. My insides curled up a little bit.

"Need a ride home later or do you have your own car?" Zoey asked.

"Sure, I'll take a ride. I don't have a parking pass yet."

"I'd say we could hang at my house, but I have a dentist appointment at four. Maybe tomorrow?"

"No worries. I'm going to hang at my mother's catering kitchen for a few hours. She cooks out of the Presbyterian Church on Elm."

"That's right on the way. Your mom is a caterer? That's cool."

"Yeah, she and her sister just opened a gourmet-dinner delivery service. They call it Dinner, Dear. The idea is to provide three-course gourmet meals as commuters get off the train."

"Oh, right. I think my dad has picked up from them a couple of times. Delish. So, hey, maybe you'll come over tomorrow after school?"

"Sounds like a plan, as long as my mother doesn't need me at work."

"Whatever works. Either way is fine," she said, and walked off down the hall.

Chapter Four—Dinner, Dear

The minute I saw the clutter on the countertops, I knew it was going to be awhile before I got home to Kelly Green or my homework. The stainless-steel countertops were covered with food, spices, and disposable containers.

"Hello, hello," Mom called out. She was cutting carrots into pretty flower shapes. My Aunt Allie stood by the sink, rinsing off strawberries. I waved to everyone.

"Hi Ivy," Allie said. "How was your first day?"

Ethan was peeling potatoes at the counter. He flashed me the peace sign and grinned, two years of braces paying off with a straight pearly smile. "You survived, huh?" he asked, dimples deepening.

"Yeah, barely," I groaned. "How'd things get so crazy messy here?" Seeing all the food and wrappers strewn around the room, it was obvious that my mother really needed as much help as she could get.

"I'm here even though I do have a ton of homework," I announced. I was dying to curl up in bed and check out Bryce's Insta account and any Facebook posts, but I would never let my mom down. With Carly at Blue Hills, my mom needed my help, and this was my chance to show her that she could count on me.

"What can I do?" I said, hoping my fake cheer would fool them into thinking I was more interested than I felt. "Any news on Carly?"

"Nothing yet, honey. We can go see her later. For now, I'm inundated with cooking. So much to do, but it's all good." Mom smiled, but it was a tight, pursed look. I knew she was worried and tired.

"Come on, dig in. You can finish tossing the salads," Mom said.

I didn't want to disappoint her, but I really needed some time to myself to think about Carly's situation, as well as school, all the people I just met, and what the heck I was going to wear tomorrow. However, I concentrated on being agreeable and plastered on another fake smile.

"Don't worry, Ivy." Ethan pointed to a pile of folded aprons stacked in a plastic bin. "Wouldn't want you to get your cute first-day-of-school outfit covered in flour." He puffed out his chest and I noticed the Dinner, Dear logo of crossed spatulas on the apron over his lavender shirt that still managed to look pressed and fresh.

I definitely did not want to get my clothes all dirty, but it was inevitable. Mom not only needed my help, but I'm sure she wanted me around, now that Carly was away.

"How's the new girl doing?" Mom swiped a lock of hair from her eyes and left a smear of oil on her forehead, smoothing out the worry lines for just a moment.

"I'd give the day a six out of ten." I grabbed an apron and set Carly's old book bag in a corner.

I pulled the apron over my head, careful not to get the neck loop caught in my hair.

"You just get highlights?" Ethan handed me a hair tie. "We don't want hair in the food."

"As a matter of fact, yes, just last week. You like?"

"Yeah, you look good as a blonde. Maybe I'll get a few streaks myself." He mock posed and made a *Vogue* face. I laughed.

"So, what time do you want to head out to see Carly?" I asked.

Mom cast me a weary look. "We can visit after seven. She's just getting acclimated, so it might be better if we wait a day."

"You know, Mom, I have a zillion things to do at home and schlepping to the middle of Nowheresville, Connecticut, is really not what I want to be doing, but we should go. I'm sure she'll want us, even if a big part of me doesn't think she deserves us right now."

"Ivy, Carly is suffering," Mom said.

"I know," I said.

"Can I count on you to be supportive and understanding? That's what Carly needs right now."

"I'm down with it, Mom, but let's hurry, OK?"

"Is Carly going to get better?" Ethan asked. He had left his potato chopping station and stood next to his mom.

Allie put her arm around him. "Carly is going to be fine. I know it."

"I hope you're right. I couldn't take another struggle," Mom said. Just two years apart, she and Allie had led parallel lives. They had gone to the same college, married and then divorced around the same time, had us together, and now they've started Dinner, Dear together. Allie kept the books and helped Mom cook, and Mom created the menus, found recipes, and wrote down shopping lists.

"'There's nothing more we can do right now," Mom said. She stared hard at Allie, whose straw-colored bangs fell in front of her eyes. Allie nodded ever so slightly.

Out of nowhere, I started to cry. "Mom, I want to see her tonight." Wow, I was really feeling all the feelings at once.

"Oh honey, this is such an emotional time for all of us. Let's get going. I have a special delivery we have to do first, and then we can head over to Blue Hills."

Allie smacked her lips together and shook her head toward my mom. "Remember, Ivy, your mom is tired too. She hasn't slept very much lately." I felt Allie's smooth, lean biceps press around my shoulders and chest for a moment as she embraced me.

My mom came over to me and wrapped her sticky, wet, flour-covered hands around my waist and grabbed Allie's hand and squeezed it for a second. "I'm OK," Mom said.

"Don't, Mom. You're getting me all dirty," I pulled away.

"Sorry, honey. I'm rushing to finish the orders and making extra chicken cutlets."

"So, who'd you meet today, sweetie?" Allie asked.

"A girl named Zoey Marks."

"Zoey Marks?" Ethan tucked peanut-butter chocolate-chip cookies into sandwich Ziploc bags. I snuck a cookie and popped it into my mouth.

"Hey, stop it." He swatted me away with his apron. "I know her. She's cool. Did she tell you about her brother?" His eyes moved back and forth from me to his mom.

"Ethan!" Allie called out. She slashed her neck with her fingers in the universal sign of "cut."

"What?" he said, throwing his hands in the air.

"What?" I echoed, looking expectantly at Ethan.

"Nothing. She had a brother who died. I'm sure she'll tell you herself."

"Are you kidding? How'd he die?" I said, but really I was thinking, How sad. All we had talked about were the kids in school.

"She'll tell you," Ethan muttered and turned to go. "I have to go to the bathroom." I noticed Allie pass him a dark look.

"Help Allie and Ethan organize the food, please," Mom ordered me. "Don't forget to color-code the containers." She threw her hand up to her head and more flour puffed on her hair.

My mom looked young. The only makeup she ever wore was clear gloss, which I noticed she had on now. Flour stuck to her lips. Her cat-like green eyes were bloodshot. Maybe we were all super tired today, and who could blame us?

"We just need to load and deliver the food to the train station and then you and I can drop off the turkey and stuff, go see Carly, and then, maybe, just maybe, I can get some sleep." My mom rested her head against the wall for a minute.

"Sam," Allie addressed my mom. "Ethan and I can do the station delivery."

"That would be great, actually," Mom answered, tossing some extra rosemary and thyme into a small baggie. I got a whiff of the herbs and was immediately reminded of Thanksgiving. Last year we had spent it with Allie, Ethan, and our grandparents upstate.

"Why would anyone want a turkey dinner in September?" I asked, stacking green dessert containers into a plastic tub with rope handles.

"I don't know, but they pay well, so we're doing it," Mom said.

We filled the rest of the containers with food, some for the train station and the rest for this ridiculous Thanksgiving dinner. Along with the day's regular menu—one complete meal with salad, sides, and dessert each evening—my mom and Allie had cooked a turkey, gravy, stuffing, fancy cranberry salsa, an amazing honey-and-lavender sweet-potato soufflé, and molten lava cakes.

"It's just like Thanksgiving in September. Any leftovers?" Ethan was standing next to me, stacking the salads and the couscous for tonight.

My mom shook her head and Allie laughed. "No, but there's plenty of chicken cutlets."

"Not the same, but OK. I'll call you later," Ethan said to me.

"Are you sure you don't need me to drop off the special dinner too, Samantha?" Allie asked again. "You really look like you're going to fall on your face."

"I feel like it, but I need to make nice to Flora. She wants to see me ringing her doorbell, arms full of food."

"Well, screw her. I am your business partner and your sister." Allie crossed her arms.

"Well, unfortunately, she specifically requested me, so let's indulge her. Hopefully she'll keep ordering our food. We need the money now more than ever." Mom picked up a big carton filled with double-stuffed sweet potatoes. "Carly loves these," she mused sadly.

"Well so do I, Mom."

"I'm sorry, honey. I know you do." My mom stiffened up for a moment and looked around the room, frowning. "So, Allie and Ethan will deliver the daily dinners. Ivy and I will drop off the Thanksgiving food and then go visit Carly. We can clean up later, I guess."

"Stop it, Sam." Allie put her arm around my mom. "Ethan and I will get this kitchen in tip-top shape. You just worry about Carly."

"Thanks, Al." As she headed out the back door of the church kitchen, the gleaming appliances seemed like a rebuff to the gloom and pessimism we were trying to stave off.

I hurried after her. How could she forget that the sweet potatoes were my favorite too?

IT WAS STILL LIGHT at five thirty when we drove through the village and then up the hill toward the fancy part of town. We turned into a long, tree-lined driveway with open iron gates flanked by stone posts, and drove past an enormous ugly metal sculpture on the lawn. It looked like a giant orange menorah, but clearly it was supposed to be something serious.

Every window in the oversized white colonial was adorned with elaborate trim on top. Shiny copper gutters ran across the length and down the corners of the house. There were already four cars parked in front of a three-car garage.

We pulled up behind all the cars and my mom clicked open the hatchback door. As we walked to the rear of the car to pick up the packages, the side door of the house swung open.

Two teenage boys stood in the entranceway, smiling broadly with open arms.

My face felt hot. I imagined it was bright red. My stomach did a somersault. Standing in front of me was Bryce Houston, flashing his bright white megawatt movie-star smile.

"Hi, we can take it from here. I'm Bryce." He winked at me for the second time that day. "And you're . . .?"

"I'm Ivy," I said, my eyes squinching. I felt that tug in my tummy again. He was cuter than ever, up close. I couldn't take my eyes off his, and we both stood there for a second, grinning like idiots. I cringed. I was still wearing the apron. I pulled it off and threw it into the backseat.

"Great! Thanks," Mom said. "Take these boxes and I'll go back to the car for the rest of it with . . .?" she hesitated.

"I'm Jonathan," the shorter boy said.

"OK, Jonathan, come with me."

Bryce looked at me and I pursed my lips, trying not to smile too widely. He was tan with broad shoulders and long arms and legs. The other one, Jonathan, who I assumed was his brother because they looked alike, followed my mother to the car. Jonathan was skinny and his shirt was ripped. His jeans looked dirty in the light of day.

Bryce led me into a modern kitchen. All the stainless-steel appliances looked new and unused. From the back windows I could see the buildings in town and the mountains across the river. I kept sneaking glances at Bryce.

"Just set the food over here," Bryce said, grabbing more containers from my arms. "Whoa, it's heavy. What did my mom order?"

"Thanksgiving dinner with all the trimmings."

My mom walked in; Jonathan trailed behind her, balancing three long plastic food containers. She placed the box of chocolate molten lava cakes on the light-gray granite countertops and tossed a big bag of chocolate chip cookies next to it.

"Can I have one now?" Jonathan grabbed a lava cake from an open box.

My mom's face tightened. "They really need to be reheated. Maybe snack on the candied nuts?"

Jonathan ignored her and stuffed a whole mini cake into his mouth. Chocolate sauce oozed down his chin, and he used his hand to wipe his face. Gross, I thought.

Bryce frowned. "Jonathan, get a napkin, would you?' To me he said, "Just ignore him. He thinks he's still at the frat house."

"What frat house?" a chipper voice said, and Phoebe Li, barefoot and in shorty shorts and a very thin T-shirt, walked into the kitchen. Best friends? Really? I also questioned Ethan's other comment about Bryce being a bit of a jerk. He seemed super nice to me.

"Hey, it's Ivy, right?" She peered inside one of the containers as though it were hers. "Mmm, looks delish."

"Uh yeah," I said. "We met in the cafeteria this morning."

A petite blond woman entered the kitchen. She wore a long gauzy skirt and a matching oversized yellow silk top. Initially, she appeared much younger than my mom, but as she came closer, I could see fine lines around her eyes and pulling across her upper lip.

"I love the smell of Thanksgiving." She turned her perky little nose up in the air and inhaled deeply.

Bryce poked the end of his finger into a box. "Mom, this food looks amazing."

"I know. That's why I order it, right Sam?"

My mom nodded and Bryce's mom continued to gush.

"Samantha Green's food is going to take over this town," she said. "Hi, I'm Flora." She stuck out her hand toward me.

"I'm Ivy. Nice to meet you," I said.

"Flora, Ivy is my younger daughter. She started at Marble Springs today."

"What year, dear?" Flora asked.

"She's a senior, Mom, like us," Bryce said. "We all just met."

"Welcome to the neighborhood. I'm sure Bryce and Phoebe will introduce you around." Flora nodded her head eagerly. "Right folks?" she gestured toward them.

"Absolutely," Phoebe said. "Listen, this all looks so good. Wish I could stay." Phoebe headed toward the back door and slipped on her designer flip-flops.

"Flora, I'm just getting to know your lovely sons and, uh, your daughter?" my mom hesitated.

"No, no, I'm just a family friend." Phoebe jumped in. "But I'm always here. Bryce, thanks again for the calc help."

"Take some of this, dear," Flora said. "I know you love cookies. They starve you at home, don't they dear?"

"Close to it. I'll take two for the road and eat them in the car. My mom will go ballistic if she thinks I've been eating sugar."

"Don't tell her that we indulge your sweet tooth over here." Flora handed Phoebe two of my mom's chocolate chip cookies wrapped in a napkin.

"I won't. Nice to see you, Ivy." Phoebe took the cookies and waved goodbye. She hugged Bryce and tried to hug Jonathan, but he ducked. "Wipe your chin there, slugger, and for once, try and behave!" she said to Jonathan with a stern look.

"You tell him, dear," Flora said, not smiling. "He won't listen to us."

"Bye," I said, crossing my arms as Bryce shut the door behind her. Everyone watched her leave.

"Well, Samantha," Flora said, bringing us back to the delivery. "You've met the boys, who will be eating the majority of your amazing food. Jonathan is back from college for the weekend." I saw her glare at Jonathan for a split second but then immediately smile at my mom. She looked at me. Flora's skirt swished as she moved toward Bryce and tenderly rested her head on his shoulder for a moment.

"So, you're new, huh?" Jonathan sneaked behind my mom and stuck his hand back in the chocolate-cake box. "Good luck to you."

"Jonathan," Flora enunciated. "Stop eating the food. It's for later."

"Ha!" He licked his fingers and walked out of the room, oblivious to his bad manners.

"Kids can be so difficult and embarrassing sometimes, you know? That is, when they're not being amazing. I hope I live long enough to see them discipline their own children," Flora said.

"Hmm," my mom mumbled, with a quick sidewise glance at me. Flora Houston was lucky she had both sons with her for dinner. We both nodded politely.

"Samantha, this food looks fantastic," Flora announced, as she peeked into the containers and used a fork to spear a small piece of turkey. "I will personally make sure everyone in town knows about you and your sister. Thank you so much for bringing this over. We're all set, unless of course, you'd want to see the rest of the house. We just renovated upstairs."

"I'd love to see the house, Flora, it's beautiful, but we're kind of in a rush."

"Just pop upstairs for a minute. You've got to see the TV embedded in the mirror. It's very cool."

"OK, but honestly, we don't have a lot of time." My mom's face pinched.

"Stay down here, the tour is boring," Bryce said to me. Again, my gut twisted a little.

"Okay," I mumbled. I bit my lip.

My mom followed Flora and I followed Bryce into the adjacent family room, joining Jonathan. I sat down at the far end of the sofa from Bryce. Jonathan lounged in a recliner near me, scrolling through his phone. I didn't know what to say, so I avoided eye contact and looked around the room, noting all the pretty candles and framed family photos, and lots of books.

"We don't have to watch the news if you don't want." Bryce flipped the channel away from CNN. He stopped clicking when he came to an old rerun of *Friends*.

"I love *Friends*," I said, looking away.

We stared at the television like we were witnessing breaking news. I crossed and uncrossed my legs, then folded them up underneath my butt until I realized that my feet were on the sofa, so I quickly put them back down on the ground.

"Um, so, do you know where you want to go to college?" I asked, desperate to find some common ground with him. I twirled my hair for a second then stopped and sat on my hands so I'd be still.

"I was going to apply early decision to Johns Hopkins. That's where Jonathan goes, but he's really screwing up there and I'm afraid his record will ruin my chances."

"Stop exaggerating. You think because I had to leave a frat house for one lousy weekend it's going to mess things up for you? You give me way too much credit," Jonathan said.

"He's probably right," I said. "Anywhere else you like?"

"Cornell maybe, but everyone applies there. You?"

"Cornell," I said, and we both laughed. "Maybe Vassar. My sister goes there." Ugh, I didn't mean to bring her up. I checked my own phone. We really did need to leave if we were going to see her tonight.

"How old is your sister?" Bryce asked.

"Carly's going to be a junior. She's traveling now." The fib felt like a lump in my mouth. I didn't like lying, and I was bad at it too.

"Cool. Where?"

"Oh, all over." Shit, I was now mired in my own lies and I didn't know how to get out from under them.

"I know a Carly from town." Jonathan was now eating the candied nuts from the mason jar we brought, and he had a box of gummy bears by his side on the chair.

"She went to Preston too, and now she's at Vassar. I doubt you know her," I said.

"No, I do, I think. She's pretty hot if I remember right."

I ignored his compliment to Carly and for a second wondered under what circumstances they might have met. "I really doubt it. She worked all summer as a nanny and now she's away." The lie continued to burn in my throat. Thankfully, Bryce changed the subject.

"Hey, I'm going to a friend's house after dinner. Want to join me? I'll introduce you around." He looked down, for the first time seeming a bit unsure of himself.

"Ugh, wow, that's so nice of you to ask, but it's the first night of school. I'd better go home with my mom. Maybe another time."

"Sure, another time." He returned his gaze to the television and we sunk back into silence for a few moments.

Oh my God, I thought, I blew my chances with him. He was sweet and charming and I didn't want him to think I wasn't interested, but I had to see Carly.

My mom called out from the front hall. "Ivy, we're leaving."

I stood up. "I'll walk you out," Bryce said.

"Nice meeting you." I waved to Jonathan, slumped in his seat, now drinking a beer.

"Bye," Jonathan said.

Bryce held the front door open for me. We stopped for a moment under the vestibule, several feet away from the car where my mom and Flora were waiting in the driveway.

"Thanks. Funny that we don't have any classes together." I looked up hopefully.

"Well, you know, it's all about what team you're on. I'm on A team and I'm guessing you're on B."

"Yeah, I'm on B. Maybe gym or something?"

"I'll look for you tomorrow." He held my gaze.

"Thanks." I could barely form words. Oh wow, I liked this guy.

When we reached the driveway, my mom hustled me into the car and turned on the ignition. I waved at Bryce and then turned toward my mom.

"It's not even six, we're good to go, right?" I asked the minute we were on the main street. "I'm sure she wants visitors."

"You still want to go? I can drop you off at home and you can wait till tomorrow."

"Of course I want to see Carly. It's just I have a ton of things to do tonight, but I want to go. I can help you drive if you want." I thought about Bryce's party offer. That would have been fun too.

"I'm OK, honey. We don't have to stay long. We'll just say hi and give her some cookies."

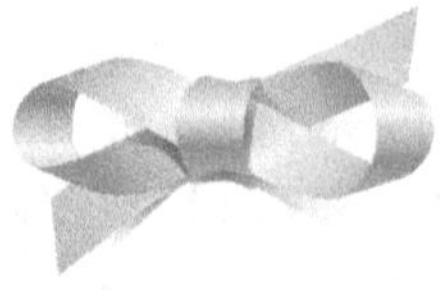

Chapter Five—First Visit

It took nearly an hour to go from Marble Springs to the small rural town in Connecticut where the psychiatric hospital slash rehab was located. Mom kept calling it a facility, but I knew it was a fancy hospital for people with drug addiction problems and psychiatric issues. I was kind of scared to see what kinds of patients were there. I tried to reassure myself that if Carly was there, it had to be OK.

As we drove down the main hospital driveway, I could see several large modern buildings as well as lots of smaller cottages. People in light summer clothing rocked in chairs on the cottage porches and chatted with each other.

We parked next to the big white-painted brick reception hall, a stately building with more than one stone fireplace stack. Oversized sculptures dotted the grass and as we walked toward the front door. I noticed more people sitting in small clusters along the many wooden benches placed along the stone paths and on the grassy courtyards. I heard someone laugh, and then I thought I heard another voice crying.

We walked into a large, modern anteroom. Two identical-looking professional women in dark skirt-suits and tightly pulled-back hair sat behind the reception desk at the front of the room. My mom spoke confidently, and a little too loudly. "Hi. We're here to see my daughter, Carly Green."

"And you are?" the lady on the right asked, with a smile meant to make us feel comfortable, but of course my nerves were frayed and I looked away. I didn't know how I was supposed to act in such a place.

"I'm Samantha Green, her mother, and this is her sister, Ivy Green." My mom stood straight and clearly enunciated her words, like she knew what she was doing. She didn't appear at all uneasy about being here.

Around the oversized open foyer, there were scattered seating areas with sofas and coffee tables and lots of potted plants. In one corner of the spacious atrium were several bookcases and cafe tables and chairs. It looked like a Starbucks.

The face of one of the ladies at the reception desk suddenly went blank. No more eye twitching or smiling. She stared at us. "Visiting hours till nine. Let me buzz her counselor and she can take you over to Carly's cottage. They should be just about finished with dinner. Have you been here before?"

I shook my head. I tried not to stare at the many adults with odd mannerisms that were walking by. Some twitched, others skipped, several shuffled along in Ugg slippers. A few people were talking really loudly, and others walked with their heads down, shoulders slumped, some mumbling quietly. A few looked like they could use a hair wash. Everyone had a companion, someone dressed in tidy clothing—a skirt or khakis—versus the obvious patients who were mostly wearing sweats or workout gear.

Within a few minutes, a tiny young woman in her twenties walked over to us. Her ponytail swished back and forth and her little nose seemed to be sniffing around the room. As she got closer, I saw that she wore no makeup and only tiny gold studded earrings as jewelry.

"Hi, Ms. Green. This must be Carly's sister, Ivy? Am I correct? I'm Joanie Latham, Carly's counselor."

"Hi," my mom said, forcing a tense smile. "Please, call me Samantha, and yes, this is Ivy."

"Hi Ivy. So nice to meet you. Carly's told me a lot about you already. She's going to be very happy to see you. She had a good first day."

"Good day?" the words got stuck in my throat. I glanced at my mom. Her body was stiff and her face frozen with that annoying false smile. "What does that mean? She nearly OD'd yesterday," I said.

Joanie Latham nodded. "I know it must be rough on you, not knowing what is happening to her, but she's where she needs to be right now. We allow family to visit right away as long as the patient isn't in any kind of crisis, but don't stay too long. It's best for Carly's acclimation and recovery if she sees her family for short visits and then gets right back to the work of getting well."

"Well, we're ready when you are," Mom said.

I felt like I was a character on a TV show set in a hospital. I couldn't quite connect to the reality of where we were. I felt a fog over my head, but I tried to act normally. I copied my mom and forced a smile.

"I'll walk you both over. In the future, during visiting hours, you can sign in directly at her cottage."

We followed Joanie to one of the outlying white clapboard cottages behind the reception hall. She led us through the front door and off to the left into a dining room. I noticed Carly right away. She was at one of many bridge tables set up in the room, sitting with two other women, one about her age and the other looking closer to my mom's age. The dining room was painted beige with a mauve-trimmed wood panel. Old-fashioned pictures of horses, barns, and fields dotted the walls, and an elaborate chandelier hung above.

All the tables in the room were full of women ranging in age from teens to gray-haired grandma-aged ladies. Some were obviously visitors like us. They had their coats on and their pocketbooks clutched close to their sides.

"Remember, she may seem a little different in this environment. Just be yourselves." Joanie squeezed my wrist. "Family support is the most important aspect of the healing journey."

Carly looked over toward us. She waved and left her table. She looked skinnier than usual. She usually ran three to five miles a day. I didn't know if she was confined to the cottage or would be allowed to run along the paths.

"Hi, hi, hi!" She giggled for a second. "Welcome to my home away from home." She ran into my mother's arms. I stood back with Joanie and watched my mom and sister cry, holding each other in a tight embrace.

"I'm so sorry. I'm sorry. I'll make it up to you. I'm going to come home soon. I promise. Ivy"—she broke away from my mom and gave me a hug—"thank you for coming. I really appreciate it."

"I'll be right over here." Joanie pointed to a table and chair in the corner.

"Mom," Carly said, taking my mom's hand. "I can't believe you're visiting me in rehab. In a hospital. I'm so sorry," she repeated.

Carly then led us to the living room area off of the dining room. There was a fireplace with a brick surround and the room was decorated with two big, cushy sofas and a couple of floral-printed upholstered chairs with high backs. It looked like someone's personal living room.

We sat down, and Carly continued to cry in earnest. "Please bring me some of your cookies and brownies, Mom. The food is for shit here. It's all heavy pasta and casseroles. Gross."

"You look really thin," I said. "You know, I say that in a good way."

"Oh yeah," Carly held up her shirt and showed me that her skirt was big around the waist. "I'm thin all right, but it's no cause for jealousy, that's for sure. Ivy, so far the food sucks, and the shampoo makes my hair lank and brittle. Can you bring me some Pantene? I swear, I gotta get out of here ASAP."

"It looks lovely here." My mom held Carly's hand.

"Yes, it looks lovely here, Mom, from the outside looking in, maybe." Carly pulled away. "It looks like a fucking country club, I know. I get it, but we all know it's the loony bin. People are more than drug abusers here, they're schizophrenic and bipolar, and the worst is Borderline Personality Disorder. Do you know it? Those people are impossible to talk to. Most patients are dual diagnosis. They do drugs *and* they're psych patients."

"You are not being very kind, Carly," Mom said.

"Come on, Mom, lighten up. I swear, I'm not a real drug abuser. I definitely was beginning to want the oxy a little too much, but I can get it under control and fast."

"So why are you here, then?" I asked. Seemed like an obvious question.

"You guys caught me by surprise at the hospital. I felt like I had no choice but to agree to go, but I could do a daily outpatient program. I don't need to sleep here, not really."

"But you're here, so why don't you get the most out of it?" Mom encouraged. "Joanie seems nice."

"She's fine. We sit around and talk about when we started taking drugs. I'm the least offender here. Most of these ladies have been doing H and coke and taking narcotics for years."

"How long are you here for?" I asked. I could see all the ladies in the dining room, picking at apples, drinking coffee, talking with each other. There were a few older men in the room, obviously fathers, and one young guy in his twenties, maybe a brother. We were alone on the sofas though. I stared hard at Carly. Except for being super skinny, and the bad hair and dark circles under her eyes, she mostly looked the same as always to me. I had to agree with her. Why was she here?

"I don't know. They say anywhere from forty-eight hours to a week or more; depends on how I do."

"Listen, Carly." Mom hesitated. "Just give it your all. Go to meetings. Participate in group. Learn all that you can. Drug abuse and alcoholism is hereditary, and we have it in our family."

"What? Who?" I piped in. "I don't know anyone who seriously abused in our family."

"Mom, what are you talking about?" Carly asked, crossing and uncrossing her stick legs. She wore a boho-style skirt and a white

T-shirt with flip-flops. She could have been going to a street fair for a music festival.

"You know, relatives in the past have dabbled and struggled with alcohol and drugs."

"Who are you talking about, Mom?" Carly asked. My mother twisted in her seat. She looked away from us.

"You know, your Uncle David, my younger brother, he's never really been able to give up pot. Who knows what else he does?" My mom still couldn't look at us. Her eyes were fixed on a piece of paper on the table.

"Everyone did drugs in the '80s. Who are you really talking about? The key to recovery is honesty," Carly said.

"I guess I'm thinking about David." My mom couldn't look us in the face. She played with a tissue in her lap and bit her lip while she spoke. "I'm just saying, get the most out of this stay, and then hopefully you'll never have to come back."

"Mom." Carly shook her head. Her mouth crinkled up. She looked at me. "Do you know what she's talking about?" I shook my head no, but I began to think about who my mom might be referring to besides my Uncle David. We hardly ever saw him because he lived far away in Arizona and always asked my mom for money when he called.

"Mom," I began, "are you implying that Dad has a history of abusing drugs?"

My mom avoided looking straight at either Carly or me. She said, "Not exactly, although he has done his share of drugs and we all know he likes his vodka." She pretended to fluff up a pillow on the sofa. "I'm just saying that while you're here, do the work."

"I'm here, aren't I?" Carly sat up straight. She gently lifted up my mother's chin, and she spoke softly but enunciated her words, not glancing away. "I've committed to one week, that's it. Let's see how it goes. I've made some bad choices."

The three of us were silent for a few beats. We could smell the residue of dinner from the dining room, a mixture of onions and ground beef. Food-service staff dressed in blue chinos and white shirts and hats were clanking dishes as they cleaned up. Several women headed up the center hall staircase.

"Is your room upstairs? Do you have a roommate?" I asked.

"Yeah, all the bedrooms are upstairs. My roommate is a forty-five-year-old lady addicted to Percocet and oxy. She used to be a professor of psychology at a community college. She's been hospitalized three times this year for drugs and bipolar disorder."

"Wow, that's crazy." Realizing the absurdity of what I just said, I forced a fake laugh. "No pun intended. I hope she gets better."

"I know, right? It's a little scary. There are no locks on the bedroom doors. I had trouble sleeping, imagining that someone might barge in the room at night."

"Carly, you are being ridiculous. It's barely been one day," my mom said, frowning. "You are safe here. Remember what Melanie at the hospital said; this is one of the best rehabs around."

"I know that, Mom, but everyone here has a story, and some of those stories involve abuse. I'm just trying to protect myself. Honestly, I'm in the best shape of anyone here."

"Carly, what does that even mean? Everyone in this place is on equal footing. You're all here to get well," my mom said, looking around the room as she spoke. "Patience is a virtue, remember that."

"Stop it, Mom. Ivy and I have all your adages memorized, but I'm the one here, not you, and not her," she said, pointing right at me. "I'm the one with the family curse, not her."

"Harsh," I said. "Who's talking curse? Mom just mentioned Uncle David's pot habit and Dad's love of a good shot of Tito's. Not the same thing."

"You don't know that," Carly said. She waved at a young woman our own age who was heading onto the porch with another woman, a little older, maybe in her thirties. "I'm trying to tell you that I have the least amount of issues of all the women in this cottage. I'm not crazy. I've only had one incident, maybe two if you count a few over-the-top drunken high nights, but I will be fine. Can we talk about something else for a minute? All I think about and talk about here is sobriety. While you're here, tell me about home. Ivy, how was your first day at school? Marble Springs all it's cracked up to be?"

"Yeah, it's fine," I mumbled. I felt suddenly claustrophobic in the room. I wanted to get in the car and drive home already.

"And the new house? How's my room look?"

My mom smiled a big, warm, genuine grin. "Your room at home looks just like you left it. Kelly Green sits by the door. She misses you."

Joanie Latham suddenly appeared in the doorway. "Visiting hours are over," Joanie said.

"I miss Kelly Green too." Carly laughed and gave me a quick peck on the check and we fist bumped. "Love You Like a Sister," she said, using our special gesture. We had been doing this since she first went to college. The first time Carly said it to me, I told her, "But we *are* sisters." She said, "I know, but even if we weren't. I love you like a friend and a sister. Sometimes we just say each letter, like we would text it, L-Y-L-A-S.

I knew if she could muster up a smile for "LYLAS" she was doing all right. Carly hugged my mom and said, "I'll be OK. Don't worry."

My knees felt wobbly from all the stress of the visit. When we got in the car, neither of us seemed to know what to say, or if words were even necessary, but after five minutes, I felt compelled to comment.

"Wow, that was something. Do you think she really needs to be there, or could she have done this as an outpatient, like she said?"

"I think Carly is where she needs to be," Mom replied, staring at the road as she drove, hands gripping the wheel. "We'll see how she does. Sometimes people seem really good at first, motivated and energetic to get well and sober, but then they fall back into old habits. That's the danger."

"Uh huh," I said. Then we both remained quiet. My mom put NPR on the radio and we drove the rest of the way home listening to *The Moth*. The stories were a welcome distraction.

As soon as we got home, I ate two pieces of chocolate caramel and went up to bed. After washing up, I sat cross-legged in bed in my pajamas with my computer perched on a pillow in my lap. Kelly Green doggie-snored softly. When I checked social media, I saw that Bryce Houston requested to follow me on Insta. My tummy tightened and flipped. I hit accept and my gut did another somersault. Something's up with him too. I think it's called a crush.

Chapter Six— Zoey's Story

Zoey drove fast with the windows down in her Subaru, flying up the hill to a historic three-story green and yellow and orange Victorian house with a wraparound front porch that faced the Hudson River in back. Her house had flower boxes on the windows but no flowers in them. I pushed away the memory of Carly zipping us to and from school and focused on making Zoey my new friend. I had spoken to a few of my old friends from Preston recently, but the connections seemed to diminish with every text. We were all so busy in our own lives. But I couldn't have guessed that those relationships would wither so fast.

As we drove to her house, we played the "name game" and figured out common friends from all over the place, even summer camp. Gentle and heartfelt, Zoey asked me about how the dog adjusted to the new house, how my mom was doing on her own; she even asked if my mom was dating.

"No, not lately," I said. "I guess she's gone online in the past and has dated here and there. She's been single since I was little."

"Did you ever wonder why?" Zoey asked gently, the freckles on her nose merging together when she talked. She was obviously trying not to push too hard. I appreciated her sensitivity.

"Not really. She's always been highly focused on us, on me." I wasn't ready to talk about Carly yet. "She had a boyfriend for a while when I was in like fourth grade or something. We all went to Disney together with his kids. A total disaster!" I laughed out loud just remembering that terrible trip. "We fought the whole time and it was about a hundred degrees at nine in the morning." Now she's probably just too busy to date, between the move, starting Dinner, Dear, and of course, Carly.

The shades were drawn in the kitchen as we walked into the house. A woman I assumed to be Zoey's mom sat slumped at the long kitchen table by the window. She barely looked up when we came in.

"Mom, Mom," Zoey said loudly, in an attempt to rouse her mother. "This is Ivy. She's new."

Mrs. Marks looked carefully at me before speaking so softly I could barely hear. "Nice to meet you, Ivy."

"How come you're home? I thought you were going to try and go to work today?" Zoey said.

"Maybe tomorrow." Mrs. Marks wore no makeup and her collarbones jutted out from a wrinkled white blouse.

"OK. Hope so. We're going to the basement to watch TV." I smiled at her mom, but she had already looked away, out the window.

"Come down and say hi if you feel like it, Mom." Zoey lightly touched her mom's shoulder. I noticed Zoey frown for a second before leading me downstairs.

Zoey's basement was humongous. On one side of the gigantic playroom was a home theater with stadium seating for six and what was obviously a retractable screen at the ceiling. On the other side of the room was a glassed-in professionally outfitted home gym. Next to the gym, an indoor half basketball court

"You must throw some crazy parties down here."

"We used to, but not lately." Zoey came toward me and we sat down next to each other on the sectional. "Truth is, Ivy, my family isn't doing so great. You obviously noticed that my mom is a bit out of it."

I leaned in toward Zoey and touched the top of her hand. It felt awkward but also the right move. Zoe continued talking softly. "My mom's really depressed. I don't know if anyone told you, but I had a brother who died this year. Nick was nineteen. He OD'd. I wanted to tell you myself before you heard it through the grapevine."

An image of Carly lying in the foyer flashed in front of my eyes. For a split second I imagined her dead instead of in the hospital. "Oh my God, Zoey. I'm so sorry."

"Thanks. It's still pretty raw. We were close growing up, but he had drifted in the past few years, once he got into drugs."

"I totally get it. Actually, my sister is in rehab now. Oxy."

"Ugh, sucks. Hope she makes it. Nick had just gotten out of rehab when he relapsed. It's really hard."

"Yeah." I looked down. I missed Carly, felt badly for her, and was also so incredibly angry with her. Why did she do this to herself and to our family? And then I felt sorry for her again. I knew she would rather have been home or back at college. Zoey and I looked at each other and then we both looked down, tear drops falling down both our cheeks.

"What hospital?" she asked.

"Some fancy place in Connecticut. Blue Hills." I felt oddly guilty that Carly was alive and Zoey's brother was dead.

"Oh yeah, I know it. Nick was there once." Zoey paused and took a deep breath. "My family hasn't been the same since he died. My other brother just plays video games all day long and runs ten miles a day. My dad doesn't talk and stares at the news all night. And my mom cries all the time. She hasn't gone back to work yet. She has a big job in Manhattan and I think it would give her an important purpose and help normalize our lives again. At least to a new normal."

"My mom tries to keep busy so she won't think about and worry about Carly all the time. I know she must be afraid, but she doesn't show it. We went to see Carly yesterday."

"How was that?"

"It went all right, I guess. Carly hadn't been abusing drugs for all that long. Or so she says. I don't know what to believe anymore. I didn't even realize how much she was getting high until she told us the truth the other day. She definitely wants help, so I'm hopeful."

"That's a good sign." Zoey squeezed my hand tighter. I squeezed her hand back.

"I guess there's a reason why we found each other," I whispered. "Tell me about Nick."

"Most people avoid mentioning him. It's like they're afraid I'll burst into tears. Maybe I would, but I'd rather they ask about him than pretend he never existed. So, thanks for asking." Zoey's eyes widened and she nearly laughed, probably from nerves. She giggled in between sentences but it was a kind laugh, a sweetness that oozed out, no matter what she was talking about.

"I know what you mean," I nodded. "Lately my old friends don't ask about Carly and they're mostly drifting away. Any new friends I make won't ever know her before this."

Zoey wiped a tear off her cheek and gave me a brave smile. "Nick was tough and loud, always trying to fit in and get people to like him. He loved to show off his singing and acting talent. He had a fantastic voice and he loved being the center of attention. Two years ago, he fell off a ladder and hurt his back and busted his knee. He started with Oxycontin and got hooked almost immediately. He continued using even after his injuries healed. He stole from our house and other people's medicine cabinets. Eventually, he started buying on the internet and through connections all over the area."

"That's terrible. Carly used oxy after she hurt her ankle. Someone told her it was better than Tylenol with codeine. She just told us that she couldn't stop taking it."

Zoey closed her eyes for a second and put her hands together in front of her heart. I thought I heard her whisper, "Please, God," but I couldn't be sure.

I bit my lip and picked at one of my cuticles. "You must really miss him," I said.

"I do. In Nick's memory, I started a drug prevention club at school. It's part of a national group called SOAN. It stands for Stop Opiate Abuse Now. Maybe you'll join?"

"Sure," I agreed, but I really wasn't certain I wanted to be a member. I didn't want to be known as the girl with the sister in rehab.

"You don't sound very convincing. No pressure. You don't have to join."

I swallowed hard. I was thinking maybe I could take a backseat role and not hurt Zoey's feelings.

"Maybe I can help with social media or something. I'm good at that."

"Anything would be great. We need to spread the word about how common oxy and heroin abuse and overdoses are, even in nice towns like Marble Springs."

I would do whatever Zoey asked. I wanted to be her friend. I liked how real and genuine she was, how openly and honestly she shared her story with me.

"I'm sure people know about your sister, don't you think? This is a small town."

"Probably. I try not to think about it."

"I understand." Zoey got up and pointed the remote at the TV. "OK, shall we try and move on? It's not going to be easy, I can tell you that."

Zoey flicked on the television and a large screen lit up on the far wall. She hit a DVR'd episode of *The Bachelor*. It seemed kind of ridiculous that we could switch so quickly from talking about drug overdoses and the death of her brother to *The Bachelor*, but actually the change was a relief.

I crossed my legs and tried to get comfortable. I felt large and bulky on the sectional sofa, but maybe it was just the experience of sharing with someone new that made me feel so exposed.

"What do your friends say about what happened?" I asked, staring at the TV.

"Some never mention him at all anymore, like it's taboo, but they always ask me, 'How are you doing?' That's their way of asking."

"Sounds awkward. Are they nice?" We weren't really watching TV.

"Most of them are really sweet. A few are bitchy and a little self-absorbed."

"Yeah, I know the type."

"I guess. I mean, I have friends in all groups. I like to mix it up. What about you?"

I picked up the remote and changed the station to CNN and paused, reading the headlines at the bottom of the screen. I cocked my head and pursed my lips, trying to exude a confidence I didn't really feel. "In my old school, I guess you could say I was a big fish, but in a very little pond."

"Marble Springs may not be as small as Preston, but it's still a pretty small pond. Did you have a boyfriend?"

"I did, but we broke up when I told him I was switching schools."

"That sucks. Did you like him?" Zoey bounced up and down in her seat. She had a lot of distracting energy. Watching her made me want to get up and move around too, but I sat still and tried not to fidget.

"He was OK. I don't miss him, though. How about you? Anyone special for you?"

"Nah, I haven't liked anyone enough. I would like to get a few guys onto SOAN though. We need a good mix."

"I can ask my cousin Ethan." I volunteered Ethan without thinking twice. He was a do-gooder and would help anyone who asked.

"That'd be great," Zoey said. "A few of my girlfriends joined SOAN just to be nice and supportive, but I get the sense that mostly they want to talk about who's using and who's in trouble, not to mention that membership looks good on college applications."

"Hmmm," was all I said. I didn't want to commit to something that identified me as someone who had this problem in my life. I wanted to change the subject altogether, so I got up and walked across the room. "Amazing gym," I said, eyes on the glass-enclosed professional set of machines and weights.

"Thanks. My mom used to be a gym fanatic. I don't think she's been down here since . . ." Zoey looked away from me and focused her eyes on the elliptical machine. Snapping out of her reverie, she asked, "Are you hungry?"

"No, but I can always eat." Even though it felt forced, I moved toward her gave her a big hug. Our boobs mushed together and we both pulled away and smiled. "So glad we met," I said.

"Me too. Glad you left Preston, even if you had to do it senior year."

We went upstairs to find snacks. Zoey's mother had relocated to a sofa in a cozy corner of the cozy kitchen. She was curled up in a fluffy yellow blanket with her eyes closed.

"She's on leave from her job," Zoey whispered to me. "She's the CEO of an advertising agency."

Her mom looked peaceful. "I can't even imagine what she went through," I said. I thought of my own mom, screaming her head off at Carly every time Carly came home wasted. "Do you want to die?" she'd yell, and Carly would wave her off and say, "Mom, I'm not going to die." But what did Carly know? It happened every day to normal people from good homes like ours where the family members loved each other.

"She's on a lot of medication, mostly antidepressants, but it doesn't seem to make a difference." Zoey began opening cabinets, pointing to cookies, chips, and candy. "We keep the cupboards stocked, but in this house we all starve out our sadness rather than eat our way through it."

"I can understand that," I said, but I really didn't. I had a bad habit of eating my way through my problems and stress. "What about your dad?" I filled my arms with the food she offered—a small container of cookies-and-cream ice cream, hot fudge, M&Ms, and some seltzer to wash it all down.

"He's zoned out too, but at least he goes to work." Zoey took a large hunk of white-and-purple-frosted birthday cake out of the freezer, unwrapped the cellophane, and zapped it in the microwave oven. Twenty seconds later, the icing dripped off the plate. It looked delicious. We both took as much junk food in our arms as possible and brought it all downstairs.

"What about your family?" she asked, once we were back in the basement. We dumped the food on an oval glass coffee table and sat on the sectional.

"Everyone has a story, I guess," I said tentatively.

Zoey slurped her ice cream and ate a huge piece of the cake. I cut myself a big piece of cake too. I loved a good food frenzy.

"And yours is?" she urged.

"I don't know where to begin," I said. "It's complicated and annoying."

"I have all afternoon," Zoey said, leaning back into the sofa, putting her feet up on the coffee table.

I usually tried to avoid talking about myself because people always had so many questions, but because Zoey had shared such personal information with me, I felt I owed her something.

"The short version is that my parents are divorced and my dad lives in Florida. He left when I was little. We don't hear from him very often."

Zoey made a face. "Sorry." She scooped cookies-and-cream ice cream onto the vanilla cake with white-and-purple icing. "My younger brother," she said, pointing to the writing on the cake. It said Happy Birthday Michael. "His birthday was last week, but he didn't want to celebrate. He won't talk about Nick, just keeps running and playing his sports."

"Oh God." Her story just got sadder and sadder.

"Sorry, I didn't mean to go back to all about me," she said. I loved people who didn't just talk about themselves. Zoey definitely was empathetic and not self-absorbed.

"It's fine. I'm done. My mom lost her big corporate job a few months ago because they were downsizing the company, and so we sold the big house and I switched schools. It's all fine."

"Well, it's not really all fine, is it? How's Dinner, Dear going? I told my dad that I met you and he wanted me to relay that he loves the Thai short ribs."

"Those are good. Their business model is popular, my mom tells me. People love the idea that they can get off the train, pick up a bag full of warm or at least room-temperature food, go home, and have a full meal with their family. She works with her sister, Ethan's mom. I think it's going to really take off."

"Me too. My family loves the lemon rosemary chicken and parsnip whip."

"Yup. It's my favorite. She's been making it my whole life." I gestured with my hand toward the glass-enclosed half basketball court. "Do you ever play?"

"No, I hate sports. My dad loves basketball. He used to host games on Sunday morning for his friends." She paused and stared at the hoop. "But not lately. Do you want to shoot some baskets?

"Are you kidding? I suck at sports. Literally, I'm a total klutz. I also can't draw, carry a tune, or play an instrument."

"I guess you get by on your good looks." Zoey laughed, and I noticed that her bright green eyes twinkled when she was happy. "Are you into acting at all? We do a one-act play in the fall and a musical in the spring. I can't carry a tune, so I usually try out for the fall play."

"Mmm, maybe." I didn't really like getting on stage in front of people, but at this moment, I felt like doing everything Zoey did.

After we demolished all the cake and ice cream, Zoey drove me home. When we pulled up to the curb in front of my house, I got out of the car. The warm September breeze prickled my neck and mosquitos buzzed near my ear. I looked up at the double-doored duplex house we were renting. It was a far cry from Zoey's impressive Victorian with all the authentic colors and trim, or even our old house, which was a big split-level. This two-family rental needed a paint job on the outside and new carpeting in the living room. But we had a river view from almost every room. That was what convinced Mom to take the place when she saw it for the first time.

"My mom says that everyone has baggage and there aren't any porters to carry it for you," I said.

"Yes, but mine is a steamer trunk and yours is more like a small overnight bag." Zoey gave me a wan smile and she shook her head sadly for a moment.

"Here's another one of my mom's favorite sayings," I said. "You don't know what goes on behind closed doors."

"In what way?" Zoey looked at me, perplexed.

"That means don't think everyone else is all super cool and happy just because they look that way on the outside. We're all a little bit confused, only some people are better at hiding their baggage than others."

"That's for sure." Zoey still had both hands on the steering wheel like she was going to take off any second. "Want me to pick you up and drive you to school tomorrow?"

"That'd be great."

"I'll be here at seven fifteen. Hey, let's take a selfie together and post it."

I came around to her side of the car and we posed, smiling silly into the camera. As she drove off, I stood outside the house for a few minutes, thinking about Carly and Nick, Zoey's brother. I felt so incredibly grateful that Carly was working hard in the hospital to get well.

When I went inside, I sent Carly an email.

Dear Carly, I hope you're doing OK and feeling stronger. It was great to see you and we will try and come again this weekend. Things are OK with me. Being the new girl isn't as bad as I thought, which is good. I'm crushing on a new guy. See you soon.

Chapter Seven—Around the Reservoir

On Saturday morning, my mom was dressed in yoga leggings and a Namaste logo T-shirt when she brought me lemon ricotta pancakes on a wooden tray with foldout legs.

"I love these pancakes," I gushed, sitting up straighter in bed and taking a big bite of the fluffy pancakes.

"I know." She hopped onto the bed and scooted me over. On the tray was also a mug of hot Earl Grey tea, a small pitcher of syrup, a cup of raspberries, and a glass of milk. I dug back into the pancakes.

"Mmmm, delicious, Mom. What time are we going to see Carly?"

"I think later in the afternoon. We can bring her some dinner. I have some cooking to do this morning and Bryce Houston's mom put in a big order for tomorrow. Have you seen him around at all?"

"Yeah, I saw him a few times in the halls."

"His mom is a little wacky but a great customer, and she's helping spread the word about Dinner, Dear. Did you have fun with Ethan and Zoey last night?"

"Yes. We went to the mall, had some pizza and saw a movie, then went back to Zoey's house. There was a party, but they didn't want to go." I had really wanted to go to the party. I was hoping that Bryce was going to be there, but I had to go along with Zoey and Ethan.

My mom picked up my fork and took a big bite of the pancakes. She smacked her lips together. "What are you up to today? I have yoga and then I'll start cooking with Allie."

"Guess I'll go for a run first, then do some homework before we go to the hospital. Do you want my help in the kitchen?"

"I think we're good. We did a lot of prep work yesterday." Mom smiled, but I could tell she wasn't feeling as cheery as she pretended. Her eyes looked tired and her skin, dry and flaky.

"Hey, you OK?" I asked.

"I'm fine, just trying to take care of business. At the hospital, we may meet with her counselor and talk about her care plan and future discharge."

"OK. I sent Carly an email, but she hasn't written back." I shoved the tray of food to the side and hopped off the bed. Mom lay back against all the fluffy throw pillows and snuggled with Kelly Green. I gave the dog a squoosh on the butt and then dressed quickly in black leggings and a bra and white T-shirt.

I looked away from her as I spoke, staring out the window, noticing some kids riding their bikes toward the river and seeing the puffy clouds float by. "Mom, do you think Carly will be able to get clean? It's really hard once you start using, isn't it?"

I turned back around and saw that Mom's body had stiffened and she'd closed her eyes. When she opened them, she looked into my eyes and didn't blink.

"Yes, I do. She has a lot of obstacles to overcome, but I have faith in her. She is determined to succeed."

"Zoey said her brother had just gotten out of rehab when he OD'd."

"I know, honey. Allie told me. Zoey's brother's death was a tragedy, one that never should have happened. I know this may sound naive, but Carly's different. She's gonna be OK. She has all of our love and support and the assistance of professionals. Let's focus on the positive. It's all we've got." She got up from the bed with Kelly Green in her arms, and came to me and hugged me with the dog between us.

I had always been in the shadow of Carly because she was older and the more outspoken and demanding of the two of us. With her gone, I was spending more time with my mom, and I liked it.

"OK, so text me when you want to leave for Connecticut. Maybe we can go to the mall afterward."

She sighed. "Maybe. We'll see how we feel."

I grabbed Kelly Green and headed over to the reservoir. The weather was 70, sunny, and breezy, so it was the perfect day to be outside. Young couples with baby carriages, teens on rollerblades, seniors in baggy sweatsuits, and a ton of runners in shorts and T-shirts were on the two-mile circular path around the artificial lake.

I was walking for about five minutes when suddenly I felt someone tapping on my shoulder. I whirled around. Standing there with a toothy smile was Bryce Houston.

"Hi. Cute dog." He bent down to pat her on the head. A jogger with ear buds nearly tripped on them.

"Oops, careful. Her name is Kelly Green," I said, moving to the side of the path.

"Kelly Green. Cute name, like the color, huh? And you're Ivy Green, like the vine? Creative parents."

"Well, they named me, and I named the dog. What are you doing here?"

"Just hanging. My house is over there, behind the trees."

His hair was oiled back and he was in jeans and flip-flops. A shiny gold chain peeked out from the neckline of his green polo shirt, which nicely matched his hazel eyes. The chain was a bit much, if you ask me. Very disco '80s. He was a bit too polished, not my usual type. My last boyfriend was more mismatched and edgy. But looking at Bryce, I couldn't help but smile at him. My stomach did flip-flops just being near him. He looked me right in the eyes and touched my upper arm for added emphasis. Bryce oozed warmth and sex appeal. He really, really seemed to want to talk to me, be with me.

Through the early-autumn canopy of green and yellow, I thought I saw the roofline of his house. I put my hands by my side and smiled so hard my cheeks hurt. We both rocked back and forth on our feet and stared at each other.

I pulled out a plastic sandwich baggie. "Want one? They're butterscotch chocolate-chip oatmeal cookies."

"Yum," he murmured, scooping up several broken chunks as well as the tiny crumbs. "Did you make these?"

"I melted the butter, does that count?"

Bryce held his hand in front of his lips as he chewed. "Yup. Mmmm. What are you doing out here?"

"Just taking a walk. And you?"

"My parents always have people over, so I left."

"Did you eat the food from the Thanksgiving dinner? My mom makes the best stuffing, right?"

"Yeah, it was good. Can I join you?"

"Sure." Inside, my mind raced ahead and my stomach bounced up and down. It was like there was a beam of light connecting us. He was drawn to me and I was pulled toward him.

"It's a big loop. I come here when I want a break," he confessed, as we began walking.

"Is that often?" I felt the pitch in my voice rise and I was talking extra fast. I did that when I was around new people or excited.

"Naw, but lately, my mom's had a lot of company and Jonathan is home and he always creates chaos."

We walked slowly around the lake, allowing people to pass us. The path was damp and my sneakers slid in places on the dirt. When I breathed in, the clear air felt crisp in my nose.

"Gorgeous day out," I said nervously.

"Really? Weather chat?"

"Well, literally, it is a gorgeous day, right Kelly Green?" I spoke in my silly, high-pitched dog voice, embarrassed but also so thrilled to be with Bryce that I didn't care if I sounded like an idiot.

"I remember meeting you years ago," he said, and winked at me. "You showed up at my bar-mitzvah party with Jordan Kurtz, am I right? I thought you were adorable then. Now you're just plain hot."

My cheeks turned red and my legs wobbled. He was flirting for real. "I don't believe you. You ignored me," I said, trying to act cool.

"I did? What a mistake. How about a second chance?" Bryce's dimples deepened and a lock of shiny hair fell in front of his eye. He pushed it aside with another brilliant smile.

I loosened the leash and Kelly trailed off into the brush. Bryce and I grinned stupidly at each other. He leaned in and for a second, I thought he was going to kiss me. It was too soon. Thankfully, he looked away and we began a second loop around the reservoir.

"What's the real reason you left your house?" I asked.

"I came out to get high."

I tensed. "Literally?" I said in a squeaky voice and cocked my head to one side, squinting into the sun.

"I take it you don't smoke?" Bryce had both hands in his pockets and walked on with a little sway.

"I don't care that you do," I said, not sure that's how I felt. I pretended to examine something on Kelly Green's ear. I don't judge others, but I wanted to keep drugs out of my life for now. With Carly in rehab, it didn't seem right to do drugs or have them around. But it was only weed, I rationalized. What's a little pot on a Saturday morning at . . . I looked at my phone. It was only ten thirty in the morning.

"It relaxes me, actually." He puffed out his pockets with his hands. I could see he was holding something on the right side. Then, he leaned in toward my face and smiled harder. My heart fluttered.

We kept walking and then stopped in the middle of the path and allowed some runners to pass. Bryce took my hands in his. They were soft. We both went quiet and stared at each other. I felt self-conscious, but I was unable to look away. My stomach did that weird topsy-turvy thing again. My mouth felt dry and I panicked for a second. Did I have bad breath? I hadn't showered or used deodorant that morning. I hoped I didn't smell bad.

Bryce kissed me. His lips were lush and smooth, like satin. I inhaled and noticed that Bryce smelled delicious, like pine trees after the rain, strong and clean. First he kissed gently. I kissed him softly back, but then he got more insistent. I felt his tongue tentatively push through my lips and whirl around mine. At that moment, Kelly Green yanked on the leash and I stepped back, putting some distance between us. The whole intimate exchange lasted barely thirty seconds but it was intense and a little scary fast. Slick, that's what Ethan called him.

"Kelly, Kelly," I called out anxiously.

"She's one heck of a guard dog." Bryce moved in close again and gave me a peck on the lips. I kissed back. The back of my neck felt warm and my toes tingled. I could have kissed him a lot longer, but there was something about his insistence that made me uncomfortable.

We walked and talked along the dirt path. He told me about his teen tour to Costa Rica last summer and I told him about my dad in Florida.

"Love Boca," he said. "Both sets of grandparents live there. We go twice a year and my mother says she hates every minute, but secretly I think she's always looking around, wondering where she's going to live when she's old. Hey, do you mind if I light up?"

My body stiffened. Carly used to always ask that, "Mind if I smoke? Mind if I light up? Have a light?" Not everyone went from smoking to abusing, I knew that, but the smell of marijuana made me feel stressed, which is ironic since it's supposed to make you chill.

I said I didn't mind, and really it was fine, but I wondered why he needed or wanted to get high when he was with me. He took a few puffs off of a compact vaporizer. We sat down by a stream that led from the lake to the woods, and we finished the butterscotch cookies. He held my hand. His palm was smooth like a baby's. It felt like we had known each other for a long time.

"So, how has it been so far at Marble Springs? It can't be easy being new as a senior."

"It's OK. Ethan's been a huge help. He's introduced me to a few people and Zoey's great too. I met all her friends."

"And you met Phoebe Li. She's part of that crowd."

"More like the head of it, as far as I can tell." I noticed how firm his biceps looked, popping against the fabric of his shirt. I felt the urge to put my finger to one of his muscles, but I resisted. Too much, too fast, I thought, even though it felt natural to be together.

"People are jealous of her. If you really knew Phoebe, you would love her," he gushed. "We do math together every week. You should join us."

I had to laugh at that and allowed a little giggle to escape my throat. "Really? I always need help with math." I gulped and then decided to go for it and ask the question I had been wondering since I first saw them together in the hallway. "Did you two ever date?"

"Are you kidding? No way. One, she'd never look twice at me, and two, she'd never look twice at me."

"Oh." I smiled at him. I didn't know what to say that wouldn't be an insult. Of course Phoebe wouldn't date Bryce. He's adorable but hardly the same look as the six-foot-three quarterback she's currently hooking up with.

"I know what you're thinking. It's OK. I'm just too short for her. I'm only five foot ten." We both laughed.

"I thought five ten was on the tall side." I said.

"It's pretty average. But honestly, Phoebe and I are just really good friends."

Kelly Green scampered by our feet, occasionally sticking her nose and paws in the water and then quickly jumping back.

"You're so beautiful," he said, touching my hair.

Adrenaline raced through my veins and I forgot all about his weed and the rest of the world.

"Want to go out? Maybe for dinner?" he asked.

"You mean a real date?" I couldn't wait to be with him again.

"Yeah, a real date. I'll even feed you. I need to scoop you up before the rest of the boys at Marble Springs discover you."

I could only nod my head up and down. His charm intoxicated me. The only problem was a little nagging fear in the back of my mind that he was a little too fast, a little too shady about the weed, and a little too ostentatious. I stared at the chain. I pushed my hesitancy aside and looked at him, inhaling that fresh pine cologne again. I felt fluttering inside my chest and I was aware of an alertness in my demeanor that I could only attribute to excitement and allure. The chemistry between us was like an electric current.

"See ya, Ivy Green, Kelly Green."

"See ya, Bryce Houston."

• • ✿ • •

WHEN I ARRIVED HOME, my mom and Allie were sitting at the dining room table, reams of paper and piles of magazines strewn around the coffee table. They were drinking tea and going over menus. "We'll go to the hospital in about an hour," my mom said. I must have made a face because she immediately finished with, "You don't have to come with me, Ivy. It's OK if you don't go this time."

"Nah, I'll go. Of course I'll go." I felt my face slacken. I actually didn't want to go. The whole afternoon would be shot. All this attention on Carly was taking a toll on my homework and time I spent doing pretty much nothing. "Maybe the mall?" I suggested again.

"Maybe. Let's see how she's doing. Who knows how we'll feel when we leave."

"Maybe is your favorite word, Mom." I slunk up the stairs and didn't wait for a response.

My lips felt swollen from all the kissing and I ran my tongue over them. I went to my room and immediately FaceTimed with Ethan.

"Hey," Ethan said. He was crossed-legged on his bed with a bowl of ice cream on his lap.

"That looks amazing." I said.

"It absolutely is." He gulped down a spoonful.

"Your mom's here." I fiddled with the strings on my sweatshirt and tried to get comfortable on my own bed. "We're going to see Carly in a bit."

"Yeah, I know. How is she?"

"I guess she's OK. I'll let you know later. I wanted to tell you something. I just spent the morning at the reservoir with Bryce Houston."

"You're kidding, right? He's gross, Ivy." Ethan peered at me through the screen, his brow furrowed, his mouth all scrunched up.

"Why would you say that?" My heart sank but my brain tuned in. One side of me was mad that he was slamming Bryce and the other part of me wanted to hear more because it justified that teeny-weeny voice in my head that said to watch out.

"Cuz it's true. Supposedly, he gets around and does a lot of drugs."

"Supposedly. And supposedly, I think he really likes me."

"That may be so, but watch out. He can't be trusted."

"Maybe you're just jealous." Bryce's description of Phoebe came to mind.

"Really? You want to go there?"

"No, I'm sorry. That wasn't fair. You're just pissing me off. I tell you I like someone and you tell me he's no good."

"Well, I'm trying to help you out. Literally, I think he supplies weed to half the football team and most of the cheerleaders. That's the last thing you need." His fists were balled up beside him and his face was beet red.

Before I could temper my emotion, I raised my voice. "Literally? Really, Ethan? I don't think so. He may smoke weed once in a while, but he's a nice guy. I think I would know." Obviously, I would know nothing at this point, but I stood up for Bryce anyway.

"I wouldn't be so sure of yourself. You had no idea what Carly was up to until it was nearly too late."

"That is mean, Ethan. We have done everything possible for Carly and this is not about her. I'm sorry I told you anything at all." Tears welled up and I got off the bed and walked away from the screen.

"Don't shut me out. I don't want to fight with you. If I don't tell you the truth, who will? I just don't think he's such a smart choice for a boyfriend. He could be trouble and you certainly don't need that in your first week at a new school."

"I think you may be overreacting, that's all." I stayed in my corner of the room, away from the computer.

"I don't think so," he said. "I'm sorry I got you upset. Talk to you later." The computer hummed and I could tell the screen went dark.

Ethan and I fought and made up over and over in our lives. We'd get over this one too, but I was mad that he was so judgmental about Bryce and scared that there may be a glimmer of truth in what he was saying.

Chapter Eight—Blue Hills

We took the back roads to Blue Hills, passing horse farms and cow pastures as we drove.

"We're almost there," my mom announced cheerily. "I expect a lot more people today since it's a weekend. Don't be scared if you see some of the patients looking a little out of sorts. Many of the residents are battling multiple mental illnesses."

"Mom, I get it."

"I know but, while this place looks like a country club on the outside, it's not. I did my research. This is one of the best adult drug rehab and psychiatric hospitals in the country."

"Thanks. I got an email from Carly. She's really excited that we're coming."

"I am too, honey, but I have to be realistic. Carly has a long way to go."

"Aren't you supposed to say, 'one day at a time?'" I quoted one of the hospital pamphlets I had picked up the first time we were here.

"I don't know what I'm supposed to say." She sighed, or more like guffawed, and continued to stare straight ahead. Her hair was unkept and she didn't have on her signature lip gloss. It didn't look like she was getting a lot of sleep, and I guess I couldn't blame her.

We parked in the lot directly next to Carly's cottage and headed inside, stopping at the desk with a sign that read, "Visitors please register upon arrival."

A young girl in workout clothes greeted us. "Hello, may I help you?"

"Hi. We're here to visit my daughter, Carly Green."

"Yup, Carly, she's cool," the girl said, tilting her chin toward the right. "She's over there."

"Thanks." My mom waved to Carly. I waved too and Carly stood up and smiled, motioning that we come toward her. She looked calm and rested in yoga pants and a long white cotton workout shirt. The ache of missing her stabbed at my heart. I wanted to bolt over, but I shuffled behind the lady who walked slowly toward Carly. As we got closer, my mom walked faster and took Carly in her arms.

"Carly, my baby." She hugged her for a long time, like she was never going to let her go.

I stood next to them for a few seconds, staring at my feet.

Carly, tears in her eyes, gently pulled away. She looked at me and forced a smile. "Hey, is that my sweater?" I was wearing her beige Irish knit crew neck and her tight jeans again.

"You snooze, you lose." I hugged her and for a moment felt how Mom must feel. I didn't want to let go. I wanted to take her home with me, just like this, hugging our way to the car, not losing contact. I could feel the bones in her back and it made me squeeze even tighter, like I could hold the pieces of her in place. If we stayed connected, we'd both be able to keep ourselves together, like Humpty Dumpty.

She patted the sofa next to her and we all sat down. "You remember Joanie, my counselor."

"We're all very encouraged by Carly's dedication." Joanie, who was sitting next to her, squeezed Carly's upper arm.

"That's great, honey." Mom smoothed some hair off of Carly's forehead and touched her cheek. "How are you feeling?"

"I'm good, hardly any withdrawal symptoms."

"Carly has told us so much about what a terrific support team you are for her," Joanie said. "She is going to need all of your help when she returns home and reintegrates into the community. I understand you've recently moved to a different house."

We nodded. Carly talked about the program, the group therapies, and her cottage mates. I thought she looked one hundred times better than she did when she was admitted. Over the summer she had lost a ton of weight. Now I understood that she had been taking drugs that diminished her appetite.

One night last year when we were waiting for Carly to come home and my mom was particularly distraught, I said to my mom, "We have to leave it to the universe."

"Ivy." My mom scoffed and made a mad face at me at the time. "The universe has nothing to do with Carly's reckless behavior. Carly needs to be more responsible."

"What I meant, Mom," I tried to explain, "is that we can only do what we can do."

"I'm her mother. I can do more," she said to me, that night and many nights over the summer.

"Your room is ready for you at home," I told her. "You'll like it."

"Thanks." Carly looked more like her usual energetic self. Her eyes were bright. Her skin was pink and clear. "I feel like I never even moved in. How's that guy you emailed me about?"

Bryce's twinkling, winking eyes and his charismatic smile flashed in front of my mind's eye. An image of the vape appeared in my head. This was not going to be easy, I reminded myself, looking around the rehab center. I shook my head. "We just met."

"I know, but you seemed into him in your email. Heavy crushing." Carly's knees bounced up and down. She looked back and forth from me to my mom.

"Let's focus on your progress, shall we?" my mom said with a wink. "Don't worry, Ivy, I'll be asking plenty of questions on the ride home.'

"It's not always about me," Carly laughed. "For once I want to talk about Ivy."

"Really?" I said.

"It's nice to see you and your family laughing," Joanie, the counselor leaned in toward Carly. "We think that Carly should be ready to go home soon."

"Great," I said too loudly. "When?"

"Ivy, shhh." My mother used her arm to push me back in my seat. "Carly will return home when she's ready. No one's rushing her."

"I'm not rushing her," I said. "I'm not, Carly. I just want you to figure all this out and come home when you're ready."

"Of course," Joanie said. "We're already working on the best therapeutic discharge plan for her. Carly will talk with me and her psychiatrist and we will re-evaluate at the end of the week. There are lots of options to maximize success. For now, I'll say goodbye and let you three visit alone."

I had to admire Joanie's tact. No subtleties. After she left, we sat together for another five minutes and then we walked outside.

"Have you heard from Dad? He said he was going to try and come see me." Carly looked away when she spoke about our dad. She was very tight with him, unlike me.

"I don't speak to him," Mom replied, lips pursed, eyes averted. "Have you heard from him?"

"Yes. He said he'd try to come up around Thanksgiving,"

Mom picked up her pace and clutched her fists. "I know you enjoy seeing him, honey." I was sweating. I wished I had worn shorts and a tank top. I saw someone jogging on other side of the property. This place was so weird—part dry-out, part asylum, part spa. I corrected myself. I knew that despite its rarefied looks, Blue Hills was not a spa or a country club. It was a locked hospital. I felt ashamed that I had even forgotten for a moment why Carly was really here.

"And I know you like to pretend he doesn't exist, Mom. My therapists say I need all the family support and collaboration possible. I emailed with my advisor at school. If I go back next week, I'll be able to catch up. Any longer and I'll have to take off a semester."

"Carly." My mother bit her lip again and stopped on the path. Tears glistened in the corners of her eyes. Her mouth went tight. We both looked at Carly. What did she want us to say? What wouldn't ignite an argument?

"What does your therapist think? Next week seems a little quick to rush back to college, especially one where there are a lot of temptations."

"Mom!" Carly raised her voice but wasn't quite yelling, yet. "There are drugs everywhere. I'll be fine. I am fine."

My mom enunciated every word. "We need to work together with your team here. Let's take this one day at a time. God forbid you relapse."

"Mom." Carly's voice was tense and I could tell she was trying not to yell. I glanced around to see if anyone was looking at us. There were lots of clusters of family groups, but no one was paying attention to us. I assumed everyone was living out their own family drama. "That's insulting. I'm here to get clean and stay clean. I not gonna relapse." She stood with her hands on her hips, eyes blazing.

I motioned us toward a bench underneath an oak tree. In the distance, I could see the glassed-in building that was the gym. Squinting, I could make out some people moving on the equipment.

"Hey, is that the gym over there?"

"Don't try to change the subject," my mom snapped. "We need to work with the hospital and Vassar and set up a program for recovery."

"I am recovered, Mom. I am never going to do drugs again. There are people in my group with friends and relatives all who OD'd on heroin and oxy and I am not going to be one of them, I promise."

She can't promise a damn thing, I thought as we continued walking. I wanted to be with Carly, but I didn't want to deal with her when she was angry and defensive. I wanted the sister of my childhood. The girl with the Barbie dolls and teddy bears, hanging out in my bed watching animal shows.

"I have a friend whose brother OD'd last year," I volunteered. I wasn't sure it was an appropriate comment or the right time, but I've wanted to tell Carly that since I met Zoey.

"Who?" She whirled around and looked at me. "From home?"

"Yeah, his name was Nick Marks."

Her face crinkled up. She put her hands in front of her eyes and she began to cry. "I knew him." I put my arm around her shoulders and my mom did the same. Carly cried hard. She blubbered. She blew her nose.

"We used to meet up by the riverfront and party. He was a nice guy. Thankfully, I'm still here. One of the rehabilitation opportunities they talk about here is to speak to other kids in crisis about rehab. I may do that when I'm home. You know, high schools and afterschool clubs."

"That would be awesome. There's a group at school called SOAN, Stop Opiate Abuse Now. They're trying to organize a speaker. Maybe you can help," I said.

"I would love it." Carly wiped her eyes and nose in the tissue my mom offered. "Seriously Mom, the usual stay here is forty-eight hours to a week. I want to get out of here and reclaim my life."

"OK, honey. I only want your complete and full successful recovery." Another patient waved to us as he and his parents walked by. Carly enthusiastically waved back.

"That's Oliver, isn't he cute? We've been hanging out a lot, watching TV and stuff."

"I thought you're not allowed to fraternize when you're in program," I said.

"Yeah, that's part of the AA program, but we're just friends." Carly was still waving at Oliver and smiling broadly. "For now, anyway."

"Glad to hear that." My mother looked at her watch. "I think it's time we head back. Carly, you look healthy, and more importantly, you seem like you're on the right track."

"Thanks, Mom." She punched my shoulder playfully. "I miss you, Ivy. And stop wearing all my clothes. You'll ruin them." Carly was laughing but I got scared. It's uncanny how she always knew what I was doing. I smiled back at her.

On the way home, my mom and I stopped at our favorite Mexican restaurant in town. The comfort of a spicy chicken-and-guacamole burrito with lots of shredded cheese on top helped distract us from thoughts of leaving Carly behind a locked gate. She said she was committed to a sober life. I hoped she meant it.

I avoided the topic of Bryce throughout dinner, but as we waited for the waitress to process the credit card, I felt I had to say something.

"Mom," I tentatively began, my voice catching in my throat. "I really like Bryce so far, even though we've only been together once, but there's something I need to share with you about him."

I thought I saw her hands grip the edge of the table. "What is it, honey?"

"Ethan thinks he does drugs, maybe even gets them for his friends."

"Oy," my mom said. The waitress delivered the credit card receipt and Mom signed. We both stood up for a second, but then my mom sat down again and so did I.

"What makes him say this?" she asked.

"I don't know, rumors I guess. He felt he had to tell me what he heard. What people say about Bryce," I said. We looked into each other's eyes.

"That would be a problem," she said. "Especially for Bryce, but you'd want to think twice about dating him if this is the case."

"You're being awfully calm about this, Mom," I said. I stood up again. I wanted to get out of here. I felt like the air was suddenly too hot. I needed air. "We've only just started to talk and see each other, but I think he's interested in me, and I like him too. I just wouldn't want to do anything that would jeopardize Carly's recovery."

"Of course not. And I don't want you to jeopardize your social life, especially in a new school. You have your own challenges, Ivy. I know that. It's not easy being the new girl in your senior year. And I'm sorry you have to deal with all of this . . ." Mom's voice drifted off.

We began to walk toward the car. "Mom, don't say you're sorry. I understand why we had to move and it's fine, really." I didn't know if it was fine yet, but it definitely wasn't as bad as I thought it would be.

"Why don't you see how things progress with Bryce and assess as you go along. How about that for a plan?" Mom said, unlocking the car doors with the fob.

We drove home listening to music, and we didn't mention Bryce again. When I got into bed, I sent Carly a good night text.

Keep up the good work. I miss you, but want you to get strong. xoxox

Right before I shut out the lights, my phone buzzed. It was Bryce on FaceTime.

"Hey." He was in his bed, wearing athletic shorts and a bright-yellow T-shirt.

"Hey." I wore my old beat-up tank top, and I wasn't wearing a bra. Not a good look. I yanked the blanket up to my chin. I picked at my cuticles. My toes wiggled under the blanket. I hoped he couldn't tell how nervous I was.

"Just wanted to say goodnight. It was great hanging with you today," he said. "Thanks for the delicious cookies. I could've eaten another twenty."

"Me too. I'll bring you more next time."

"Deal." He was smiling and his eyes sparkled. I noticed his hands sat quietly in his lap, unlike mine.

We didn't talk long, but when I woke up the next day, the first voice I heard coming through my phone was Bryce's. "Good morning, Ivy Green."

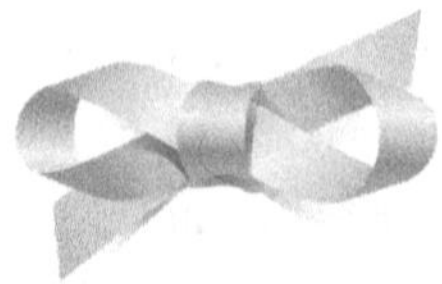

Chapter Nine—Phoebe

At the end of the next day in school, I was looking around the halls for someone familiar. I was hoping to catch up with Zoey or Ethan, but I didn't see them. I had bumped into Bryce in the hall after math class and he walked me to English. I gave up and headed out the door, figuring I'd take the bus or walk.

"Hey."

I turned and looked but only saw a swell of people heading out the door behind me.

"Over here, it's me, Phoebe." I turned back around. In front of me, down a few steps toward the front of the school, Phoebe Li was waving, her red fingertips gently fluttering back and forth toward me. I ran down the stairs.

"Hey." I tried to sound nonchalant like her. Why was she alone? Where were her friends? Where was her boyfriend? I wondered.

"Need a ride?" she asked, smiling broadly, white perfect teeth gleaming. "Or is Bryce driving you home?"

"Huh?" I muttered. It sounded so strange to hear his name spoken aloud and so out of context. "Uh, no," I recovered. "Why would he be driving me home?" I prompted.

"Duh, I don't know, cuz he likes you? Cuz you like him? I can tell." Phoebe held her head high when she spoke. She walked fast and grabbed my elbow, pushing me out the door.

I agreed and for a moment, stared at her. Phoebe was nearly perfect, really and truly. Small frame but tall enough to exhibit stature. If I was five foot four, she had to be five six, with long legs and graceful arms.

I compared my flabby middle to her narrow waist, obvious in a tight tank top and shorty shorts on this warm September day.

"My car is over here." Phoebe's friendly, lilting voice interrupted the cautionary voice in my head. We got into her little white Audi convertible and she quickly drove out of the parking lot.

"Don't you have dance practice or something?" I asked her while we drove. She didn't initially ask me where I lived or where I was going.

"No practice today."

"Cool. Ugh, you can drop me at the Presbyterian church, if you don't mind. I'm going to help my mom."

"Oh right, the food thing. Cool. But, would you mind if I stop at the supermarket before I drop you off? I want to pick up a few things."

"Not at all," I agreed. "In fact, I'll text my mom and see if she needs anything." Phoebe drove to the fancy gourmet market in the center of town, not the giant supermarket I had in mind. She took a number and we waited our turn.

"What do you want? I know your mom makes amazing food, but here, we can pick and choose a little of this and that. I love the lobster salad and the fried chicken. Don't tell anyone though. I'd be crucified if anyone knew I ate fried chicken."

I hung back, noting all the cookies, cakes, and pies on the other side of the cash register. This store was obviously my mom's competition, offering so much more in one place. I bet my mom could easily make all of these foods and do a better job too. I tried to memorize some of the more appetizing items like the BLT on a croissant or the honey-infused baked chicken. It all looked amazing.

"Want anything?" she asked. "I'm just picking up a few snacks." She grabbed a big bag of the sea-salt milk-chocolate caramels and my mouth watered. She also ordered a container of lobster salad, two big fried chicken thighs, and some shrimp.

"Cookies?" she asked me. I nodded and she ordered two each of glazed butter cookies, chocolate-chip peanut-butter cookies, and cream-cheese chocolate brownies.

"Let's go," she said. I couldn't believe how easily she signed the receipt for $125, like it was a dollar. That kind of money was nearly my family's entire grocery bill for the week, maybe two weeks these days. The store was so fancy and the customers all looked dressed up in boots and cool handbags. No wonder Dinner, Dear was taking off so quickly; not everyone could afford this kind of food.

"Do you have time to sit in the park and eat it with me? I hate to dine alone," she mimicked.

I nodded and looked at my watch. It was just past three. My mom was expecting me, but I didn't want to say no to Phoebe. I was thrilled she wanted to hang out with me.

"I get so hungry after school," she said in the car. "My mom would go ballistic if she saw me eat all this, but I don't care, it's soooo good."

"My mom makes amazing brownies too," I said, as we headed toward the park that faced the river. "And her balsamic glazed chicken is to die for."

"I'll bet. We've ordered from Dinner, Dear a few times. We love it. My mom is wild about no sugar, no oil, no salt, so you can imagine how dull our food is. She orders it online from some disgusting healthy company in Vermont."

When we got to the parking lot, we got out and walked toward the picnic tables facing the river. Phoebe's little shorts were riding up her tiny little butt. I thought I looked OK when I got dressed in the morning, tugging Carly's shorts up my waist. I felt the button dig into my bellybutton. Hanging around Phoebe made me even more self-conscious about my body than I already was. She talked a lot about food and weight. As if reading my mind, she complimented me.

"You probably don't have to worry about your weight at all. You look great in those jeans."

"Thanks. They're my sister's, actually. Since she went to school," I lied, "I've been wearing all of the clothes she left home." I couldn't look Phoebe in the eye as I spoke, knowing full well that Carly would have a fit if she knew I was lying about her and that I had borrowed liberally from her closet. But honestly, wearing her things made me feel close to her. The worn-in softness of the fabric and whiffs of her perfume were so familiar. In some weird way, I felt like I was with her.

Phoebe spread out all the food on the small area of wooden planks between us. The wood was rough under my thighs and I squirmed on the bench, hoping I wouldn't get a splinter. "Well, it looks great on you," Phoebe said. "I gotta tell you, our friend Bryce really likes you."

"Really? What makes you say that?"

"Dig in. Help me with this. I can't bring it home and it's too good not to eat." Phoebe handed me a plastic fork from the bag. I checked my phone for the time. I needed to go soon.

"Bryce and I are good friends," she said. "I've known him forever. Our moms are on all the same charity committees. He's a great guy, kinda geeky in a cool, chic way, if you know what I mean."

"Kinda," I said, "but what's his deal? I can't figure out who he hangs with in school. He's not an athlete and he's not a nerd and he's not a druggie."

"Whoa, well, he's not a druggie, but . . ." Phoebe plowed the lobster salad into her mouth. She had only ordered sample sizes of everything, but there was a lot and she was eating quickly. She shoved a forkful of a fried tempera shrimp into her mouth and held out the fork for me to take a bite.

"But what?" I asked, trying not to talk with my mouth full. My mind wandered away from Phoebe for a second and I thought about Carly, out there in rehab instead of college. Was she going to blow a whole semester? I didn't know. I wanted to visit her again. I wanted to reassure her that I was here for her, that I could help her.

"No buts. You know, we all party and sometimes Bryce is the one who can score. At least for me, anyway. Don't tell him I told you that. I mean, we all just party for fun, nothing serious. Bryce is really a good guy. You should go out with him."

"Really? How do you even know he wants to go out with me? He just met me."

"Of course, he told me," Phoebe said with a giggle. She kept eating. People in the park walked by and kids zoomed past us on scooters. It was getting closer to dinner time. I really needed to get to my mom, but I wanted to ask Phoebe more questions.

"What did he say? By the way, this lobster salad is yummy." There were only about three bites left in each container. We moved on to the cookies.

"I know, I love bingeing on Gourmet Garage food. The cheerleaders get boring chopped salad with chicken every Thursday night. It's ridiculously predictable."

"Not to be a pest or anything, but really, what did Bryce say about me?" I pushed because I was feeling nervous and excited about the idea of Bryce. I was a person who liked having a boyfriend, someone to call or text me all the time and someone to walk the halls with during the day and go to games with on the weekend.

I wondered what Phoebe meant exactly about the drug use. I hadn't really thought about what it would mean to do drugs with friends while my sister was in rehab. I imagined Googling, "Is it OK to date a drug user when your sister abuses narcotics?" Uh, probably not.

Phoebe's shiny hair swung back and forth by her neck as she rolled up the garbage. We had nearly finished all the food. Only a half a brownie and a glazed cookie were left. Before I could stop her, she hurled them into the river, practically whacking a duck on the head.

"Why are you doing that? I would have taken it home," I said.

"If I don't toss it all right away, I'm afraid I'll continue eating and we've both had more than enough, right? We can always get more tomorrow." She let out a nervous laugh.

"Yeah, that's true," I mumbled. She may go to Gourmet Garage on a regular basis, but I didn't. Anyway, I'd just ask my mom to add sea-salt milk-chocolate caramels and chocolate-chip peanut butter cookies. I was lucky, I had a built-in Gourmet Garage at home.

"So, do you think Bryce is hot? He told me he thought you were super hot."

"Really? No way. What else did he say?"

"Nothing really. His old girlfriend dumped him at the beginning of the summer before she went on teen tour, so he's been looking for his next conquest. You definitely fit the bill, new girl and all. Would you go out with him?"

"Probably," I said, trying to sound nonchalant. "I like his gelled hair, but the gold chain is a bit much, don't you think?"

"Yeah, I can't get him to take it off. I told him it was way too '70s, but he doesn't care. Wait till you see his bath-product collection. He's really a girl when it comes to beauty supplies. Can I tell him you'd go out with him? He's gonna ask when I tell him we hung out today."

"Sure." I forced myself to look at Phoebe and not bat an eye. "I gotta be honest, I'm not so into weed, but I really like him a lot already."

"You have good taste. Bryce is so fun and so sweet to his girlfriends. I wish Wes was half as nice to me as Bryce."

I looked at her again. Her beautiful face suddenly seemed flat, drooped. Her dark eyes cast down and I noticed she frowned for a moment, but just one second later, she looked up again and brightened. "Bryce is awesome."

We walked to the car. I stood still by the passenger side door. "How come you two don't date, then?"

"I could never date Bryce, are you kidding? We're just friends. I didn't mean to sound negative about Wes. He's great, really great. We're in love."

I didn't believe a word she was saying. Just like all this binge eating had some undertone of desperation to it as well. Phoebe was clearly one of those popular, pretty girls who had to show a positive, perfect image all the time. And I guess I was trying to do the same with her.

I couldn't decide if I liked Phoebe as a person or not. I definitely was going to do my best to be her friend though. She was too popular to diss, but I didn't feel completely comfortable being my true self around her. I was always second-guessing myself, questioning whether or not I was saying or doing something right or wrong. It was nerve-racking to always wonder what she thought of me, but maybe we just didn't know each other well enough yet. With Zoey, the closeness was immediate. We just got each other right away, but with Phoebe, I felt uneasy.

Phoebe drove me to the church and I got out of the car, anxious to run inside and help my mom.

"See you later," I said.

"One sec." She popped her window down and looked at me expectantly. "Are you free next Friday night?"

"I think so," I said. Maybe she was going to invite me out with her and her friends.

"Oh great, that would be awesome." She started tapping on her phone.

"What'd you have in mind?" I tried not to sound too needy. It would great to fit in with the popular crowd at Marble Spring. I couldn't deny it; I did like being popular.

"Oh, well, actually, hold on, I'm texting my friend that you're free." I wondered which friend she was talking about. Most of the popular girls seemed like fun, from the little I had spoken to them at school. One or two might be a little airheaded, but I could deal with that.

"So, you remember my friend Annie, the one in our drama class?"

I nodded and Phoebe kept talking, hardly taking a breath in between sentences. "Well, we're all going to see Taylor Swift in a couple of weeks and she needs someone to babysit her little sister so she can go with us. Do you think you could do it?"

I felt like she just punched me in the gut. How could I have been so stupid and thoughtless. I'm not her friend. I'm just the new girl who might be able to babysit.

"Oh wow, Taylor Swift. I love her." I thought that might be hint enough.

"Us too. We've seen her every year. Sorry, I wish I had an extra ticket."

"Me too." My heart sank.

"Well, let me know. We're desperate."

Not my problem, I thought. Maybe Carly would be around then and we could try and get cheap tickets, or even Zoey, unless she was already going with Phoebe's group. I forced a fake smile for Phoebe. "Sure. See you later."

"Bye. Thanks for joining me," Phoebe said, waving as she took off down the street. She had no idea she had just insulted me.

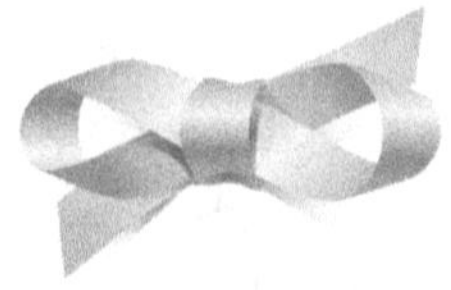

Chapter Ten—Date Night

On our first real date, Bryce wore a blue button-down and dark jeans with loafers, no socks. His hair was once again glistening with gel.

I had agonized over my outfit, consulting with Ethan on FaceTime. Eventually I settled on my typical uniform of jeans and a red silky top from Carly's closet.

"Wear heels," Ethan encouraged from his own bedroom to mine via computer.

"They are so uncomfortable," I moaned.

"That's the point, girlfriend," he said, laughing. "You'll look and feel sexier in heels and you know it." He was right, and I ended up grabbing a pair of Carly's black low-heeled booties.

My mom was wary when I told her I was going out with Bryce.

"I thought you liked his family, Mom," I said, confused because she made such a big deal about Flora Houston being so important to her business.

"I do, it's just . . . I don't know. I hear he's very . . . I don't know, in my day we'd say he was fast."

"What does that mean, exactly?" I asked. She never really answered, because Bryce arrived. He said hello and shook her hand when she opened the door. My mom was overly polite and friendly. I wondered what her misgivings were, but I didn't dwell on them. When I saw his face lit up with a smile and twinkling eyes, I melted inside.

He immediately leaned in and kissed me hello. "Bye Mom," I called back. Bryce took my hand and walked me to his car. He opened the passenger side door of a deep-blue Porsche.

"Really?" I smirked.

He winked and I was hooked. Once we were seated, he reached into the middle console and yanked out a leopard-print hair holder and offered it to me.

I pulled my hair into a ponytail as he revved up the car. "It's my Dad's," he said.

"The car or the scrunchie?"

"Cute," he laughed, his dimples deepening again. The car was excessively clean and smelled like astringent. Bryce's flashy demeanor was his least appealing feature, but I pushed the thought away. So what if he was a little ostentatious? I felt a heady rush of adrenaline explode in me when I was near him. I relaxed in the seat and he drove down the parkway alongside the Hudson River. The wind whipped against my face and my ponytail swished back and forth.

We rode south toward the bridge. Whenever we hit a red light, Bryce turned his head toward me and smiled. He turned off at Penny Bridge, a small, artsy village nestled into the side of the Palisades hills along the river. Crafts and clothing stores dominated both sides of the street along the river's edge. Candles twinkled in windows and antique mirrors hung on the walls of the shops.

Bryce had made a reservation at Zen Café, a small, intimate restaurant at the edge of town. The hostess led us to a corner table, passing through the dark main room with elaborate crystal chandeliers and two tall red candles sparkling on each table.

During dinner, we talked about ourselves. He spoke about summer camp and his family vacations. I talked about moving to a smaller house in a new town. I told him I liked where we lived now because I could walk to town and school if I wanted to.

After dinner, a young musician named Giselle played guitar and sang folk songs about childhood and families. Bryce reached over and held my hand and smiled when he realized I was singing along. I knew all the words because they were the songs my mom always played in the house. At nine thirty, Giselle finished her first set and Bryce suggested we take a walk along the river.

We followed a path that ran the length of the peninsula, which outlined the town of Penny Bridge. I inhaled the pine and spice of Bryce's aftershave. It was strong but I liked it. When we were far enough away from the village, Bryce reached into his pocket. "Want to vape?" he asked.

"No thanks." I tried to keep the disappointment out of my voice. "Do you smoke a lot?" I asked, avoiding eye contact.

"Not really. It relaxes me. Don't worry; I'm completely under control. I actually have better concentration. You sure? This is very mellow stuff."

"I'm good. Uh, I'm just saying, will you be OK to drive later?"

He took a puff. "Absolutely."

Now would have been the moment to tell him about Carly, but I didn't trust what his reaction might be. It was one thing to vape but quite another to have a girlfriend with a sister in rehab. I was pretty sure there were no drugs allowed around a person recovering from drug abuse.

During the second song set, we held hands in front of the fire. Giselle's beautiful, husky voice lulled me to close my eyes for a moment and I nearly drifted off in the middle of the restaurant.

Bryce had his arm around me and kissed me on the lips. When his soft skin touched mine and his tongue gently eased around mine, I ignored all of my doubts about him. I could only think about the electricity coursing through my body, making my skin tingle and causing me to forget about the rest of the world.

The waitress came by with the dessert menu and a sample tray of sweets. Bryce and I both immediately pointed to the profiteroles with chocolate icing.

"Let's share an order," he suggested. Our spoons clinked whenever they touched and we scooped out all the ice cream from the chocolate-coated puff pastry.

"You look gorgeous," he announced, and I believed him for all of a split second. I knew I wasn't a raving beauty. I had the kind of open, pretty face that fit in most anywhere. I was good looking enough to hang with the popular girls, but I was not so amazing looking as to be in the ranks of the Phoebe Lis and her immediate circle. But with one kiss, Bryce made me feel accepted.

On the way home, Bryce kept the top down. "It's a little, windy, do you mind?" I asked when it got too cold for comfort.

"No worries, whatever you want." He flashed me that megawatt smile again and closed the roof.

At a red light near home, Bryce took out his vape pen again, taking a quick hit before the light changed. I looked away, grimacing. If he was ever pulled over and drug-tested, he would fail miserably.

"You've been smoking all night, but you don't really seem wasted."

"I have a very high tolerance," he said. "I can drive high, study high, I even took my ACTs high and got a 32."

"Yeah, but you'd fail a drug test.

"I'm fine, don't worry about it."

"I'm not worried; it just seems like you smoke a lot." People always thought that it didn't matter that they smoked weed and no one noticed, but it did. When Carly told me about all the times she had been high and I had no idea—at her high school graduation, at synagogue, at family counseling sessions—I was shocked and hurt.

"Do your parents know you get high?" I asked.

"Probably. Weed isn't really a big deal in our house. Why does it bother you so much?"

"I guess cuz it's still illegal in New York state. I don't want to get stopped."

This would have been the perfect opening to tell him about Carly, but I didn't.

As we got closer to home, Bryce began to slow down. One block before my house, he pulled off the main road down a lane I never knew existed. He stopped at a small dirt parking lot facing the river. The lights of the bridge and the twinkling stars illuminated the sky. I sighed.

"Want to go for a walk?" he asked, taking my hand in his across the console.

"Sure." It was close to midnight. I hoped my mom wasn't waiting up.

Bryce got out of the car and came around to open mine. We kissed deeply by the side of the car. His mouth tasted musky, like the weed. Our tongues intertwined and I could feel his hands pressing on my back. I slowly forgot about the rest of the world. Bryce took my fingers and kissed each one of them. "Hmm, delicious and cold," he said. "This is good, right?"

"Yes," I said, slipping under the magic haze of his attention and touch, but as soon as I remembered the vaping, I questioned being with him. It was very confusing. I was the girl with the sister in rehab. This just didn't seem right.

"You're like no one else I've ever been with. So funny and smart and self-effacing. You have no idea how cool you are," he said, slipping a hand under my shirt. The warmth of his hand against my cool back made me shiver. I moved in closer to him and he squeezed my body.

"Flattery will get you everywhere," I laughed. "Right now, I'm more than cool, I'm actually freezing."

"If you're cold, I'll take you home."

We kissed again and without realizing what was happening, I started to cry.

"Hey, are you OK? What's wrong?" He kissed my cheek where the tears were dripping.

"Nothing's wrong. I'm happy, that's all. You're the first good thing that's happened to me in a while."

"I feel the same way," he said, and he brought me in close again. "And we've only just begun." He started to sing a song that the singer sang at the restaurant.

"White lace and promises . . ." I gingerly continued.

"How do you know this song?" he asked.

"Just an old song my mom sings when she cooks."

"You do it better than the lady tonight. Sing some more," he encouraged.

I hummed a bit of the old 1970s Carpenters song for Bryce and surprisingly, he hummed right along.

We sang the line from the song, "Just the two of us," and giggled together when we forgot the words, but we were comfortable and secure with each other in a way that neither of us had expected from the evening.

Bryce walked me to the front door and kissed me goodnight. Ten minutes after I had changed into warm flannel pajamas and brushed my teeth, the phone buzzed. Bryce was singing, "and yes, we've just begun . . ."

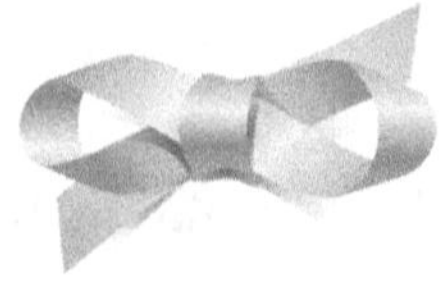

Chapter Eleven—Namaste

"We're doing this," Ethan said, when I let him and Zoey in the door that morning.

"Sure, but we're bringing the dog too. That way I know Zoey won't make us hike too far."

"Are you kidding, that dog can hike miles around you," Zoey said, grabbing a piece of toast off the plate on the table. "Anything good to eat? Where's your mom?"

"She and Allie went to see Carly. And there's cake in the fridge."

"Cool. Why didn't you go?" Zoey said.

"I don't know. I've been already and Allie wanted to go this time."

"My mom loves Carly," Ethan said, rummaging through the fridge, elbowing Zoey out of the way. "I think she prefers her company to mine."

"That's not true." I said. "But she does love Carly, that's why I didn't feel so guilty skipping out. I think Carly's coming home soon, anyway."

"That's amazing," Zoey said, pushing Ethan out of the way. "Move over, Ethan. I just want a little something before we go. And do you have any good snacks we can take with us? God forbid we get hungry while we're out."

"Ha! You're my kind of lady," I said. "There are cookies already wrapped up in the bag, and my mom cut up strawberries. Let's go."

Zoey and Ethan stepped away from the fridge and I added more cookies, some cheese, and raspberries. "Where are we going?" I asked.

"We're going to see the largest indoor Buddha statue in the Western Hemisphere. It's really cool," Zoey said.

"That sounds amazing. Where is it?" I said, slinging the insulated tote bag over my shoulder.

"About a thirty-minute drive, I think," Zoey said.

"OK, let's go." I laced up my bright-red running sneakers, the ones that had more tread than my old ratty tennis shoes. I was looking forward to the day and maybe talking to them about Bryce. Ethan clearly didn't like him, and I wanted to know exactly why.

After about fifteen minutes, we stopped at a deli for coffee. "I'm getting a donut, anyone else want one?" Zoey asked.

"Nothing for me, thanks," I said. "I think we packed plenty from home. I'll pick on the berries."

"Watching your weight for the new boyfriend, huh?" Ethan teased.

"Uh? Why would you say that?" I let Kelly Green wander away from the car on the leash so she could pee.

"I know what it means when you watch what you eat," Ethan replied.

It was maddening that Ethan noticed everything about me. And I knew that he didn't like Bryce for whatever reason he drummed up. I could tell he disapproved. Tough luck. I felt my tummy tingle just thinking about our kissing last night.

Zoey went inside the store, with Ethan following. I stayed outside with Kelly Green and let her walk around a little bit. When they returned, loaded up with a bag of warm, crispy cinnamon donuts, Ethan went right back to the topic of Bryce. Like Kelly Green biting onto a pair of my sweaty socks, he wouldn't let go.

"What boyfriend?" Zoey said, holding out the donuts to me. "Bryce Houston? Gimme a break. He's not going to be your boyfriend, is he?"

I took a little round donut, the sugar falling off my fingers. Mmmm, I bit into the warm, mushy dough, losing all sense of restraint. "I don't know." I kicked up some dirt by the car. "And what if he was? What's wrong with him?"

"Nothing and everything," Ethan announced firmly. "He's full of himself. He's pretentious. Enough said."

"Wow. You really don't like him, do you?" I kicked more dirt, feeling a little deflated, but I wasn't about to show it. "So far, so good. He's really sweet, actually."

"Really? Sweet? Is that the best you've got? Boor-ring," Ethan said.

I took another sugary donut from the bag. They were mini-sized, I rationalized. Ethan stressed me out. I struggled to come up with adjectives to adequately describe my feelings about Bryce. I wanted Ethan and Zoey to understand that I felt some kind of weird chemistry with him. I felt like we got each other, but I didn't want to sound corny.

"We're into each other. It's kinda cool." Kelly Green stood at my feet, nose in the air, smelling the still-warm donuts.

"Boooo . . . ring," Ethan scoffed.

"Leave her alone, Ethan." Zoey held out the bag to me. "Another?"

I grabbed yet another donut, counting the enormous calories in my head. "Yeah, leave me alone. It's none of your business, actually, and even if I wanted to share with you, now you've made it impossible."

"I'm just watching out for you, Ivy," Ethan said. "I've seen this movie before. Bryce Houston is a player and he does drugs. Hell, I think he sells them too, at least to his friends."

Zoey got into the driver's seat. "There are a lot of rumors about Bryce Houston. Dealing drugs is just another one. Maybe he does sell to his friends, who knows?" Zoe said. "Mostly, people talk about Bryce because they're jealous of his money. He does flaunt it a bit, you have to admit."

"He's not that bad," I said, head down. "Come on."

Ethan hopped into the passenger seat and I got in the back. "Let's get going," Zoey said as she started the car.

I looked at my phone and saw that Bryce had texted. "Want to grab dinner again tonight?" he wrote.

I texted back, "I'm on a hike, not sure when we'll be back."

"Is that him?" Ethan said, shaking his head again. "Really, Ivy. I can tell you're already a goner."

"He doesn't really sell to the cheerleaders, does he?" I asked. "Cuz that would be bad and really disappointing."

"Really?!" Zoey drove quickly, keeping her eyes on the road. "Ivy, he's got a reputation of being a bratty rich kid who gets drugs from his friends down county and sells or maybe he gives them to his friends, specifically Phoebe. I don't know if that's true or not, but it's what people think. Hell, everyone has to get their drugs from someplace. Nick got his from the heroin users by the river and now he's ended up dead." I felt a big fat lump my chest. Carly knew Nick. She might have gone to the river once in a while too. It easily could have been her dead too.

"I'm sorry," Ethan muttered. "I didn't mean to bring up Nick."

"You don't have to be sorry. I brought him up. I think of him all day, every day. I can't help it. One day he was here and the next, he's gone forever." Zoey's voice faltered. She kept her eyes on the road but I could tell by the stiffness in her shoulders that she was upset.

"Did he ever go to Blue Hills, where Carly is?" I asked.

"Twice, actually," she said. "He flunked. My parents sent him to Blue Hills, and some other fancy place in Mississippi, and finally, they just put him in City Hospital. They said it didn't matter where he went if he didn't want to get well."

"You sound so pragmatic," I observed.

"Fake it till you make it, baby. Actually, I'm numb. I don't know what I think or feel about Nick's death other than it was a waste of a brilliant life."

"Brutal," Ethan said. "I'm so sorry."

"Didn't I just say? You don't have to be sorry. It's worse when people act like he never existed. Anyway, we were talking about Bryce."

"Zoey, if you feel like talking about your brother, we're here for you," I said.

"I'm good. Let's move on. Let's focus on you and why you want Bryce Houston to be your boyfriend."

"I don't have a good answer to that question. I barely know him, but I do like him. He's sweet and thoughtful and he buys me candy bars."

"And I'll say it again, boooo-ring." Ethan was laughing.

"And you think he's hot?" Zoey snickered from her perch at the wheel. "Cuz that's kinda key. You gotta wanna do him."

"Zoey!" I squealed, laughing and bouncing Kelly Green off my knee. "Yes, I think he's hot. Do I want to have sex with him? Is that what you're asking?" I had already thought about sex with Bryce and I knew I was way ahead of myself. I definitely felt turned on around him, that was clear. I definitely enjoyed making out with him, another plus in the right direction. But did I want to "do" him?

"Who talks like that anyway?" I said, laughing.

"What about the drugs?" Ethan asked. "That can't be good with the Carly situation."

"I'll have to figure it out as I go along. So far, you're just repeating what sounds like rumors."

"I think it's all true, if we're being honest," Zoey said. If I were being honest with myself, I'd have to agree with Zoey. Rumors usually contained more than a grain of truth to them.

"One day at a time," I said, trying to end the conversation.

"How appropriate that you quote the motto for the AA and NA alcohol and drug programs," Ethan remarked.

"Come on, let's stop fighting and get into zen mode," Zoey said.

"Please," I said and nodded.

"We're not fighting. We're discussing." Ethan turned and put his hands together in front of his chest. "Namaste."

"Namaste," Zoey and I said in unison.

I leaned forward and gave him a kiss on the cheek. "Thanks for looking out for me. I'll let you know if we need to call the drug task force."

We parked at the bottom of the monastery and walked a short distance up an inclined path lined with statues, each one inscribed with an inspirational thought at the base. I stopped to read a few lines here and there. Mostly, I thought about Carly and how much she would enjoy the serenity of this place.

We got to the top of the hill, and the Buddha appeared framed in its enormous temple.

"Oh my God, it's so huge," Zoey said. "Let's go in." The Buddha was as tall as a four-story building and as wide as a house.

"I can't with Kelly Green," I said, pointing to the No Dogs sign.

"No worries," Ethan said. "You go first and I'll watch Kelly Green."

Zoey and I removed our shoes and separated as we walked inside. I felt the glow of spirituality settle around me as I gazed up at the enormous Buddha, which filled the entire hall. It was encircled by thousands of small statues of the Buddha on a lotus terrace.

Around us, tourists milled about the outskirts of the temple, and religious people knelt closer to the Buddha. I wasn't religious and I certainly wasn't a Buddhist, but I was awed by the power of such an immense statue. Looking up at the serene face of the Buddha, I silently said Namaste and Thank you. I figured that would cover all the appreciation and love I was feeling for my family and friends. We were all lucky to be alive.

As I walked out, I grabbed a few pamphlets about the monastery and the Buddha. I wanted to come back here with Carly one day soon.

On the way back, Zoey asked if we would mind stopping at the cemetery where her brother Nick was buried.

"You don't have to get out of the car if you don't want. I just want to say hello. It's right near here."

"Of course," Ethan agreed immediately. "Do you want to go alone? We can stay in the car."

"It's OK if you want, but no worries if you don't. It's kind of a weird ask, I get that."

"Not at all," Ethan assured her. "We're here for you."

"Thanks, but I'm good either way."

We pulled off the road at the Mount Ida cemetery and Zoey drove up a windy hill, with flat gravestones all around.

"This is a Jewish cemetery," I commented.

"Yeah, my mom is Jewish and she considers us kids Jewish."

"Same," Ethan and I said in unison. And then we both said "jinx" together. Old childhood habits die hard, I realized.

The three of us got out of the car and stood silent for a moment. "You guys don't have to come with me. I just need a minute."

"Do you want some privacy?" I asked.

"No, it's OK. If you want to see his grave, I don't mind. I just don't want you to feel pressured."

We walked down the little path and stopped in front of a grouping of stones. Several of the stones had inscriptions with Zoey's last name, Marks.

"Nick is buried with all the grandparents and great aunts and uncles. They probably never heard about heroin or opiates," Zoey said.

"Actually, even the Sumerians used the poppy flower to help with pain," Ethan said.

"Huh?" I asked, hurrying my pace to keep up with Zoey. I was beginning to sweat under my armpits and at the nape of my neck. We had been walking outside all morning.

"People from the earliest civilization, in Mesopotamia. You really should know that." Ethan flaunted his knowledge with a silly grin.

"How do you know all this?" Zoey asked, kneeling in front of the one grave that didn't have a marker.

"You should too. It's on the AP exam," Ethan said.

"Do you want us to be quiet now?" I asked. Kelly Green scampered around the graves. I noticed that to our left was a whole group of children who had died very young.

"I'm going to say a silent prayer," Zoey said. "It doesn't mean anything about death, but it's the one prayer I know."

"Go for it," I said. "Do you want me to pray too?"

"Only if you want to for yourself."

We all remained silent for a few minutes.

Afterward, when we were walking back down the dirt path, Zoey said with a straight face, still no tears, "I miss him a lot."

"I'm so sorry," I said, immediately regretting it. "Ugh, I mean, I'm sorry to say I'm sorry. I hate that phrase. I'm here for you, that's what you need to know, always."

"It's OK, I know that. Thanks for being here. I'm so glad I met you two."

"Same," Ethan and I once again said at the same time. And then we mouthed the word "jinx" to each other.

"I don't know what I believe in," Zoey said, her shiny red hair glowing in the sunshine. "But I do know that we have to take care of each other. I hope Carly recovers fully and lives a life that my brother won't. Carly will be OK, Ivy. We'll help you to know how to best help her. That's my promise."

"Thank you." I started to cry and we all hugged each other. I was so lucky to have these people by my side. "I can't wait for you to meet her."

We stood by the car for a few minutes longer. We looked toward Nick's grave and we all bowed and said, "Namaste." And then Ethan said, "Peace." And I said, "Love." And Zoey said, "Strength."

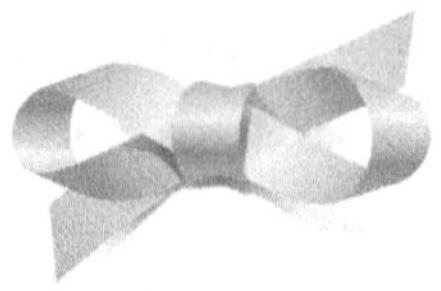

Chapter Twelve—Homework

While I was packing up dinners for my mom, I noticed Bryce's family featured prominently on the schedule. I smiled, just thinking about how much Bryce was going to love the chocolate layer cake. I shook my head, trying to cast off thoughts of rehab and getting high. They didn't go together.

"How's it going with Bryce, honey?" my mom asked, while pressing hard on the plastic containers to seal the food. She looked refreshed today; her hair was in a ponytail and her peachy skin glowed.

"I really like him a lot, but . . ." I gritted my teeth and debated how much I wanted to share with my mom. I was afraid to say something she'd hold against me later.

"But what?"

"But . . ." My voice quivered. I wanted to share, but I chickened out. "I don't want to get too attached. We're going to college next year."

"That's true. Have you started on your college applications? What are you thinking? Do you want to look at more colleges?"

"I don't know. I think we saw enough in the spring. Anyway, I don't want to talk about it now."

We finished loading up the food and arrived at the station just in time for the 5:33 commuter train from Manhattan. Everyone was so happy when they came to our car to pick up their dinners.

"Dinner, Dear meals are our favorite!" one woman exclaimed. Another said, "I wish I could afford this every night."

"How about catering on the weekends?" a man in a Stetson hat and cowboy boots asked. "I'm having a Southern barbecue for some friends.

Would you do it?" He looked like the man in the yellow hat from the Curious George books.

She asked when he was having the party and then agreed to a Southern barbecue with all the trimmings, like ribs, grits, okra, collard greens, and lots of rich buttery cornbread.

"Mom," I asked her, after the guy had driven off, "do you even know how to cook that stuff?"

"Not at all, but I'll figure it out with a little help from Google. Wanna help?"

"Sure." I liked working with my mom when she was creating something new. "Are you going to see Carly later?"

"I told her we had to skip tonight. Too busy."

"OK, hope she's cool with that."

"Honey, I have visited her as often as they let me. We have to let her do the work. She thinks she'll be discharged soon."

"I know, but it's already been two weeks, longer than she thought she'd be there."

"Thank goodness for that. She's receiving a lot of much-needed therapy and support. She's gonna need us more when she gets home."

Later, when I got to Bryce's with all of their Dinner, Dear food, both his parents met me at the door. Marty, Bryce's dad, grabbed the boxes and tins of food out of my arms and took them to the counter. Flora hugged me and gave me a quick peck on the cheek.

"Go on upstairs, sweetheart," she said. "Jonathan's home. The boys are in the playroom on the third floor."

Hmm, I thought, Jonathan was home a lot. When I go to college, I'm not going to come home every weekend to see my mom.

I climbed the stairs and headed toward the attic door. As I walked by Bryce's room, I couldn't help but notice all framed posters of fancy, expensive sports cars. He can be ostentatious; Ethan was right about that.

I went upstairs to the third-floor playroom. There were two desks side by side on one side of the room and a large TV in the middle, with all kinds of electronics on a table in front of a sofa. Game space. Bryce came toward me and kissed me on the lips. Jonathan waved from the window seat. He was a watered-down version Bryce—shorter and not as good looking and definitely not as fit.

We walked toward Jonathan. The boys had a lit vape and were standing by an open window. I frowned and walked to the other side of the room, pretending to study some framed family pictures. As I walked around, Jonathan held out the skinny metal tube, offering me a hit. I shook my head no and continued staring at the knickknacks in the room.

After they finished, we went downstairs. Bryce took my hand and led me to his room. On his desk, Bryce had a photo of himself and his brother on a boat somewhere tropical. He had several books propped up with bookends. I asked him why Jonathan was still home, but he ignored my question and kissed me instead. I inhaled his irresistible piney scent and felt goosebumps form on my arm.

When we were together like this, all my doubts melted away and I could think about nothing but the flutter in my tummy. He moved me closer to the bed and we sat down, lips locked, tongues tangled. I could taste his spearmint ChapStick . . . and a little bit of the leftover THC from the vape. Yuk. I pulled back.

I fingered his gold chain and couldn't resist asking, "This is so interesting. Where did you get it?"

"My mom gave it to me," he said. I was glad I asked before I said something insulting.

We lay down on Bryce's bed, our legs entwined and our chests pressed together. He swirled his tongue around in my mouth. The weed taste was mostly gone. It felt good and warm and I loved being so close to him. I nestled my chest close to his chest, his leg falling in between mine. Bryce moved his hand under my shirt. I shivered, goosebumps rising all over my arms. He kissed me intensely, tongue moving further back in my mouth. His hand pushed higher up my shirt and his fingers slid under my bra. I took a deep breath. I could hear him breathing hard too.

Suddenly, the door burst open and his dad walked in. Bryce and I immediately sat up straight and rearranged our clothes. Marty was really tall, at least six foot five, and also a bit overweight. He took up a lot of space in the middle of the room.

"Oh, sorry, I forgot to knock first." My face turned red. I couldn't look up at first, but I knew I had to say hello. I forced myself to smile and quickly realized that he didn't care that I was laying on the bed with Bryce.

"Hi," I said, trying to sound at ease.

"Dad, a little privacy would go a long way, please," Bryce stammered.

"I said I was sorry. Really. My bad. Anyway, dinner's on the table. Come on down," he said, addressing me.

My face still felt red like a tomato and I struggled to keep a straight face. I wanted to roll off the bed and hide under it.

"Join the Houston comedy hour—if you dare, that is." Bryce's dad smiled and his face was full of deep laugh lines. He seemed to be a friendly, gregarious man. He obviously didn't care one bit about what we were doing on the bed.

Downstairs, Flora had laid out a beautiful dining table laden with fancy dishes and silverware. She served my mom's Dinner, Dear food on oval porcelain platters.

"Why are we in the dining room?" Jonathan asked, chewing on his carrots, food visible in his mouth.

"Jonathan, don't be rude," Flora said. "Ivy's here. It's a special occasion."

"Mom," Bryce began, "Jonathan literally just got kicked off campus, for like what, the third time? I'd hardly call that a cause for celebration." Bryce was also talking with some bread tucked in the side of his cheek.

"I fucking did not get kicked out," Jonathan said as he stood up. He lowered his voice and addressed me directly. "I'm just taking a break." He reached down and took a bit of garlic bread but remained standing. His eyes were dilated from smoking and I wasn't one hundred percent sure he was processing the conversation.

"Jonathan's going back right after midsemester break," Marty said.

Bryce shrugged his shoulders and smiled at me. I didn't really care why Jonathan was home or for how long.

"Ivy, don't let my brother fool you," Jonathan snapped. "He's the hothead in this family, not me. I'm fine. I'm just taking a few weeks off to get some shit done."

"What happened to fraternity rush, then?" Bryce wouldn't drop it. I could see that Jonathan was getting more and more agitated. Flora kept blinking and tapping her fingers on the table.

"That's enough, boys," Marty said.

"You mind your own damn business. I can't wait till you go to college. Let's see how many fraternities rush you," Jonathan said.

"Boys, we have a guest. Please stop fighting," Flora said softly. "Let's have a nice dinner, OK? How do you like Marble Springs High, Ivy? It can't be easy to transfer your senior year."

Bryce grinned from his side of the table. All eyes were on me. "I like it a lot," I said, with as much enthusiasm as I could muster.

"And there's me, of course." Bryce pursed his lips and winked at me. I smiled back. My toes tingled and I felt my heart beat a little faster. I licked my lips and remembered how soft Bryce's lips were when we kissed. A jolt of energy surged through me and my stomach did its usual flip-flop. I definitely saw a few red flags with him, the drugs and rumors for sure, but I couldn't help but love being around him.

"Are you working on your college applications?" Marty asked me. "Do you know where you want to go?" And then the conversation returned to a familiar track. For the rest of the meal, we talked about colleges for Bryce and me and about my mom's company and other easy topics. Flora served my mom's chocolate cake with vanilla-bean ice cream for dessert and that put everyone in a better mood.

Later, back in his room, this time with the door locked, Bryce told me what happened. "My idiot brother just got kicked out of school again. This time he threatened a kid in his fraternity and the police were called. He's so fucking stupid, he doesn't know when to shut his mouth."

"Oh my God." I looked left at him, surprised at the violent nature of his brother's behavior.

"He also had a knife on him. My mom said it was only a dull butter knife from the cafeteria, but when he showed the knife, the other kid reached his arm out to grab it and then Jonathan stupidly pushed him. The kid fell backward and hit his head. And then went to the hospital for scans. He's fine, but of course the incident was reported to the school, and they have requested that Jonathan return home for a while. Jonathan is a walking time bomb," Bryce admitted sadly. "He's a disaster waiting to happen. I just know that one of these days we're going to get a bad phone call. It's just a matter of time."

"That's a terrible thought. Is something seriously wrong with him?" I asked.

"I don't know. His issues have issues. He never means any harm, but somehow he finds trouble wherever he goes. He can't shut up, and he can't keep his hands to himself. That's one reason I'm thinking of not applying to Hopkins. I don't want to be around his mess."

"I get it," I said, and I realized that now would be the right time to tell him more about Carly and where she is, but I didn't. "Is he mentally ill?" I said instead.

"I don't know. He's always been a little unsteady, but he's my brother, you know? I'm used to it."

Wow, I thought, you really don't know what goes on behind closed doors. Flora Houston always appeared calm, like everything in her life was perfect, but apparently not. Jonathan sounded really unstable, and it scared me.

Bryce asked me to stay and do homework with him and Phoebe, who was on her way over. I agreed, mostly because I didn't want to leave him alone with her.

We set up in the dining room. Phoebe was equally as bad at math as I was, but I was really surprised at how smart Bryce was and how he quickly broke down the problems in more easily understood parts.

"Surprised ya, did I?" Bryce said.

"I never doubted you for a moment." I smiled at him and he winked back.

"Hey, you two, I'm still here," Phoebe said.

"We know," Bryce said, laughing, and I marveled at his white teeth and deep dimples.

We studied for about an hour. It was getting close to ten when we closed our books. Bryce's dad came downstairs just as we were getting ready to leave.

"Look at my son with two gorgeous gals," Marty joked when he sauntered in to sneak another piece of cake. "Don't let it go to your head, Bryce."

"Dad," Bryce said, "you're embarrassing me."

"You, embarrassed?" Phoebe laughed. "Never."

"Right, it's pretty hard to embarrass Bryce," Marty said with a smile.

"Dad, come on. Don't scare off Ivy. She hasn't known me for that long."

"Now's the time to run, Ivy," Phoebe said. "He may seem like the ideal boyfriend—good looks and brains—but watch out."

"Come on, Phoebe, not you too. Don't believe a word they say, Ivy. I'm a great boyfriend. You'll see."

They threw around the boyfriend word like it was rice at a wedding. It felt like all the blood seemed to flow faster through my veins and into my heart. I wanted to be his girlfriend, but I didn't want to give too much away. I shrugged one shoulder and made a coy face.

Bryce walked us to the driveway where his car and Phoebe's were parked.

As Phoebe was about to drive off, she lowered her window. "Hey Bryce, any chance you can get me some of the good stuff for the Taylor Swift concert at the end of the month?"

I looked at her, my mouth askance. I knew enough to stay quiet. It was all true, then. Not only did she smoke, but she relied on Bryce to supply her with weed. I was so stupid. Of course, rumors were usually partially true.

"Sure, no problem. Just don't get pulled over with drugs in the car," Bryce said.

"Ha ha, I won't. It would be fun for the concert and then we're having a sleepover all weekend."

"So, you found someone to babysit for your friend's little sister?" I asked.

"Yeah, no worries. Did you get a ticket?"

"I didn't really try."

"Want me to take you?" Bryce asked brightly. "I just love Taylor Swift."

"You ass," Phoebe said, laughing and rolling up her window. "You hate her, don't lie to Ivy. See ya." She drove off down the long driveway and past the gates.

"I don't hate Taylor Swift," Bryce said after Phoebe left. The chilly late-September air reminded me that fall was definitely here. I wrapped my arms around myself for warmth. Bryce noticed and moved closer, putting his arm around me.

"Wow, that was shocking," I said, settling into his warm, sturdy frame. I felt his breath on my neck.

"What's shocking? That I like Taylor Swift or that Phoebe smokes? Really, most people do. It's better than a lot of other stuff kids are doing these days."

"Well, yeah," I scoffed. I couldn't look him in the eyes, so I stared out into the night, toward the woods. "It is better than oxy or heroin. But really, is that the right comparison?"

"I didn't know you were so uptight," Bryce said, kissing me behind my ear. I felt a tingle run up my spine in spite of my hesitations about his drug use and dealings.

"I'm not." I swiveled away. "I just didn't expect it of her. She's so . . . so . . ."

"So what? So pretty? So rich? What does it matter? Most high school kids smoke weed."

"I don't. I could, but I choose not to. And by the way, are you a dealer?" I said, finally managing to ask the question that's been on my mind for so long. I kept looking past him, toward the darkness. He turned my chin toward him so I was forced to look him in the eye.

"I'm not a dealer, Ivy. I get Phoebe what she wants once in a while. Maybe you should give it another try. Relax a little."

"No thanks. I'm just surprised, that's all. She doesn't seem the type, but I guess the point is that there is no one type of person who does drugs. I should know that better than anyone." I was gearing up to tell him about Carly, but it felt so hard to spit the words out. I didn't want to burst any kind of happy bubble around the newness of us. Having a sister in rehab or a psych hospital was just not part of that perfect scenario, although to be perfectly honest, neither was his disastrous brother.

He spoke his words very carefully, keeping his eyes locked on mine. "You're right. You can't stereotype people or put personalities into little boxes. We all smoke or use drugs for different reasons. I'm not saying they're good reasons, just admitting the reality of drug use. You don't know Phoebe. She looks like she's got it all together, but her parents put a lot of pressure on her."

"Aren't we all under a lot of pressure? I don't know anyone whose parents don't harass them about their grades and college." I was cold, standing outside for so long, and I put my hand on the door handle, hoping Bryce would get the hint, but he kept talking about Phoebe.

"Hers are different. They are stuck on her being a dancer or an actress. They punish her if they find candy in her bag because they don't want her to get fat. Her mother sends out her head shots to acting agencies without her permission."

"First-world problems. You're very protective of her."

"I feel bad for her, that's all. Just because she is always smiling doesn't mean she's happy all the time. Fake it till you make it, ever hear that expression?"

"Yeah, like Insta—the facade is all a big lie. She didn't even think to ask me to join her friends. I was just a potential babysitter."

"Why would you say that? She didn't have a ticket for you. When is it? I'll get us tickets." He looked at me with incredulity. He had no idea why I would feel the way I did.

"Why do you protect her so much?" My heart beat faster. I felt sweat forming under my arms.

"We're close friends, that's all. I care about her. Come on, let's go."

When he drove me home, he pulled into a spot in front of the house, but he didn't turn off the engine. The car was warm and I felt my heart melting just a little bit when he kissed me across the stick shift. He drew me into him, but the stick shift was in the way. We kissed for a long time before I gently pushed him away with a warm smile and a last smooch.

He made a pouty face, but sat back in his seat. Then he brightened and said, "Hey, do you want to take a ride down county with me tomorrow? I have a quick errand to run and I'd love your company."

I quickly ran through the day's empty agenda in my mind. "I don't see why not," I said. "Sounds good."

"OK, great. I'll see you around eleven tomorrow morning. Meantime, I'll ask my dad about the Taylor Swift tickets. It'd be fun with you." I smiled and he continued talking. "Please don't be mad about the weed or Phoebe. Neither is very serious."

"Bryce, I haven't told you something."

"What is it? You can tell me anything." He held my hands, which were sweaty and a little clammy. I felt nervous to share with him, but it finally seemed like the right moment.

"I didn't know how to tell you this, so I've been putting it off." He nodded as I spoke, encouraging me to finish. "My sister, Carly? She's not traveling. She's in a rehab place in Connecticut. She nearly OD'd on oxy over Labor Day weekend."

Immediately, I felt an intense sense of relief and release spread across my shoulders and down my back. It felt great to be completely open and honest with him. Surprisingly, he didn't flinch or look surprised.

"I know," he said gently.

"What do you mean you know?"

"I've been waiting for you to tell me yourself."

I squinted and pursed my lips. My hair fell in front of my face and I didn't bother to push it aside. I bit my fingernail. "Who told you?"

He leaned in close to me and took my hand. "Ivy, it's a small town. People know shit. It's OK. I don't care that your sister is in rehab."

"Well, do you see why I'm so hyper about drugs?"

"Obviously I get it, but what happened to her has no bearing on me."

"You can never do drugs around her, ever." I looked at him straight in the eyes, pleading with him to understand the severity of what I was saying.

"Of course, I would never. I'm not an idiot. How is she doing?"

"Carly? She's doing great. I think she'll be home soon. Wait till you meet her. She's beautiful and athletic and smart. She's my rock star."

"You miss her, huh?" Bryce's voice dropped to a near whisper. His hand was caressing my arm.

"I do. She's my best friend." I brushed my wet eyes with my hand before more tears could gather.

"She'll be OK, you know that, right?" Bryce's green-gray eyes were bright and he looked so sincere.

"I think so. Who told you, really, who?"

"It doesn't matter."

"I want to know."

"Phoebe told me," he reluctantly admitted, looking away from me when he spoke.

"Phoebe? It figures." I could feel the leather seat hard under my butt and I wanted to get out of the car. Shame rippled through my skin and I felt hot. I should have known that people talked.

"I'm so glad that you've finally told me." He leaned in for another kiss. I gave him a peck and moved back.

"I'd better go in."

"You're not mad, are you?" he asked, head cocked to the left like a puppy.

"Of course not," I said tensely. "I'll talk to you later or tomorrow. Bye."

I closed the car door and ran into the house. The lights were off in the kitchen and living room. Only a small antique floor lamp shone in the dining room where my mom clicked away on the computer keyboard.

"Have fun?" she asked, glancing up from the computer.

"Fun is not exactly the word I'd use to describe doing homework, but hopefully my math grade will improve. Bryce is good at calculus."

"That's a step in the right direction. Or should I say an x and a y equals the right equation?"

"Very funny. Whatcha doing?" I peered over her shoulder. "Ewww, who's that? He's gross."

"Nobody. I'm just fooling around on some dating sites. Gives me something to do at night."

"Let me see. I'll pick someone for you."

"It's OK, my Prince Charming isn't online tonight. Let's go to bed." She was laughing, but I could sense the disappointment in her voice.

In bed with Kelly Green by my feet, I struggled to concentrate on the rest of my homework. Bryce pinged me on FaceTime. As soon as I saw his face, I felt my cheeks get hot.

"Hey," he whispered. "Are we OK?"

"We are." I beamed at him. We talked for a little while until I felt myself falling asleep.

And in the morning, before my eyes were even open, he buzzed again and said, "Good morning, beautiful."

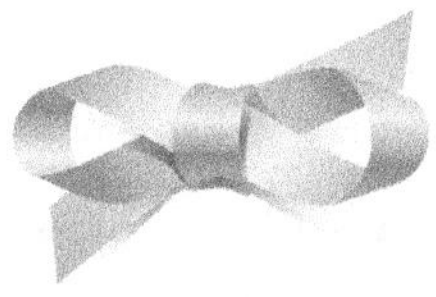

Chapter Thirteen—The Deal

I sat down at the kitchen counter and helped myself to a piece of vanilla cinnamon French toast my mom had left out on a plate.

At exactly eleven, Bryce beeped his horn. For a split second, I thought about changing into leggings. These jeans were way too tight, but I didn't want to keep Bryce waiting, so instead I smeared a last bite of French toast into the maple syrup, swallowed it whole, and took off. Kelly Green stared at me with her wide, pleading eyes. I shook my head. "No dogs allowed, little bear. Gotta go."

"Honey, will you be back by two? We're supposed to see Carly later today," my mom yelled from upstairs.

"I'll try, Mom, bye." I ran out of the house and hopped into Bryce's car, bending gingerly so I wouldn't hit my head. I pulled the safety belt across my washed-out pink cotton peasant blouse and buckled in. What a mistake to wear these stupid skinny jeans. They were killing me. I smiled at Bryce. He hypnotized me with those pearly white teeth. My grin widened and I felt hot and excited, but my stomach killed. When he looked the other way to back onto the street, I carefully undid the top button of my jeans and exhaled. Phew, that felt better.

"So, where are we going?" I asked. "And why?" Bryce zoomed off down the street and onto the highway, heading south.

"I promised some friends at school that I would try and score for them," he said.

"Oh my God, are you kidding? You asked me to go with you to pick up drugs? After what we discussed last night. Bryce, really?"

"Come on, one thing has nothing to do with the other."

"Actually, buying drugs from someone is kinda a big deal. You're making me an accomplice."

"I am not. We're going to my friend's house in Scarsdale, hardly a crime scene. Just picking up what Phoebe asked."

"So you buy for her?" My neck felt warm. My cheeks turned red. This couldn't be happening. I had a sister in rehab. I can't have a boyfriend who has a problem too. "What's the story with you two anyway?"

"We've been best friends since we were little. Please don't worry about this. We're going to my friend Dauber's house. Wait till you see it. It's amazing."

"More amazing than yours?" Everything about Bryce was enticing except the pot smoking. Bryce turned me on not just because he was cute, but because he had this kind of charisma about him. He was full of warm, loving energy. I loved that about him.

"It's all good." He gave me another one of his enchanting smiles. His dimples deepened and I melted in my seat. I liked him. A lot.

"Jonathan wanted to come with me but I said no. I thought a drive together would be fun. It's a gorgeous Indian-summer day." He was right. It was warm out. The leaves were just beginning to turn. The water along the Hudson River reflected shiny sparkly light. The day was perfect.

"Does Jonathan have a real diagnosis?" I asked.

"I don't think so. He's been on different drugs for a while though. Some for ADHD, some for anxiety. He's a weird dude. What can I say?" Bryce kept his eyes on the road and zipped along the Saw Mill Parkway, heading south toward the city. "I'm not gonna lie, he's always pissed people off and had trouble making and keeping friends. Things just got worse as he got older."

Bryce turned off the parkway and we drove through a perfectly manicured town with big Tudor-style homes and oversized brand-new houses set back from the road by big front lawns. Many of the houses looked like estates and had hedges growing along the edge of the lawn and sidewalk.

Bryce rang the video doorbell affixed to a stone tower at the end of the driveway. A buzzer went off and the elaborately scrolled metal gates parted like the Red Sea. We drove up to a circular driveway in front of a huge white house with pillars across the entire front of the house.

"Kinda looks like the White House," I observed.

"It's not small is it? I wouldn't be surprised if he had a helipad in the backyard," Bryce said.

We followed a bluestone path toward the backyard. His friend Dauber greeted us shirtless at the door of his white pool house, a miniature version of the big house. Dauber's real name, I learned, was Doug. He was tall, with sculpted abs that I could easily count.

"Hey, Dauber," Bryce said. "This is Ivy."

We both said hi.

"What's happening, dude?" Dauber said. "I'm here all day, just hanging. I just rolled a blunt." Dauber slurred his words. He was wasted at 11 a.m. "We've known each other since, what? We were eight? Nine years old?" Dauber said.

"Something like that," Bryce agreed. I thought of Carly, who must be in the middle of a therapy session or talking with other patients who suffer with drug-abuse issues like her. What was I doing here in the midst of a drug deal? It made no sense.

The guys sat together on a low-slung white modern sofa. I sat across from them in an oversized, overstuffed upholstered chair. I just sat there, still as could be, folding and unfolding my legs, hoping my blouse covered my unbuttoned jeans.

"What can I get you?" Dauber offered. "Bloody Mary? Mimosa? The bar is stocked. I have everything."

I poured myself plain seltzer and began to pace around the large living space.

Dauber got up and walked to the fridge. He pulled out a small canvas zip-up bag. "Want a hit? It's a smooth-as-silk sativa, really good. Very, very mellow. Just makes you feel creative and loving. And the high doesn't last too long either, so you can get right back to your day." Dauber held out the fat blunt at me. I shook my head.

"Why don't you try it, just once," Bryce got up and encouraged, his dimpled smile accentuating his good looks.

"Bryce, come on, you know I don't."

"I know you haven't," he said, wrapping his arms around me, "but I think you could. How else will you relate to what your sister is going through if you have never used drugs yourself?" He motioned me over to the sofa and chairs, where Dauber had sat back down, smoking and rolling joints. A bunch of little round tin containers sat on the side of the coffee table.

"What kind of nonsense logic is that? And I've gotten high before. What do you think, I'm some kind of Puritan? I just don't like how it makes me feel."

"OK, suit yourself. I'm not trying to corrupt you or anything. I actually think it would help you not only relax a bit, but also help you be a better support to Carly. She's coming home soon and you will be able to relate."

I thought about his fucked-up logic for a second. I looked at Dauber. He sat back, put his hands behind his head, and smiled at me.

"It's really easy on your nerves. I promise. You'll hardly feel it, but you'll experience an easiness of mind and spirit for a little while, and then the cloud will lift and you'll feel relaxed. Try it. It can't hurt."

I stiffened and sat up straight. "Fine." I reached across the coffee table and took the blunt from Dauber's fingers. I had tried weed a few times in my life. "Give it to me."

I took a long inhale off of the joint. It even tasted smooth and light. "Are you happy now? I'm not some socially awkward nerd at a party."

Bryce put his arm around me and pulled me in my chair toward him. "I never said that, Ivy. I think you're the coolest girl I've ever met, and the prettiest, I might add. I just think if you were ever going to smoke, this weed is one of the best highs money can buy."

I stared at him and looked at Dauber, who had closed his eyes and looked like he was taking a nap. "I'm fine. It feels fine." And it did. I kissed Bryce on the lips and enjoyed the feel of his soft skin against mine. I felt really alert, but calm. I felt like I understood everything Bryce was saying to me. It made sense for me to try this pot, to remember the feeling of high so I could better understand how Carly got lured from one drug to the next. I wouldn't do it again any time soon, but this was fun.

We sat with Dauber for another hour. He played some good music. He showed us his house, which was like something out of a Kardashian show. My high was lovely and then it was gone before I even made it to the first-floor powder room. I could appreciate the lure of the weed, but I also could understand how someone might take it to the next level and then the next and then the next.

Just as we were getting ready to leave, Dauber handed Bryce a small Ziploc. "Take these. I'm sure you can get rid of them. Ms, about seventy-five Gs. Worth about $500 but I'll float ya. I got them for someone but I won't be able to get rid of all of it."

"Okay, but it could be a while or not at all, is that cool?"

I had no idea what they were talking about, Ms and Gs, but it was pretty clear that they were exchanging drugs for cash. I tried to catch his eye and motion with my head, but he avoided my glance.

"No rush," Dauber said.

I didn't know the full extent of this drug deal, but I was pretty sure Bryce was buying for Phoebe and maybe her friends too.

"Hey, tell your brother that I've got for him too, the next time he's home."

"Jonathan's home this weekend but he has to lay low. He got busted again. I'll share, no worries."

Bryce took my hand and we stood up.

"Thanks for stopping by. Nice to meet you, Ivy. See, nothing bad happened to you," Dauber said.

"Nope, I'm alive. Nice to meet you too." But I didn't really feel like it was nice. I felt like I had betrayed myself and my mom and Carly too. On the other hand, I had liked the feeling of lightness and the way my thoughts had coursed through my consciousness for a little while. I was confused about my reactions.

Back in the car, heading home, I asked, "What the heck just went down?"

"What do you mean?"

"Do you sell drugs at school? Is Dauber your dealer?"

"Ivy, you've literally got to chill out. I barely do drugs myself," he said, as he took a long inhale on the vape in his right hand. "He had some Mollies."

"Aren't you afraid you'll get caught?" I stared out the window at the parkway as Bryce sped up the road. We were nearly back in Marble Springs, already past the bridge, but I wanted to talk about this.

"By who? I don't have enough drugs in this car to make a cop blink. Once in a while I help Dauber get rid of extra stuff. Most of the time, it's just weed."

"Whatever. I'm not going to start an argument." I had to figure out a way to reconcile in my heart and my head how I felt about dating a hot boy with a drug issue. How could I possibly introduce him to Carly? How could I face Carly at the hospital now? Well, I was sober. And dammit, most teenagers got high without a problem. I mean, Carly certainly wasn't asking me to be clean and sober all the time just because she had to be.

"I'm sorry if you didn't have a good time," Bryce said as he pulled into town. "I thought it might be fun, but I understand why it might not have been for you."

Thankfully, my mind was clear now and I felt energetic. "Honestly, it wasn't exactly fun, but it wasn't terrible either," I said. "He's a weird dude, Dauber."

"He's got it going on, that's what he's got. He's rich and good looking. His parents leave him alone. Wait till you meet his girlfriend. She's hot as hell and real as shit. She's defines the word cool."

"Hmm, and how would you describe me?"

"You're pretty perfect, you know," Bryce said.

I laughed. After his good looks, his gold chain was the first thing I noticed about him and the one thing I hated. His car was flashy. His hair had shiny gel in it all the time. But he really was a sweetheart.

"OK, you're redeemed," I said, still giggling. "You know, I just feel kinda bad about smoking."

"Why? You liked it, didn't you?"

"It was OK. I got a little buzz, but it's the whole Carly thing. It feels wrong . . ." I let my thoughts drift off into the space between us in the car.

"You smoking a little weed and Carly nearly ODing on oxycodone are two completely separate universes. You have to see that, don't you? Taking a few hits once in a while is like sipping chamomile tea in the afternoon. It's harmless, is what I'm trying to say."

"I know, but it's not nothing, Bryce. I can't be high around my sister, ever."

"And you won't be." He drove into my driveway and we both got out of the car. He came around to my side and held me. "It's OK, Ivy," he whispered into my ear. The hair along my neck stood up on end. Below my waist, everything bounced around, and it felt like my whole body was having a party. We kissed for a long time. "It's OK. I'll watch out for you."

Bryce came into the house with me. My mom acted pleasant to him but slightly reserved. He probably didn't notice that she was being a little bit stiff, but I could tell she was holding back. She was wary about people who were too showy. If she only knew where we had just been and what Bryce had stashed in his car, she'd kick him out of the house faster than the speed of light. I kept thinking about that bag of drugs.

Just as he was about to go home, Ethan and Zoey showed up.

"Everybody, this is Bryce. Bryce, do you know Zoey and Ethan?"

Zoey gave him the once over, noticing his clothes and his hair. "Yup," she said with a wry look at me. "We've known each other forever." The three of us and my mom stood around the small kitchen. It was more of a galley kitchen and we were very close to each other.

"Hi, I'm Ethan."

"Hey." Bryce spoke loudly and reached out to shake Ethan's hand. Taken by surprise, Ethan hesitantly offered his hand, but he looked dubious.

"Anyone hungry?" my mom said as she headed to the fridge and started carting out leftovers. She placed plates of artichoke-and-eggplant dip and homemade flatbread on the dining room table.

"I love when Ivy has friends over. Bryce, this is the same food your mom picked out for your family. Hope you won't get sick of it."

"None of us could get sick of your food, Samantha." Bryce winked at me and smiled broadly at my mother. His charm definitely got under my skin but I could tell that my mom wasn't as smitten as me. We moved into the dining room and sat down.

"We love it at our house too," Zoey said, frowning. "Dinner, Dear meals are really the only decent food we've had lately." She picked up a chip and smeared it with dip. "Hey, Bryce," Zoey said. Her auburn hair looked freshly blown out around her face. When done up, Zoey looked gorgeous. I could tell from the curve of her mouth and the slant of her smoky green eyes that she was about to start digging and I wasn't going to like it. I was right.

"We share a mutual friend, you know. Phoebe."

"Where are you going with this?" I asked. "They're really close friends."

"I know. We've actually met before, right? I've definitely seen you at parties, right?"

"Yeah, of course. Ivy and Phoebe are also getting to be friends," Bryce said, smiling easily at me.

"So I hear." Zoey pursed her lips.

"Really?" Ethan's eyes popped out of his head. "What could you two possibly have in common?"

"What do you mean? We're in a few classes together. She's cool and so am I? Right?"

"You're so cool," Ethan said, laughing.

"I am, Ethan," I said.

"She's super cool," Bryce said. He took my hand, and my friends stared.

Ethan stood up. "Well, I'm sure Phoebe Li is a good person and a great friend."

"Thanks for your support." I tilted my head to the side and watched my mom. She was staring at us with a blank expression, taking it all in.

"I've known Phoebe since kindergarten," Zoey said. "She's not so terrible. If Ivy wants to stick her face up Phoebe's butt, that's her choice."

"What is that supposed to mean? You introduced me to everyone. They're your friends too." I looked at her incredulously.

"I'm just giving you a hard time," Zoey muttered.

My mom brought out baba ghanoush and pita triangles and placed them on the table.

"I love all this Mediterranean food," Zoey gushed.

"One of my customers requested it, so I experimented with some new recipes."

"Delish, Samantha," Bryce said, exaggerating all his words and sugarcoating his compliment.

"Sweetheart, would you like some to take home to your parents?" my mom offered Zoey. "Allie and I made way too much hummus and souvlaki. We could feed an army."

"I think my dad might eat some of the vegetables," Zoey said.

"I have a few containers of vegetable soup here in the freezer. I'll send you home with that as well. As for you, Bryce, your mom already ordered all this. She told me she was having a big party this weekend."

Bryce licked his lips and fingers. "She always has a party." Kelly Green circled under our feet, hoping for some droppings. I scooped her up on my lap. "Did she order the orange pound cake? It's soooo good. I could keep eating it and never stop."

"Thank you, Bryce. See, Ivy, moving to a new town and a new school isn't so difficult."

"Ha! Mom, you try it!"

"I have my own challenges, thank you very much," she said, and left the room again.

"Hey, sorry, but I've gotta go." Bryce got up from his chair and came to my seat. He petted Kelly. "Nice dog," he said.

I stood up and walked him toward the kitchen door. He grinned and kissed me on the forehead. I felt my cheeks turn pink just thinking about my friends watching from the next room. I hoped he wasn't going to kiss me on the lips.

"Next time," he whispered, and kissed my ear lobe. My body tingled and I felt my face flush even more.

"Mmm, next time," I whispered and quickly stepped toward my friends. "Bye," I said loudly.

"Bye everyone," he said.

"Bye," Zoey and Ethan said in unison from the dining table.

When he was out the door, Zoey was the first to exclaim, "Wow, he really likes you."

"You think so?" I asked, blushing. "He's funny." I sat down again and took a big gulp of water.

"He literally fed you cake from the palm of his hand," Ethan said, and snorted.

"He did not. He handed it to me," I said. "He's nice. He's sweet. He's cute."

"So besides all the drugs, what's wrong with him?" Zoey said. "Maybe he's just too slick for his own good."

"Or maybe he smokes too much, right Ethan?" I said, pointedly trying to provoke Ethan.

"Come on, Ivy." Ethan's smile disappeared and he turned his head toward me, concentrating on each word he said. "Someone has to remind you that a weed-smoking, drug-dealing boyfriend may not be a good choice. Not now, not ever."

"It's gossip. There's nothing to worry about," I said, a little too fast.

"Just be careful you don't get hurt," Zoey said.

"I'm always careful," I said.

"But the heart wants what the heart wants, right girlfriend?" Ethan said, repeating a line his mom always said about her own dates. "Just don't let his fancy hair and expensive gold necklace get the best of you."

"Ha, the gold chain has got to go, right? So '70s."

"Very disco." Ethan gave me a high-five. "We're OK? I'm only looking out for you."

"We're fine." I thought about telling them about Dauber's house and the morning but decided to keep it to myself. I couldn't be sure how either of them would react.

"Honey, just be ready by 3:15, OK?" my mom said, returning from the other room. "We have a four o'clock meeting at the hospital. We may be taking Carly home today."

"Wow, so soon," Zoey said. She picked at the butterscotch cookies my mom had set out on a plate. "Nick was a thirty-day guy, not that it helped any." She didn't look at me. She kept eating.

"It's been three weeks already. That's longer than she intended," Mom said.

"I hope she never has to go back." Zoey poured herself some milk. My mom caught my gaze and I looked down. I was self-conscious about my eyes. I didn't want her to notice if my pupils were still dilated.

"Honey, everyone is different." My mom shrugged her shoulders and walked closer to Zoey. She looked like she wanted to hug her, but Zoey stiffened, got up, and began to help clear the table. It was hard to break through Zoey's tough exterior. I knew she missed her brother. She talked about him often, but she didn't allow grief to stop her life at all. I didn't know if that was a healthy response, or if it was going to strike her on the back of the head one of these days, when she least expected it.

Later in the day, I texted Carly. "Can we talk?" She called me back right away.

"What's up?" she asked. "I'm just about to take a walk with Oliver."

"Ooo, Oliver. Remember, no fraternizing." I giggled, but suddenly remembered that what I was about to tell her was about fraternizing with the enemy.

"Things are going well with Bryce," I said.

"That's good. Is that all?"

"Well, I wanted to tell you something else about Bryce, you know, besides the fact that he's adorable and irresistible."

"And that is? I don't mean to rush you, Ives, but I can see Oliver waiting on the path out front."

"It's OK, not a big deal, really, but I wanted you to know, he vapes a lot. He and his brother, they smoke weed almost daily, or so it seems to me."

"And? He's a, eighteen-year-old boy in high school. Tell me something new," she said.

"It's OK?" I said. I was in my room with Kelly Green, staring at my perfume bottles. Wondering if it was time to put them in a box in the closet. They were pretty, but they cluttered up my dresser.

"It's never OK, Ivy, to do illegal drugs, that's the real answer, but the realistic answer is that most people our age have at least tried weed. It's the ones like me, and Oliver—I've really got to run—who can't control it. I did a lot more than weed. Anyway, to be continued."

"Thanks, Carly. You be careful with Oliver. You're both in recovery."

"OK," she said. "LYLAS."

"Yeah, LYLAS, Love you like a sister, sister," I said, and hung up the phone.

If she was OK with it, then I guess I was too. I texted Bryce a smiley-face emoji with a heart. LYLAS my butt, I thought. We were both treading on thin ice here and I think we both knew it.

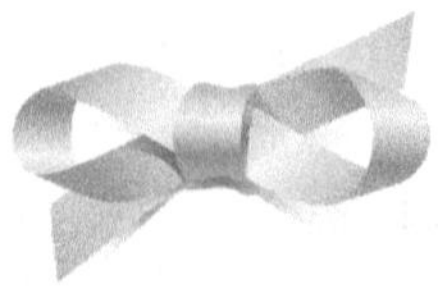

Chapter Fourteen—Carly Comes Home

We left the house late in the day, as the sun was going down. We drove in hazy twilight, and it seemed to me like we were driving into a dark cloud.

My mom finally spoke after about twenty minutes of listening to NPR. I think I preferred the distraction of *The Moth* radio show, but I guess she wanted to prepare me for what was going to happen.

"When we get there, we'll meet with Joanie one more time. If Carly is ready and the doctors clear her, she can come home."

"What's to discuss?" I asked, staring at the many horse farms we passed on the way to the hospital.

"Well, she could come home and live with us, like always, or she could come home for a few days or a week until they find an appropriate sober group house. It all depends on what Carly wants."

I didn't turn to look at my mom; I just kept looking out the window as the fields and barns flew by. I thought I had more time to figure things out—at least another day or two. I knew that smoking weed was not the worst thing in the world, but Carly needed to live in a place with no temptation, and I had to help her.

"Mom." I scratched my nose with my index finger and bit my lip.

"Yes, honey. I know it's not going to be an easy adjustment for any of us, but—"

"No, it's not that. I have a question."

"Shoot." She quickly looked at me and nodded with a trusting smile. My mom's shoulders were relaxed. She was smiling. Her hair was shiny and soft around her face. Her tone easy and unsuspecting.

"What if when Carly comes home, she encounters people smoking or drinking?"

"Honey, she's been in therapy for the last three weeks where they discuss how to handle those types of situations. They encourage each other to seek out new friends who will not tempt them." My mom tapped her fingers on the steering wheel as she drove. She bit her lip. I realized I'd inherited that bad habit.

"Well, it's hard, you know. Everyone parties around here." I stared out the side window. I couldn't look at her.

"You mean Bryce? Do your other friends smoke too?" Her voice was modulated and she spoke without accusation.

"Well, yeah, he vapes, but it's also really common at parties and when people hang out."

"Are you talking about yourself at all? It's OK, Ivy, you're right, it is pretty normal for teens to smoke pot. I certainly did when I was your age."

"Do you ever smoke now? Lots of parents do, you know."

"I know, and sometimes an old-fashioned bong gets passed around at an old-fogy party that I happen to be at, but since Carly got out of hand and even before that, I've tried to refrain. I don't want to be a hypocrite."

"Well I don't either," I replied loudly, pouting. I turned away in my seat, the seatbelt pulling across my chest like the soft Velcro restraints that were on Carly's hospital bed in the ER.

"Ivy, I'll say it again and again. No drugs or alcohol around Carly. That's a hard rule and I don't want it disobeyed."

"I get it. It won't be a problem."

"I know it won't, honey. I know you have Carly's best interests at heart. She comes first."

"Always," I muttered. I wasn't ready to continue delving into Bryce's and my own drug use. "Oh no, I left some of her clothes out on my bed," I said.

"Don't worry, I put them away. You're going to have to get used to wearing your own clothes more often. That's probably going to be the hardest part of Carly's homecoming."

"It will be my pleasure and the easiest part of her return." I laughed nervously.

When we got to Blue Hills, we went straight to Carly's cottage and signed in at the door. She and her counselor Joanie were waiting for us in the living room off to the right of the foyer. I could tell Carly had put extra effort into her appearance. It looked like she had blown out her blond glossy hair and she wore makeup, at least blush and eye shadow as far as I could tell. They both stood up as we got closer to the sofas, and Carly moved quickly toward my mom and hugged her. She hugged me next, and I could smell the faint citrus scent of her favorite Kate Spade perfume.

"Hi," I said.

"Hi, thanks for coming to get me. I can't wait to get home."

"Yes, yes," Joanie replied, her tight pencil skirt wrinkled along the bottom and her white starched blouse taut across her boobs. "The family meeting is set up in the cottage office. Carly's doctor is waiting for us there." Joanie led us toward the back of the house, down a short corridor, past a hall bath and into a small room lined with bookshelves. A big wooden desk dominated the center of the room and the doctor, white lab coat and all, sat stoically in his high-backed wooden roller chair.

My mother strode over to the desk and held out her hand. "Hello, Doctor. Nice to see you again."

"And you too, Mrs. Green. Good to see you under these circumstances rather than when we first met."

"That's for sure," Carly agreed. She nudged me over to the three client chairs facing the desk. Mom sat between us. Carly looked like she was ready to go out on a Saturday night with friends in jeans and a cute silk blouse with black heeled boots. She even carried a purse.

I shifted back and forth in my chair and crossed and uncrossed my arms in front of me. What was my role here? I wondered. Joanie sat in a chair in the back corner of the room, listening and presumably waiting for her chance to make additional comments and explanations.

"We think Carly will do well at home, with the love and support of you two," the doctor said. "She can leave now, continue treatment with a private therapist, and come here once or twice a week for group therapy."

"That sounds great," my mom said, bobbing her head up and down. She leaned over to Carly and put her hand on her thigh. "We are here for you, honey."

"Thanks, Mom. I'm going to need all the help I can get." Carly's forehead was shiny. Her eyes were bright and she appeared to be very alert. "I am ready to reclaim my life," she said.

"What about school? It's too late to start at Vassar, right?" I asked. I wanted to show my support by being involved.

"I've already missed three weeks." Carly bit her lip and tears formed in the corners of her eyes. "I'll go back next semester. Maybe I can add a couple of courses from the community college for now."

"We talked about that," Joanie said. "We believe you should take it easy and focus on recovery."

I alternated between biting my lip and biting my cuticles. I didn't really know if I was supposed to talk. In the courtyard, a small group of girls about Carly's and my ages walked by with two adults dressed in skirt-suits like Joanie.

"Those are my cottage mates," she said to me with a shrug. "One just got here last week, the other two have been with me most of the time. The one in red, she nearly OD'd too. The EMTs gave her naloxone or she would have died. She's doing better though."

"Pay attention, Carly," my mom quietly reminded.

"I am, Mom. I am so grateful for my team." She gestured with her shoulder toward the doctor and Joanie. "I'm not ready to go at this without them, so I'll drive back for group sessions, but I want to get home and sleep with Kelly Green. I miss her and my bed and my friends, even the ones I pissed off."

"I think we have a strong, positive plan in place for Carly," the doctor said. "We have daily and nightly group meetings for our discharge patients. She can see her local therapist in Poughkeepsie, and we've also put her in touch with an age-appropriate Narcotics Anonymous meeting nearby."

We sat there talking about Carly and her recovery program for over an hour. Just before the meeting was over, I piped in, asking my very important question. I needed to know what the rules were.

"What happens if Carly is hanging out with me and friends and someone smells like weed because they've been smoking on their own?"

My mother glared at me. "Didn't we just go over that in the car? No drugs or alcohol in the house or around Carly," Mom said. Carly just stared at me with no expression.

"You know, a lot of my friends use drugs recreationally and I'm worried that eventually Carly is bound to find herself around people who smoke or take pills."

"You can't control everything, dear," Joanie said, gently patting my hand with her soft fingers. "Carly knows that kids do drugs. They smoke pot and they drink beer and many, like she did, do worse, but Carly's goal is to stay away from people who engage in dangerous behavior of all types, and I know you will do what you can to support her."

"Of course," I said.

"She's worried because her boyfriend vapes," Carly announced loudly. I suddenly regretted sharing that information with Carly. I had wanted to be completely transparent with her before her discharge. Now I wasn't sure what I should and should not tell her.

"Carly!" I said. Why did she have to implicate Bryce? Damn. "That's not true," I lied for the sake of lying.

"Isn't it though?" she said. The adults and professionals just stared at us. I think Joanie was trying to suppress a disapproving pout, but my mom's face was frozen.

"Ivy, is this going to be a problem?" My mom gritted her teeth and enunciated every word."

"Oh Mom, he's a nice guy. You said so yourself. He doesn't present a risk at all. Really, you're getting hysterical for no reason." If lies were smoke, I'd be on fire right now. I could almost will myself to feel high again. No way was I going to admit to my own drug use. I mean, it was one time in the past month. Hardly a habit, right? But I couldn't stop my self-accusatory thoughts from pummeling my brain.

"I'm just trying to plan for Carly," I said.

"Let's keep this discussion central to Carly's successful re-entry and recovery, shall we?" the doctor said. "Ivy, I'm sure Carly appreciates your concern about your boyfriend and the openness of your questions. The most important aspect of Carly's recovery is that she remove herself from at-risk behavior, and that includes drugs and alcohol of any kind. Your boyfriend should not be bringing drugs or alcohol to your house, and he should not be visiting when he's high. And besides, it's illegal."

"I know. I only brought it up because I want to know what the right thing to do is. I don't even have to date him if it's too risky for Carly." I looked at Carly. "I'd do anything for you." I meant it.

"You're her sister. We know you will do everything in your power to help her get through this difficult transition," Joanie said.

"Ivy, I appreciate your support, but let's focus on my discharge. On me." Carly's eyes were clear and focused. She raised her hand to smooth down her hair. She had always been prettier than me with a cuter figure. I can live with that. I got better grades and definitely didn't get into trouble like her, but it looked like I was getting my big sister back in her best shape—inside and out.

My face turned red and I stared out the window again, away from the incriminating faces. I don't know why I brought up the subject of friends using drugs.

My mother reached over from her chair and turned my cheek toward her. "This is about saving our family, Ivy. I won't let anyone get in the way."

"I know, I know," I stammered. "I won't either. I just wanted to ask the therapist while we were here so I could understand the boundaries." I started to cry.

"Ivy, we'll figure it out, OK?" Carly said. "Let's just get out of here."

"Ivy," Joanie said, "your relationships are yours to negotiate and enjoy. But please, no drugs or alcohol around your sister."

"Jesus, I really opened up Pandora's box," I muttered.

"No, dear, what you must understand is that for Carly, Pandora's box was opened a long time ago, and she's trying to shut it down for good," Joanie said, smiling at Carly.

"Thank you, Joanie," my mother kindly said. "Let's continue with this session so we can get Carly home tonight."

"Yeah, let's," Carly insisted. I was beginning to quickly remember what it was like to have Carly home all the time. It's always all about Carly. I know she almost died. I know she had a problem abusing drugs. I was trying to help. And what do I get? I get everyone slamming into me, yelling about whom I can and cannot date. It's ridiculous, but typical. The Carly Show is always all about Carly.

. . ❦ . .

MY MOM STUCK HER KEY in the front lock and pushed the door wide open. The last time we had been on the front stoop together, Carly had collapsed and nearly died. "Carly, welcome home." My mom smiled from ear to ear. "Come in. Your sister has been working hard to make you feel welcome."

"Yeah, right," Carly glanced sharply at me. "She's been working hard at wearing my clothes and putting them back so I won't notice."

My phone buzzed. It was Bryce. I didn't dare respond until I could be alone.

"Come on in, honey. I made all your favorite foods." My mom put down the suitcase and gestured that we all go into the kitchen area.

"Everything looks so nice," Carly nodded, looking around at the white cabinets and shiny stainless appliances. "The kitchen looks new."

"Yes, that's why we took the place. Originally, Allie and I thought we might have to work out of our homes, but then we found the church kitchen. Here, have some of this beet and goat-cheese salad, and I made your favorite balsamic grilled chicken."

"Sounds good. What about dessert?" Carly asked, plopping down on one of the new counter stools mom bought the other day. I sat next to her and watched as my mom served her.

"That too, just wait," my mom said.

"Wow, Mom, you must have been preparing for Carly's homecoming all week," I said.

She put her elbows on the counter and looked right at Carly. I could have left the room for all anyone cared. "I don't want to overwhelm you, but I think it's important to get you into a routine as soon as possible."

"Mom, give me a day to settle in. I need to set up my therapies and then I'll look for a job."

"Carly, you don't need to look for a job. Why don't you think about helping Allie and me until you get your bearings?" I kinda felt forgotten, like I suddenly dropped from number-one daughter and live-in best friend to the bottom of the heap. Carly took precedence, as she usually did. Stupid of me to have forgotten the pecking order in this household.

I pushed back my chair and said, "I'm going upstairs. I'll see you when you're done."

"Don't go," Carly half-heartedly said. "Let's all finish and eat cookies in bed like always. I've missed our sleepovers. I've missed you. Cheers to sisters, remember?"

"Of course, I remember." I put out my fist and we fist bumped. "Love you like a sister, sister," I said.

"Love my girls," my mom said, finally looking up at me and smiling like she might actually remember my existence. I really had to stop competing with my sister. "Let's go upstairs now and have a slumber party," Mom said.

As we trudged up the stairs, my phone buzzed again. I ignored it.

Chapter Fifteen—TayTay

"Hey Phoebes," I said at lunch. I was sitting with her and some of her cheerleading friends in the cafeteria. They all wore their hair long and straight. They had on jeans and black ankle booties, and they wore tight sweaters. I was wearing a similar uniform, I had to admit, but flats instead of boots, and my shirt was loose.

I looked around to see if Bryce was anywhere nearby, but I only saw Ethan out of the corner of my eye. He was sitting across the room with some of his drama friends. Tryouts for the school play were next week, and Ethan was excited about his audition and bugging me to try out for a part as well. I hadn't agreed, but I figured I'd probably do it.

"Did you ever find a babysitter for Annie's little sister?" I asked, with feigned indifference.

"Huh?" She gave me a puzzled expression. Her silky black hair looked like it could be in a shampoo commercial, it was so perfectly straight and shiny down her back. Suddenly, her face lit up and she grinned. "Oh right, so no, Annie can't go. Why? Do you need a ticket?"

"Didn't we give Annie's ticket to Emma?" one of the cheerleaders asked.

"We did. Sorry. I forgot you told me you wanted to go." Phoebe put her hand on my shoulder. "Maybe next time." She then whipped her hair to the right and left, pulled out a lip gloss, and rolled the sticky, shiny liquid on her mouth.

"No worries," I said, smiling and happy. "Zoey's mom got us house-seats tickets. Row 20, center."

"Amazing. Maybe we'll see you. We have VIP passes, so we're going backstage first. Are you going with Bryce? I thought he had a college interview this weekend."

"I think he does." I flashed her my best fake smile. "My sister is going with Zoey and Ethan and me. How are you guys getting to Newark?"

I was fumbling my words. I stuck my hands in my jeans pocket and stood there sheepishly. When I was with Phoebe, something felt wrong. I didn't speak easily or stand still comfortably. I felt on edge.

She flipped her hair again and smacked her lips. "Uber. Maybe we'll see you there, k?"

Later that afternoon, in the car with Zoey, Carly, and Ethan, I moaned, "Of course, she has VIP passes. I mean, that girl can one-up anyone anytime. It's unbelievable."

"I told you," Ethan said, shining his shoe with the sleeve of his shirt. "Chatting her up in class and doing your math homework together is fine, but don't expect her to be real."

"Sadly, he's right," Zoey agreed. Her steely eyes were sharply focused on the busy highway. Carly sat up front with Zoey, and I sat in the back with Ethan, squooshed next to a huge poster for SOAN.

The SOAN conference wasn't until January, but Zoey and her group had been frantically making signs and posting on social media for a few weeks. Ever since Zoey's mother emerged from her grief, Mrs. Marks had been busy helping Zoey to organize the group. So far I hadn't done much except repost on my own Insta, but I promised Zoey that I would kick into action after the holidays.

We drove slowly to Newark in bumper-to-bumper traffic. I was starving and broke out the picnic dinner before we crossed the Jersey line.

"Here everyone, half an avocado-and-salmon sandwich and some grapes." I started to hand out the food. "And lots of butterscotch chocolate-chip cookies." I held up the gallon-sized Ziploc bag containing a dozen or more of my mom's specialty.

"I just want the cookies, please," Carly said.

"Yeah, pass them up," Zoey said, driving carefully. The row of cars moved slowly through the streets of downtown Newark as we neared the arena.

"She won't start on time, will she?" I wondered aloud.

"Definitely not," Carly said.

"Are you nervous you'll run into people you know?" Ethan asked her. He was decked out in a bright purple shirt and tan jeans. He cocked his head and crossed his legs, looking up through the center console toward the front of the car. It was nearly dark.

"Not really," Carly admitted earnestly. "My friends are more into EDM than Taylor Swift, plus most of my friends are away at college."

"That's true," I said. "I hope you have fun though."

"Of course, I will." She turned to the back seat. "Thanks for offering me the ticket. I almost feel like a regular person again."

"Did you get a job?" Zoey asked. Her fingers gripped the wheel. I wondered if she thought about her brother when she was around Carly. She never showed her emotions.

"Sort of," Carly said. "I'm working with our moms for now. They're teaching me how to cook and package, and I'm teaching them how to use social media. We're having a grand old time."

"Hey, don't knock it," I said.

Carly swiveled her head to look at me in the eye.

"Yeah, I am lucky I can work with them, and don't think I don't know it."

Zoey turned back to look at me. "She is really lucky," was all she said.

"Hey, Ivy, what college is Bryce looking at this weekend?" Carly changed the subject like she was turning the page over in a book.

"Colgate and Cornell," I said. "He'll be back tomorrow night." I picked at my cuticles. I always tore at my dry skin when I felt on edge. I hadn't taken another hit from a vape or a blunt, but Bryce always offered me a hit every time he lit up. I said no because I didn't want to feel like a hypocrite when I was around Carly, but truthfully, it didn't bother me as much anymore. Bryce insisted that it made him calm and relaxed, and I really think it did.

I remembered the trip to Dauber's house and frowned, but I wasn't about to share that story with my friends or Carly. They were already wary about Bryce and I didn't want to fuel the fire. Instead, I acted like an overbearing mother and pushed food onto my sister. "Have another cookie, Carly." I held the bag over the seat. The backseat felt sticky under my hands. I was sick of sitting. We didn't have much farther to go. I could see the sign for the parking lot right next to the arena, but the traffic wasn't moving.

"I'm fine," she sassed back, waving her fingers with a cookie in between two middle fingers.

"Ivy," Ethan said loudly from his perch next to me. It sounded like he was yelling in my ear. "Did you hear that Phoebe and those guys were planning to do X and G before the concert? That's what I heard from the girls in choir. Wonder who supplied them?" Ethan glared at me.

"Come on, just stop it," I protested, but I was pretty sure I knew who got Phoebe any and all of her drugs.

Carly didn't say a word, but her surprised face and deep, dark stare said all there was to say. She looked pissed.

"Ivy, it's one thing if Bryce vapes now and again. It's quite another if he deals."

I lied straight out. "He doesn't deal."

Zoey looked at me in the rearview mirror. "Are you sure?"

"Well no, not exactly sure," I admitted.

"What do you mean?" Ethan demanded, touching my knee with his hand for emphasis.

"I mean . . ." I fumbled for the right words. "I mean that he does smoke a lot of weed, I gotta be honest. And sometimes, he and his brother associate with people who do more."

"What are you trying to say? He deals or he doesn't?" Carly asked softly.

I felt like everyone was just waiting for me to incriminate Bryce.

"He doesn't, not really," I said, hardly feeling sure of myself. I felt badly talking about drug abuse in front of both Carly and Zoey. I thought through what I wanted to say and how I wanted to say it.

"Bryce's just a normal suburban boy who likes to get high. He and Phoebe are good friends. Of course she would ask him if she wanted to try something different or smoke something, or whatever."

Zoey sat up taller in her seat. I could tell she was paying attention to every word I said and reading meaning into how I said it, so I tried to be as clear as possible.

"Listen, he's my boyfriend and I really like him a lot. And I think he likes me a lot too." I smiled in spite of myself. "He's not a bad guy at all, and I wish you'd stop making him out to be some kind of drug dealer for teenagers."

"I'm just repeating what's said about him," Zoey said. "And it goes for his older brother too. People have seen Jonathan Houston lurking around town in his fancy convertible. Why isn't he back at school?"

"He's going back after the weekend, I think." I raised my voice for a moment but then reined in my frustration and spoke rationally. "Let's change the subject. Are we almost there?"

Zoey switched the music to Taylor Swift songs and we all sang along until were able to pull into the parking lot.

Once inside the vast arena, I couldn't believe how close we were to the stage. The audience was mostly female, of course. Wearing sequined princess crowns, little girls sat with their moms, and pre-teen girls jumped up and down together, all wearing matching feathered wings, the number thirteen Magic Markered on their hands. Girls my age were wearing everything from jeans to bright-colored short fancy dresses. I saw a few fans wearing sparkly lights, and nearly everyone had glitter all over their faces and clothing. The four of us took out our own glitter pens and painted purple and silver sparkles around our eyes and cheeks. Zoey wore a black and red short skirt and teeny tank top. Up front, I could see three stages and a huge video wall. I couldn't wait for it to start.

There were so few boys at the concert that Ethan stood out in the crowd like a celebrity. His deep, dreamy eyes were always noticed, and people stared at him. The older and taller he got, the better looking he became. He was bouncing all over the place and laughing and giggling with all the girls around us—a real showman, that's for sure.

My phone buzzed. Bryce was texting me. "Hey there, guess where I am?"

I texted back, "Ithaca?" He had an interview in the morning.

"Not quite yet. Look up toward the stage on the left," he texted.

I looked up, a funny feeling gathering in my head. Was he here? I just saw a mass of circles with all different-colored clothing. The place was packed at eight thirty. Everyone was waiting for the lights to dim and for Taylor Swift to make her dramatic entrance.

"Look to your left, next to the people with the bright-pink banner that says 'Taylor Forever.'"

Oh my God, I saw him. He was sitting right at the stage. I could see Phoebe's long black hair, her back to me.

"Guys," I said, "Bryce is here." I pointed my phone in his direction.

"With who?" Zoey wrinkled her nose, confused.

"What's going on? Why didn't you tell me you were coming tonight?" I texted. I could see him in the stands, holding his phone. He wore a blue button-down and jeans.

"He's with Phoebe and her friends." I said. "What the fuck?"

The phone rang. It was Bryce. "Surprise," he said. I could see his wide toothy smile from where I was standing, not too far back, but definitely not at the stage.

"How come you didn't tell me you'd be here?" I asked. Meanwhile, Bryce was fast-talking into my phone.

"Phoebe offered me an extra ticket at the last minute, right before I left for Ithaca, so I decided to come along and I'll drive up in the morning. I wanted to say hi. You look adorable from here."

"Uh, thanks," I muttered. "I thought we were going to go together and you couldn't get tickets, remember? And now you're here with her. It's kinda weird." I tried to keep my voice light and uncomplicated but I frowned toward Zoey. This just seemed too strange.

"Crazy story. Maybe you can come up here and stand with us."

"I don't think so, Bryce. I'm with my friends and sister. Enjoy the show." My voice was cracking. Ethan and Zoey looked at me with open mouths. Zoey put her arm around me.

"I told you he was a douche bag," Ethan said.

"Ivy, I can hear that. Don't be mad. It all happened so fast. As I was getting ready to leave, Phoebe called me. She needed something and so I stopped by on my way to drop it off."

"What did she need?" I surprised myself with the severity of my tone with him. I had never been so nasty.

"Ivy, stop," he said. "When I got to her house, she still had an extra ticket so we just decided I'd take it. No big deal."

"Bryce, why did you have to stop at her house?" My mood was shot for this concert. I thought about Carly working so hard to get well and come home. I couldn't get mixed up with a drug dealer. But my knees felt weak, looking up ahead at him. He was so cute. And it was nice of him to call and explain everything.

"Why didn't he call before he left Marble Springs?" Carly asked. "I mean, it would have been nice for him to tell you as soon as he knew."

"I wanted to surprise you here—like this," he answered. "But I guess it's not going so well. Please don't be mad, Ivy. Let's meet up after the show."

"Hang up," Ethan demanded, "or I will for you."

Just then, the lights went off and the crowd roared in excitement. I clicked off my phone and gave an off-handed wave toward his general direction. I wasn't going to allow this annoyance to ruin my night.

The stage lights suddenly blew up in pink and white and a bright laser light show shot daggers of color across the arena. Above my head, a ball of white began to descend and then move closer toward the stage and onto one of the extended white planks that were built out into the audience. Taylor Swift, in a shiny black leotard with tall high-heeled black boots emerged from the glowing orb and stood not ten feet in front of me. I swear she looked right at me. She brought the microphone to her mouth and began, "Ready for It?" The interactive bracelets we all received when we entered the arena blinked in multicolors in time to the music as she sang, with lots of beautiful dancers prancing across the multistage set.

The concert was amazing, with fireworks, aerialists, a multi-layered water fountain, ridiculously tall inflatable pythons, and even a flying serpent skeleton. I almost forgot about Bryce for bits and pieces of the performance, but when she sang "Love Story" and "You Belong with Me," my heart started to race, and I felt really antsy about our conversation. I looked up into the dark stadium seats in Bryce's general direction. My phone buzzed in my hand and I saw that he had texted heart emojis. I sent some back just moments before Taylor began crooning, "Should've Said No." Maybe I should've, too.

We danced like maniacs to every song and sang loudly, nearly yelling all the words. At one point, Taylor Swift walked out toward the audience on a raised platform and she held her hand right over my head. I was so close to her I could see the sweat bubbles on her shoulders.

The last encore was "We Are Never Ever Getting Back Together," and then Taylor said goodbye. The lights came on and I immediately looked for Bryce. He was gone from his seat. Ethan gently pushed me forward.

"Let's get to the car before we get stuck in a long line," Ethan said.

"Too late for that," Carly said. "What an amazing show."

My phone rang and I picked up immediately. Ethan continued to shove me toward the exit.

"Hey," I said, still looking in the empty seats where he had been sitting.

"Unbelievable show, right? And I'm not even a real fan. She danced right over to you. Did she drip sweat on you?"

"Eww, no. Where'd you go?" We were nearly out of the auditorium. People were swarming all around us and I held onto the back of Zoey's shirt so I wouldn't lose her.

"I'll meet you outside the arena, OK? Just for a second. Exit 10," he said.

"I don't know, Bryce. It's really crowded. I'm not the driver and I'm with people. Where did your little posse go?"

"They went backstage again. Phoebe has VIP passes for two so they're taking turns. I went before the show."

"Did you meet Taylor?"

"Are you kidding me? We had the lowest form of VIP passes. We stood around some large reception area and mingled with some dancers and backup singers. It was a bust if you ask me, but Phoebe thinks maybe after the show she'll get to meet her."

"Maybe Taylor will invite Phoebe to tour with her," I said.

"Maybe, and maybe you're out of your mind with jealousy? Is that what I'm hearing?"

"Oh shut up," I said angrily, but I recognized the grain of truth in what he was saying. "Text me when you get to Cornell tomorrow. Drive safely."

"I can't see you for even a second?" he pleaded.

Ethan gave me another push, this time stronger. "Stop talking and move it. We've got to get out of here."

I turned around and glared at Ethan. Someone bumped into me from the side and I nearly dropped the phone. "Bryce, I've got to go. I'm getting killed in the crowd. Talk to you later. You still have some explaining to do."

"Chill," he said in a whisper. "I'll talk to you later, when it's quiet."

"OK, bye." I moved a little faster, took Zoey's and Carly's hands in mine, and pushed forward, leading the group.

Ethan trailed behind, wailing, "Wait a second, don't lose me."

"We couldn't if we tried," Zoey said.

On the way back, in the pitch black of the backroads in town, I thought about Bryce being at the concert with Phoebe. It made me mad, but of course what upset me more was the implications of their connection. Were drugs involved? He hadn't sounded high, but I never could tell.

"You OK?" Zoey asked from the driver's seat. Carly and Ethan were sleeping in the back.

"Yeah, that was a great show and a great night. Thank you so much," I said.

"I wouldn't worry about Phoebe. They're just friends."

"I know." I lowered my voice and quickly turned to the backseat to make sure Carly was asleep. "I worry more about the drugs, quite frankly."

"I get it, but people our age get high. Most can handle it but some can't, like our siblings," Zoey said softly, so she wouldn't wake up Carly and Ethan. "You really like him, huh?"

"Yes, I think so. He's a little sneaky sometimes though, like tonight. Why wouldn't he have texted me before the concert and told me he was going? Why wait until we were already seated? It's weird."

"Do you trust him?" We were almost home. Carly and I were getting dropped off first.

"Mostly," I said.

"See what happens. It's early days."

As soon as she stopped the car, Ethan and Carly woke up. Carly and I waved as Zoey pulled away.

"That was fabulous," Carly said, rubbing her eyes. I fumbled for the key. "Thanks for including me. I really appreciate it."

"Of course." I wrapped an arm across her shoulder. "I'm glad you're home."

"Me too."

We went straight to bed. Around one thirty in the morning, Bryce texted, "a kiss for luck and we're on our way…"

He loved the Carpenters. Most people our age had no idea who they were. "We've only just begun," I texted back and then continued with some Taylor Swift lyrics, "And the fakers gonna fake, fake, fake, fake, fake."

"Huh?" he typed back.

I sent him a funny-faced emoji and wrote, "Just random songs ringing in my ears, that's all. Good luck tomorrow. Night."

He sent me some "Zzzz" emojis and we hung up.

In my head, the song continued, "Baby, I'm just gonna shake, shake, shake it off."

Chapter Sixteen—Tryouts

"Y ou'll love it," Zoey said about the play she and Ethan convinced me to try out for. "It's a screwball comedy and really funny."

I agreed because honestly, I thought a last-minute drama addition would look good on my college application, which was due in about a month, and I needed to beef it up a bit.

On the afternoon of tryouts, Bryce walked me to the theater and gave me a peck on the lips for good luck. As he walked away, I saw Ethan stick his tongue out in our direction.

"Hey, why are you so mean? He hasn't done anything to hurt you," I said, after Bryce left.

"That whole Taylor Swift scene was weird. I don't think he's good for you, that's all, right Zoey?" Ethan looked to Zoey, who was reading the script. She glanced up and smiled.

"I'm pleading the fifth." She rocked back and forth lightly on her low pumps. Zoey wore a billowy green silk dress, and her glasses had fallen down her nose.

"He explained why he was there with Phoebe. It was cool."

"OK, if you say so." Ethan ran his tongue over his lips. "Whatever."

"Actually, I don't care if you like him or not," I said. My cheeks felt flushed and sweat began to bead under my arms. I could see Ms. Bucci, the drama coach, standing on stage, holding a clipboard in front of her with one hand and gesturing with the other to a stocky boy from my biology class. "Let's go in and get this over with."

We made our way down the center aisle toward the front of the auditorium. Ethan whispered, "Don't be mad, Ivy. I'm just looking out for you."

"You don't have to. I don't worry about your love life," I hissed.

"That's because I don't have one."

"Shush up you two. Focus on the audition," Zoey whispered.

While I waited for my turn, I imagined it being the actual performance night. My mom and Carly would be in the front row and maybe Bryce would be sitting with them. I liked the idea of being onstage, and hoped I'd get a good part.

Ethan went first. His audition went really well. He was hysterical and had great stage presence.

When it was my turn to read, I gathered up my skirt and scrambled up the wooden stairs at the front of the stage. To my horror, I stepped on the back of my skirt as I stepped up and fell smack on my face across the stage. My nose hurt like hell and I knew my face was red, but I got up and looked at Ms. Bucci. "Ooops. Maybe we could make the fortune teller a klutz," I joked.

"Maybe," she said, not smiling. Ms. Bucci didn't look old enough to have graduated high school. She was willowy with brown and blond-highlighted hair tied in a messy bun. "No parts will be assigned until after everyone has read," she declared sternly.

Miss Bucci had me read from the early part of the play. I tried to ham up my silly lines. Zoey went after me, and she read from the fortune-teller part I liked, Madame Zenobia. I could tell that Ms. Bucci thought she was good by the way she encouraged Zoey to read more lines and speak louder. She bobbed her head up and down as Zoey enunciated all the words and exaggerated the funniest parts.

After auditions, we went to Zoey's house, flopping ourselves down on the sofas in the basement.

"Phew, glad that's over," Ethan said.

"Me too," Zoey said. "I can't wait for them to post the parts."

"I doubt we'll know for a few days," I said.

"It's such a funny play. Whoever even heard of it, *You Can't Take the House*," Ethan said, "but a good choice, I think."

"My brother used to get all the leads in the plays and the musicals," Zoey said as she walked toward the casement window, looking out at the row of bushes. "He wanted to be an actor."

"I'm sorry," Ethan mumbled, burying his head in a bag of chips as he spoke.

"Me too," I said. "Sounds like he was very talented."

"He was." Zoey came back to the sofa and lay down, resting her feet atop the back cushions. She focused her gaze on the ceiling. "Please, stop saying you're sorry. I really hate that expression. It wasn't your fault, or mine, or anyone's but his. Before drugs, my brother was a typical, normal, great guy. I mean, you have to know, he was the last person you'd suspect would get involved in drugs. It started with a busted knee and some painkillers." I couldn't tell if she was crying, but I felt tears well in my eyes.

"Carly, too, was the last person you'd suspect would do drugs. I mean, we had no idea until it was too late."

"Well, it's not too late. She's home," Zoey said. "I think we need to do something positive in the wake of all these overdoses. Let's get going on that SOAN speaker for the assembly."

"Don't we have enough going on at the moment with college applications and the play? Maybe we should push it off till spring." I really wanted to hold off on public speaking about drugs, but Zoey wasn't going to drop the idea.

"No, January is a good time for a speaker. Nothing goes on in January, and you want to stay inside. We need to talk to the principal and secure a speaker." I could practically see Zoey's brain whirring away. She kept talking. "It's really a no-brainer to set this up. We can ask someone from a rehab or from the government's office on drugs, and we can have some students speak and some family survivors tell their stories. I would do it, and maybe your sister would share her experience."

"Maybe, but she just got home. She's really busy. She goes to meetings nearly every night and she has outpatient treatment back at Blue Hills. And she's working for our moms."

"That's great. Just stay close to her. You never know what might trigger a break. I don't mean to be a downer, but you don't want this." Zoey spread her arms out, meaning I don't want her world. And I didn't.

"Let's get through the play and then we can worry about the assembly." Ethan reached over my leg and scooped up some M&M's. He only ate this much junk food when he was nervous.

"Hand me those M&M's, Ethan." I was full but wanted to plow more food into my gut. I didn't like talking about drugs and overdosing. "I'm happy to help you," I reassured Zoey. "But can it wait a little?"

"Yeah, just till after New Year's," Ethan said, nodding in agreement, and then turned toward me. "Ivy, I know you think I'm a total dick to say this, but everyone knows Bryce buys and sells drugs to his friends. It's would be kinda strange for you to organize an anti-drug speaker when your boyfriend is a big part of the problem."

"I'm not organizing anything right now." I got up and stood right in front of his face. "Seriously, Ethan, back off. Practically everyone has tried or does some kind of drug recreationally. Our point would be to educate people on the real dangers of drug abuse, opiates, heroin, fentanyl. My sister, Zoey's brother, and so many others got caught up in the most dangerous aspect of drug abuse. That's what the talk should focus on, not occasional vaping."

"You are seriously misled if that's what you think, Ivy," Ethan argued, his hand going back into the M&M's bag. I felt myself wanting more too, but I knew it was just an emotional reaction to the tension in the room.

"I just think we need to be realistic and not act like all the adults who want to ban all drugs because of the bad ones. All I'm trying to say is that getting high is part of the American culture, for teens and adults. When was the last time you got high?" I stood up, flipped my hair back, and looked hard at both of them.

"I don't know, over the summer." Ethan bit his lip, thinking. "Before Carly OD'd, that's for sure. What about you?"

I looked back toward the window casements and walked toward the gym area. Should I tell the truth? "I don't know, around then."

"I haven't ever gotten high," Zoey said. Her eyes were downcast. She picked up a throw pillow and punched it before returning it to the club chair. "Nick was wasted so much and I was scared of altering any part of my brain."

"Do you ever want to try now?" I asked. "Sometimes, you know what they say, curiosity killed the cat. It's pretty harmless, if you smoke the right stuff."

"Ivy, really? You want to go there?" Ethan popped off the sofa and came toward me. He knew I was bullshitting. I couldn't put anything past him. "You've gotten high with Bryce, haven't you?" he demanded, grabbing my arm and turning me to face him.

"You realize that smoking pot and using opiates really are two completely different animals? One doesn't necessarily lead to the other," I said.

"It's OK, I'm not mad. I just want to know. We have to talk about this," he insisted. "Tell me the truth."

"No, I haven't gotten high since Carly went in the hospital."

"You swear?" he asked, looking directly into my face. I had to look away. I focused my stare on the bag of M&M's.

"Bryce gets high a lot, OK? You're right. But I stay clear of it." There, I thought, that was sort of the truth, a little lie by omission. "But I don't always think it's so terrible. Maybe we should all try it in a safe place together. We could make sure we only used the mellow stuff that makes you feel creative and giddy but doesn't last long. We should know what we're talking about if we're going to hold an assembly about drug abuse."

"Ivy, I sort of get where you're going here—knowledge is power and all. And I don't disagree that recreational use is not terrible, but . . . I don't know, I think it's hypocritical," Zoey said.

"Hear me out." I had been mulling this over for days. "Isn't it more hypocritical to criticize drugs when we haven't really experienced them ourselves?"

"No, it's not," Zoey loudly and emphatically exclaimed. "We need to talk about death and dying. Why and how someone easily begins to abuse opiates. How the drugs are laced with fentanyl. How to get help. Where to turn, that sort of thing, not how fun it is to get high with a vape. That's irrelevant and frankly, counter to our mission."

"I think part of our mission is to distinguish between safe drug use, as in legal drug use, versus the dangers of narcotics and serious drug abuse. It's all part of the reality and the problem." I felt very sure about this, even if I wasn't so into planning a conference. I hadn't told them the truth exactly, but I thought my points were on target. "Marijuana is legal in many states."

"Maybe we should talk to a professional about that point first," Ethan said. "This has to come up all the time, especially given that marijuana is legal in Massachusetts, barely an hour away."

"Let's table this for now, OK?" Zoey said. "We can talk to the principal tomorrow and take it from there."

"Right, good plan." Ethan sat upright. "Hey, look at your phones, there's an email from Ms. Bucci."

My heart raced as I fumbled to open my phone.

"I got it, I got it," Zoey yelled. "I got the part!"

"Me too, me too!" Ethan exclaimed.

I scrolled down three lines to see the email from the drama department. Zoey got the part of the realtor. Ethan got one of the burglars. Where was my name? Then I saw it, at the bottom of the list.

I got the role of the police officer's mother, the least exciting of the female parts.

"Who got Madame Zenobia?" I asked at the exact same moment that my eyes caught the words on the screen.

"Phoebe Li! Are you fucking kidding me?" Incredulous, I stood up and stared at my friends. "I didn't even know she tried out."

"I heard a few people were allowed to read last night," Zoey said, avoiding eye contact.

"She's the least funny person I know, and the least likely person I know who would ever be cast as the fortune teller," Ethan said.

"She's so wrong for the part. I can't believe it." I paced around the room in front of Zoey and Ethan, who were staring at me like I was out of my mind.

"I believe it," Zoey said. "Phoebe gets whatever she wants, whether it's a part in a play, the lead in the spring musical—and she can't sing, I may add—or president of the student body. She's just that 'it' person. Didn't you have that person at Preston?"

"Yeah. It was me," I groaned.

"Oh, it will be fun," Ethan said. "The three of us will have a great time together. I'm pumped."

"Of course you're happy. You got the lead," I said.

"It's an ensemble cast," Zoey said. "You're going to be hysterical."

"I'm sorry for what I said about Bryce," Ethan said, his head hung, eyes looking down. "I'm just looking out for you."

"I know. And I'm sorry if I offended you about the weed. I just think we need to be realistic about what goes on in the world."

"I know," Ethan said. "But I think our focus should be on the hard drugs and what they can and are doing to our friends and family, right Zoey?"

"Exactly," she said. "Get real. You know what they say, 'perception is reality.'"

"Who said that?" I asked.

"I have no idea, but it's true." Zoey moved closer. I could smell the chocolate on her breath. "That you hang out with Bryce, who everyone knows is Mr. Untouchable, the rich kid who sells drugs and gets away with it. People are going to associate you with him and believe that you do what he does. And anyone who knows about your sister will also link you to the drug world." Zoey sat down and covered her eyes. I heard her gulp back tears.

I knew she was thinking about Nick. I didn't know what to say. I knew I had lied to them about getting high with Bryce. I was a phony. A fake, and worse, a liar, but it was too late to fess up. "Let's just drop it, OK?"

Zoey looked up at me, tears running down her face. "We can drop it, but the problem won't disappear."

"I know." I couldn't look at either her or Ethan. I wanted to vomit and my head began to hurt.

When I got home, I avoided my mom and Carly. I couldn't face them. How could I be the supportive, loyal sister I wanted to be if I was dating Bryce and using too? I went straight to my room. I needed some peace and quiet to think.

My phone buzzed just as I was dozing off. I looked up and checked the phone.

I closed my eyes and heard the phone chime the song I programmed in for Bryce, "We've Only Just Begun." I didn't answer.

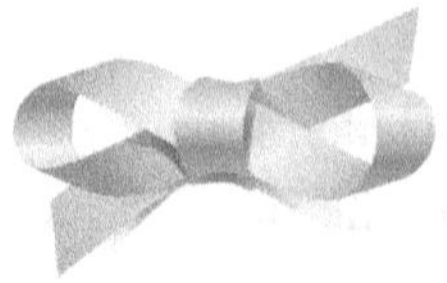

Chapter Seventeen—Spinning

"Let's take a spin class," my sister suggested, when we woke up on the first cold day of fall. "It will invigorate us both and it burns more calories than anything else I can think of." I was snuggled up in her bed, wearing flannel pajamas and a dried-up green mask on my face. Kelly Green rested between us.

"I don't want to get up, do you? And anyway, it costs too much and is too far away. Let's just walk the reservoir."

"I have free passes from Oliver," Carly said.

"Who?" I had no idea who she was talking about.

"The cute boy I met at Blue Hills. His mother works for them in the city. And no, let's take a drive to Scarsdale and take the class. It'll be fun."

Ugh, just hearing the name Scarsdale brought up a vision of Dauber's house and all the drugs. I had to shake off the bad thoughts. Carly and I hadn't done much alone together, so if this is what she wanted to do on a chilly, wet Saturday, I'd go along. "Maybe Mom wants to go too. Girls' day out."

"I'd love to join you," mom said. She was drinking her chamomile tea in front of her computer screen when we made it down to the kitchen dressed in workout uniforms of black leggings and cotton tank tops.

By the time we hit the parkway, it was 11 a.m. and we were signed up to take the last class they offered for the morning. The class was billed as "Aretha Franklin versus Taylor Swift" music.

"Something for all of us," I commented, as we trudged up the cement stairs of the studio.

"I'm so happy you included me, girls," Mom said, smiling from ear to ear.

"Really? We should have taken you to the concert," I said, and laughed.

In the low-lit room lined with five rows of identical stationary bikes, we took spots along the sides and began to adjust the settings for seat and handlebar height. Up front, a lean, bearded guy in his late twenties positioned LED candles in front of the podium bike. As I buckled in my shoes and tightened up the wheel, the teacher joked about being gay and dating in New York City. He greeted my mom personally with a Texan twang and told Carly and me to "Watch out for your tough little mama and listen to what she tells you. She's strong and smart, and that's what she wants for you too."

He meant to encourage my mom, who I imagined must be feeling a little out of place in a room full of twenty-somethings. Looking around, she was clearly the oldest one in the room but definitely not the only parent in the room. The instructor's good-humored jokes and cheer reminded me to value my mom's presence and wisdom.

During class, I thought a lot about Bryce and our relationship. I liked him, no doubt about it, but I worried about his steady influence on me. I often found myself wanting to please him instead of thinking through what might really be best, like not vaping and not watching him buy drugs for friends and his brother. It was too easy to forget with whom my loyalty needed to remain.

Carly, Mom, and I belted out our own half-remembered versions of all the songs, high-fiving each other like everyone else. Some people swung their towels around. I thought that was a little much. When we were doing the final stretch, the young instructor led a "Namaste" with a bow, and then he turned on the lights. Sweat dripped down my back and I could feel my hair sticking to my neck.

"I feel amazing," my mom said, as she stretched her legs on the bike.

"Me too." Carly's arms and legs looked spindly thin but her face was radiant and glowing from the heat and exertion of the workout.

"Hey, Ivy!" I heard a familiar voice shout to me from across the room. "What are you doing here?" I couldn't believe it. Phoebe Li walked toward me, fist bumping with the instructor as she walked by.

"I thought I was the only goofy one to drive this far to work out," she said, "but he's amazing, isn't he?" Phoebe pointed one of her long, thin, and immaculately manicured fingers toward the instructor. "You know, he does stand-up comedy in New York City."

"No wonder he's so funny," Carly said.

"That was really great." My mom wiped sweat off her brow and smiled at Phoebe.

"Carly, this is Phoebe, a friend from school and a good friend of Bryce's. Mom, you remember Phoebe." I stood up straight and pushed my hair back. I was sure I looked and smelled horrible. I had perspired and my hair felt stringy and greasy. "Great class."

"Hmm, hi," she said. Phoebe fist bumped me. We all walked out to the waiting area to put on our street shoes.

Phoebe stuffed her hands in her purse and pulled out a mint. She dug into her big black leather tote and held out three more pieces. "Anyone?"

We all shook our heads. My mom and Carly excused themselves. "See you outside," Carly said.

"What's Bryce up to today? You should have brought him. He could use a little exercise, don't you think?" She laughed and tossed her hair back then found her lip gloss and smeared it across her mouth. She never looked bad, I thought.

"Hardly," I said. "He's at home sleeping, I'm sure."

"His friend Doug Dauber lives right around the corner, d'you ever meet him?"

"Yeah," I said. I couldn't believe she was bringing up that kid's name.

"I was thinking of popping over to Dauber's to see if he was home, but I wouldn't do that without Bryce's OK. Do you think I should just drop by and ring the doorbell? Or call Bryce first?"

"I really think you should stay away from Dauber. Talk to Bryce, but I doubt he'd want you messing with his friend who happens to also be a drug dealer."

"Oh, come on, Ivy. It's harmless, you know that. Dauber's hot. I think Bryce would be OK with it. He's so easygoing and nice. He's perfect for you, Miss Goody Goody. Glad that relationship took off, with my help, I may add."

The instructor walked toward us and smiled. "Hey girls, great job. See you next time, I hope."

"Thanks, great class." I waved. To Phoebe I said, "That guy was so funny. I barely registered the workout, I was so intent on his music and jokes," I said.

"Yeah, I come here every weekend just to ride with him. I think I'm going to Dauber's."

"Do what you want. I'd call Bryce first though." She obviously had already made her mind up anyway. Phoebe was the kind of girl who always did what she wanted and took what she wanted. "Listen, my mom and sister are waiting outside for me. I'd stay out of trouble if I were you."

"Lucky I'm not you, cuz I love a little trouble now and then, but I'll text Bryce first. I'll tell him I'm interested in Dauber and want to flirt."

"Don't you have a boyfriend?" I asked. We were walking back down the stairs outside, facing the village. I could see my mom and Carly at the cash register of a coffee shop. I hoped they had bought me a cup of coffee.

"Yeah, but he's lame. Dauber's cool as hell, don't you think? Or are you so hung up on Bryce, you can't see straight? You're a cute couple, that's for sure."

"Thanks. I gotta go."

She hugged me, standing there on the sidewalk in Scarsdale.

When I met my mom and Carly in front of the little coffee shop, they were already sipping on hot drinks. Carly handed me a tea. "I share," she said. "Isn't Phoebe the one you talked about at the concert?" Carly asked. "Bryce's friend?"

I wrinkled my mouth into a frown. "She's annoying."

"Why's that, honey?" my mom said. "She seems perfectly normal and nice."

I looked toward Carly. "I think she's going to go find Bryce's friend who lives near here." My eyes wandered toward the other side of the shops, in the direction of where I thought maybe Dauber lived.

"That's so bold of her." Carly's cheeks were rosy and she smiled. She was beginning to really look more like the old healthy Carly. "What's so great about this guy?" She gestured with her hand that we should sit down on the scrolled black bistro chairs. She put down the paper cup of tea. I sucked in my breath and spit out the words I had been wanting to share with her for weeks.

My mom wanted to window-shop a little and was out of earshot. "To be completely transparent, Bryce sells drugs," I said, deadpan. "He is kind of a dealer, at least to his rich friends at school. I didn't want to tell you before because I thought it would be too tempting or something, but I think you should know the kind of guy I'm with. He's really nice and friendly and kind and so good to me and so smart, but he's also, sad to say, a druggie."

Carly's expression was blank. She didn't smile. She didn't frown. She stared at me and didn't say a word for a really long time. I glanced toward my mom. She was still window shopping. The train whizzed by in front of us, screeching to a stop for a brief moment to let off and on the passengers.

"Aren't you going to say something?" I demanded quietly so that my mother wouldn't think something was wrong.

"I don't know what to say," she said, and then went silent again. It was so uncomfortable for me to try and have this honest exchange with Carly when she wasn't giving me any feedback. I couldn't tell if she was mad or surprised or didn't care.

"Well, I told him, no drugs around you or our house. No smoking or vaping or anything."

"Uh, OK," Carly said. "I'm fine, for now. I hardly think about drugs at all."

I looked hard at her face. Her expression finally transformed. She raised her eyebrows and pursed her lips. Then she spoke calmly and clearly. "Actually, I'm not OK, Ivy. I want to take oxy every single day. From the time I wake up till the time I go to sleep. I miss it, but I constantly remind myself that it will kill me, and I don't want to die. So, I will keep pushing the thought of it away, out of my mind's eye. But it's a struggle. OK, so Bryce smokes a lot of weed."

"It's more than that, Carly. He sells drugs to people like Phoebe."

"Phoebe should be more careful with her life."

"Are you mad?" I asked. Mom was heading back toward us.

"Mad? I can't be mad about this. This is how it goes in high school. I just wish I hadn't derailed myself, and I'm so thankful that I am working toward recovery every single day."

"I'm not sure what's going to be with me and Bryce anyway," I said, half-believing my words and mostly not.

"I'm not going to fail because your boyfriend smokes pot. He's just one of many, many high school students who experiment."

"But it's more than that," I tried to tell her.

"It's OK. He's not my business. I'm not the one dating him."

"I don't want him to be a temptation. An easy call." I finally expressed my deepest fear, that Bryce would be the one to make Carly relapse. That scenario scared the life out of me. We huddled together, head to head, at the table. My mom sat down with us and put her coffee down.

"This pastry place is good, but my cookies are better, don't you think?" she asked us.

Carly sat up straight and smiled broadly at my mom. Her eyes got narrower and her blond hair looked whiter in the sunshine. "Absolutely, Mom. Your cookies are way better than any drug. I'm hooked on sugar now," she said, addressing me. "All I have to worry about is diabetes."

"Great," Mom said, not knowing what we had just talked about. I looked over toward the neighborhood of houses and wondered again if Phoebe was sitting around with Dauber.

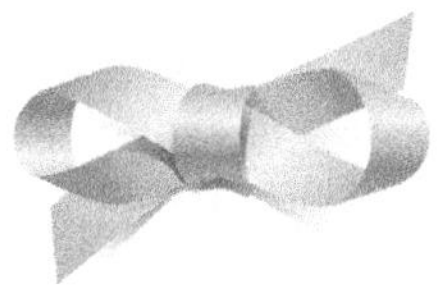

Chapter Eighteen—Interrupted

"The show is in two weeks," Ethan said, standing onstage in the middle of the house set. His pink-striped shirt that we made fun of actually began to fit the character of Merle the burglar.

"Zoey, I have the perfect skirt for your character. Do you want to borrow this tight pinstripe skirt I have? It's by Chloe," Phoebe said.

"Thanks, but no," Zoey said. "I got this." She was wearing a loose silk skirt which, to my knowledge, did look a little too cocktail dressy rather than business, but I wasn't about to argue with her. Phoebe, for her part, looked like an authentic fortune teller, in a billowy chiffon skirt with rhinestones and a sequined halter top that sparkled when the flood lights shined on her, which was often.

"Zoey, maybe Phoebe is right," Ethan said cautiously, not looking directly at Zoey as he spoke, obviously afraid of her reaction. "You might want to wear something more conservative, since you're a realtor."

"Great idea, Ethan," Zoey said sarcastically. "I'll run home and see what I've got in my closet."

"I'm just saying," Ethan sputtered.

"It's OK, I'm just saying too. I've got this," Zoey turned on her heels and walked off the stage.

Just then, I saw Bryce walk through the door at the head of the auditorium, waving toward me. I could see the glitz of his gaudy gold chain all the way from my vantage point on the stage. "Guys, I gotta run, my ride is here."

Bryce took my hand when I reached him in the aisle. "Nice outfit," he said, looking me up and down and tugging on the sleeve of my blousy top. "You're one hot mama. It's a little disconcerting."

I smiled shyly. We got to his car and he took me in his arms by the passenger door.

"I've missed you, Ivy." It had been a week since we'd been alone together. "Let's go to my house. No one's home."

"I don't know," I demurred. "It's late already. Carly and my mom are at home."

"So what? You've been with them nonstop lately. It's my turn, just for a little while, please . . ." He was kissing my neck and rubbing my back and tingles ran up and down my body.

"OK, just for a little while."

When we got to Bryce's house, he immediately led me to his bedroom, nearly pushing me up the stairs. He didn't even offer me a snack, and I was hungry. As soon as we got into his room, he locked the door and began tugging on my blouse, trying to pull down my shirt by the shoulders.

"What's the rush all of a sudden?" I backed up toward his bed and sat down, slowly unbuttoning my blouse. Where are your parents, anyway?"

"They're out." He spoke softly but with an urgency I hadn't heard from him ever. His heady scent of evergreen and sweet sweat filled my nostrils, and I kissed him hard on the lips. He pulled off his shirt and pants and then helped me off with my skirt. We both left on our underwear as we normally did, but Bryce slipped his hand into my panties and my breath caught.

We lay down on our sides and wrapped our arms and legs around other. I could feel my heart pounding against my chest. My breathing grew deeper and slower as I took in the weight and softness of Bryce's shoulders, his arms, and the hairy tendrils on his legs as they rubbed against mine. Thank God I had shaved my legs that morning. My hip bones jutted into his hips and I could feel all of him pressing on my leg. I knew what he wanted, but I didn't want it all yet.

My mind wandered for a second and I thought about where we'd be in a month or a year; probably not together, no matter how turned on he could make me feel. No matter how sweet and slow he was being right this second. A vision of me after the prom last year popped into my head. I had planned to do it just for the sake of getting my virginity out of the way, and that's what happened. So it wasn't like I was still a virgin. And it wasn't like I didn't like Bryce. I had to bring myself back to the present.

I opened my eyes and looked at him. His lashes fluttered. His lips pursed and he smiled at me. "Is this good or should we do more?" he asked.

More? Should I? What was I waiting for? "Wait, I thought I heard a car."

"Ivy, chill. I told you, my parents are gone for the night. They went to the city. I'm not going to force you to do anything you don't want to do. It just seems like it might be right tonight."

"Don't tell me to chill." I felt cold all of a sudden. I looked for the sheet or blanket under me and squirmed, trying to cover myself.

"OK, OK, I'm sorry. I'm just ready, and I hoped you were too. No pressure though. Whenever you say the word. But you know, now would be good."

"It's not a big deal, but it kinda is . . ." I wrapped the blankets around my middle and looked at him. "We're both going to college soon."

"Oh my God. That is not an excuse. We don't go to college for nearly a year."

"I know, but I don't know where this is going, or if it's going."

"Ivy Green," he said, chuckling. "You're the most gorgeous, sexy girl I ever dreamed of. I'm not going to push you, but this could be so great for us."

"By definition, I think this is what you call pushing," I said. "And now, honestly, the mood is a little bit lost."

"Jesus Christ." He got out of bed and stared down at me. "I mean really, you're the one who's broken the mood. I'm ready to go, can't you tell?" I looked at his midsection. Oh yeah, he was definitely ready to go, but I decided I was not. I pulled the blankets tighter around me.

"How about if we take a break for a second. I'm going to light up and chill, and then we can start over. This time, as you wish, nothing new on the menu, OK?"

"Oh, Bryce," I groaned. "Why do you have to get high all the time? Why can't we just be together without you lighting up?"

"Why does it bother you so much? You said you liked it," he said, the vape pen already in his hand.

"It's not that I don't get it. But I feel disloyal to my sister and what's she's struggling with. I promised to be a support, not a hypocrite. And now, I really think I should just go home." I rolled off the bed and bent down to look for my clothes. My hair fell onto my eyes and I took the hair holder off my wrist to make a ponytail. I grabbed my shirt and started to put it on.

"Come on, Ivy. Stay." He got the vape pen, then took a long drag on it.

"Take me home please. You just don't get it."

He put the pen down on the bedside table. "I don't want to fight with you. I'm sorry. I won't get high in front of you anymore. Let's get back into bed and start over. You've turned me on. Don't turn me off."

"It's a little late for that. The mood is completely lost. And listen, I'm not the boss of you. Smoke all you want. Vape. Party on, but I need to distance myself a little from the drugs. I really need to set a positive example of living drug free."

"OK, good for you. I don't need your permission to live my life, but thanks anyway. Why is everything such a big deal for you? Can't we fool around like every other normal couple our age? Does it always have to be about your sister?" He inhaled twice and then put the vape pen down on his desk and picked up my shoulders. I was tempted to lie back down. But I couldn't cave, not now.

"Listen, I don't really care that you get high once in a while, but you seem to involve yourself in other drugs for other people." I was fully dressed now. His bed was a mess of sheets and pillows. I headed out the door.

"Where are you going? I'll drive you home."

"No, I'll call an Uber. You're already high and I don't want to drive with you."

He grabbed my arm as I walked by him and he yanked me close. He was still in his underwear and still hard.

"Ivy, don't leave all mad. I'm sorry. I don't want to argue about this. You mean more to me than the drugs. Honestly."

"I believe you. Let's just call it a night and I'll see you in school tomorrow, OK?"

"No, you're mad. Come downstairs. I'll make us sundaes." He shot me one of his most charming smiles. His dimples deepened. His nose crinkled.

"I don't want to fight either. And I'm not mad. I'm confused, but I won't turn down ice cream. If you get dressed, I'll have some ice cream." I smiled at him. I had so much trouble saying no to him. I knew I should just walk away and teach him a lesson. No drugs mean no drugs, but I liked him too much.

At the kitchen table, looking out at the twinkling lights of the river towns and the new bridge in the distance, we talked about drugs and Carly and his brother Jonathan. Bryce tried to make me see the difference between what he determined was recreational drug use to what he thought both of our siblings were dangerously involved in, a drug habit veering on addiction.

"Don't you think I know that your occasional use—and by the way, it's not so occasional—is different from Carly's? But what you don't seem to get is that it all started with weed and a sports injury and oxy and then spiraled out of control. And your brother is headed down a similar path."

"How can you tell?" Bryce's face scrunched up and his mouth wrinkled, perplexed by what I was saying. "Are you lumping Jonathan in the same category as Carly?"

"In terms of a kid in trouble, yeah."

"Ivy." He shoved a heaping spoonful of vanilla with chocolate sauce into his mouth, and when he spoke I could see all the food. It was gross. I looked away. "I think we both need to worry about our own families."

"I know that." I couldn't look at him. He was talking with his mouth full. "But I can't be with someone who is smoking weed all the time and doing drug deals in Scarsdale when I have a sister struggling. I hope you never know what it's like."

"Me too. Carly's doing great, though, right?"

I stood up, surprised once again at his insensitivity. "Are you kidding me? Do you not get it? My sister is addicted to oxy. It's not what you're calling a habit. Do you know how many teenagers and other people die every year because they OD on Oxycontin and other drugs? It's a fucking epidemic." I pulled out my phone and hit the Uber app. "I'm going."

"Come on, Ivy. Don't be such a bitch." He said it without even realizing how awful he sounded. I stepped back from the table.

"Fuck you, Bryce. We're officially done." I stomped out the front door and started walking down the driveway. I couldn't bear him for a second longer. I couldn't believe I had been nearly naked in bed with him just thirty minutes earlier. Ethan was right. What a jerk.

"Come back here." He followed me and grabbed my arm, pulled me back.

"Don't touch me!" I yelled.

He stood back, pleading with me. "Ivy, I'm sorry. I didn't mean it. Please, don't leave like this. Help me to understand. You're right about Jonathan, but not because of drugs. He has a mental illness. He's bipolar, that's why he acts so weird. I was just too embarrassed to tell you."

"What? Bipolar? *And* drugs? That is a horrible, deadly combination." I walked back toward Bryce. I looked at my phone. I could see the little car heading up the hill on the screen. The Uber would be here in two minutes.

"I'm sorry about Jonathan. And I'm sorry you didn't tell me sooner, but I'm going to go. I think we need a break. Things are getting too intense. We both need to focus on school and college applications."

"I don't know, Ivy. I'm not good with temporary breaks. I can't make any promises."

He looked pathetic, standing next to me, his head hung, his hair lank and a little greasy. I'm sure I didn't look so great myself, but I tried to remain strong. "No one's asking you to, Bryce. Here's my Uber."

"Fuck you, Ivy. I'm not waiting around."

"Please don't." I got in the Uber and slammed the door. What an asshole, I thought. But why? Why was he so mean all of a sudden? Was it the weed? Is that what made his mood switch so radically? Maybe, I thought, but it's too late now for lame excuses.

When I got in the house, Carly and my mom were sitting at the kitchen table playing Scrabble. Teacups, saucers, and limp tea bags sat in front of them alongside some of my mom's best blondies. I immediately grabbed one.

"What's wrong?" my mom asked, the second she looked at me. I imagined my face was blotchy and mascara had dripped down my cheeks.

"Bryce and I broke up, for real this time," I said, talking with my mouth full of blondie. "He's a dick."

"What?" Carly asked. "Since when?"

"I guess since always." I sat down on the sofa. Kelly Green jumped on my lap and I buried my head in her fur. "Mmmm, Kelly, you're the real deal. Does she need to go out?" I could use a walk, I thought.

"No, she's fine. Honey, what happened?" my mom said gently, as she placed all seven tiles in a row, spelling "Severed."

"We're just too different, that's all. He's very chill and smooth and he likes to party, and I just can't deal with his fast lifestyle. He's Mr. Marijuana and I'm just not."

"Mr. Marijuana?" Mom asked. I looked at Carly, but she was studying her Scrabble tiles, putting some down on the board, then moving them around. It was nearly impossible to beat my mother, who knew every two-letter word and every Q-without-U combination.

"Forget about it, Mom. I'm fine. I'm going to bed." I picked up the dog and started walking upstairs, first looking at Carly's Scrabble options. I took her tiles and placed them on the board, using a Q already there. "Quiver."

"Good one!" Carly exclaimed. "Thanks. You sure you don't want to talk? We can come upstairs."

"I'm good." I trudged up the stairs, pausing in front of the hall mirror. I sucked in my breath. My hair was a mess, my outfit askew, and my makeup blotchy. "Ugh," I groaned into Kelly Green's head. "Hopefully tomorrow will be a little better."

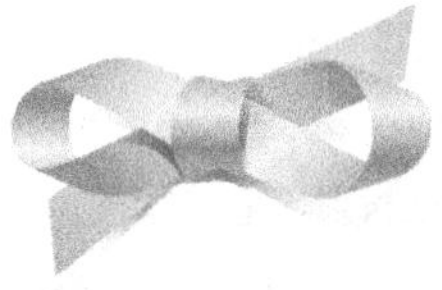

Chapter Nineteen—Rehearsal

"So, how are you doing?" Carly asked me in the car. She was driving me to play practice and then heading to a meeting.

"I'm OK." I forced a cheery smile. "I miss all the texting, but other than that, I'm fine."

"Really? Cuz I heard you crying." She placed her right hand in the middle of the front seat console and drove with her left.

"I wasn't. I'm fine."

"You definitely don't seem fine. Did you two ever have sex?"

"That's not it, but it was the instigator for the fight, kinda." I looked in my book bag for some leftover candy or mints. Just talking about Bryce triggered a desire to eat sugar.

"He's cute, but not worth it if he's a dick. Trust me."

"I smoked with him." I said solemnly.

"You did?" Carly tossed her hair around and laughed. "Listen," she continued. "I told you, most kids in high school smoke some weed, maybe do a little more. Not everyone loses control like I did. I'm not recommending drugs, not after what I just went through, but you're not a bad person for getting high once in a while. Just remember, it's still against the law in New York, and you're underage."

"I know. I'm not saying I'm a regular user, believe me." We were almost at school. "I just wanted you to know that he's not the best influence, on top of being a dick. And he's really not a dick, to be honest. He lost his temper with me, just one time."

"Well, do you want to forgive him?"

"I don't know. He called me a bitch. That's a bit of a non-starter." Carly pulled into the parking lot and we faced each other. She fingered the collar on my soft chamois shirt.

"Yeah, that's pretty bad. Hey, you're still wearing my clothes without asking." She laughed. I gave her a guilty grin.

"I needed comfort clothes. Look, I'm wearing mom's velvet sweats. I really just want to curl up and hide for a while."

"No time for that. Seriously, if you like him, talk to him. The drugs are only a problem when they are a problem. Maybe he'll cut back. Maybe he'll apologize. Figure out what you want from him and see if he can give you what you need."

"That's good advice, but I'm not sure he can comply. He's weak. He's a momma's boy." I tried to smile through my tears, but I missed Bryce. He was such a sympathetic listener and was so nice to me. Until he wasn't. Why did he change so radically in that moment? I couldn't figure him out.

"You are talking out of both sides of your mouth, girlfriend. But it's OK, you have all the time in the world to figure this out. Me, on the other hand, I gotta go. I'm late for a meeting."

"OK. Hey, one more thing I've been meaning to ask you," I said, bundling up my things and opening the door to leave. "Are you going back to Vassar?"

"I hope so."

"What do you mean? Do you think you'll be ready?" I assumed she'd pick up her old life where she left off before the drugs set in. It never occurred to me there might more delays.

"I miss my friends but I want to feel secure. As long as I'm putting my life back together, I want to make sure I do it properly."

"Seems like a plan. I decided to go ED to Columbia instead of Cornell. Thought I'd try being a city girl."

"Ooh, that's cool." Carly had her hand on the shift. I could tell she was in a hurry, but I wanted to finish talking.

"I figured you'd go back to Vassar, but it's just a Metro train line away. I hope Grandma is still paying."

"She is." Carly relaxed her grip on the shift and I let go of the door handle for a moment. Carly said, "She set it all aside for us. College is the one luxury we have left, since Dad lost his job and left."

"Thank God." I breathed heavily. I could see the air against the window. Winter was on its way.

Carly's eyes were cast down and she spoke seriously. "I think it's important that we are extra considerate of Mom. She's been through hell. I feel so guilty."

"I know that, Carly." I held my tongue and didn't say what I really was thinking.

"I know a lot of the stress was my fault, but I can't take back the past. I can only go forward." Carly started to cry and I found myself tearing up too.

"It's OK. I know it's hard," I said. "It's been hard on me too—just a little bit, anyway." I wanted Carly to know that while she was gone, a lot had happened at home and in my life. "I know the focus is on your rehab, but I have to tell you, I was really scared."

The tree limbs blew around us, litter in the road swirled along the sidewalk, and we cried like babies in our old beat-up blue-upholstered Toyota. It had been my grandmother's.

"I know and I'm sorry. Part of my recovery is to learn how to accept my culpability. Jeez, I feel the divorce was partially my fault too."

"OK, now you're just being a drama queen. You know perfectly well that they were getting a divorce long before drugs came into the picture."

"I mostly believe that, but not entirely. I may have pushed things along somehow."

"You can't take credit or blame for everything, Carly."

"Listen, I was stealing oxy from their medicine cabinet two years ago, after my own script ran out."

"And did you ever wonder why they had so much oxy in the medicine cabinet? Lately, Mom has been making these odd comments about Dad and drugs, and then she shuts down. I haven't asked her about it yet, but I'm gearing up."

"Who are you talking about? Dad or Mom?" she asked.

"I don't know. Just worry about yourself. Go to your meeting now." She blinked and started to say something more but stopped. I hopped out of the car at the curb and waved to Carly. "Sorry I brought it up." I didn't want to talk about other people doing drugs, least of all our parents.

Play rehearsal went well, although I thought Ethan clowned it up a bit too much. At one point, Zoey and I were standing in the wings while Ethan read his lines.

"Ethan's a sweetheart, really cute, but he's not as funny as he thinks. Who's gonna break it to him?" Zoey said.

"Not me," I said, laughing, and then quieted my voice. "He's a good actor. I'm glad he got a lead."

"You keep saying he got a lead, I got a lead, Phoebe got a lead. How many times do I have to tell you, it's an ensemble cast? There are no real leads."

Shuffling my feet back and forth, I said, "My part is decidedly smaller than most of the others. I don't mind."

"Obviously you mind. You've been complaining since we were assigned parts six weeks ago. Hey," Zoey said, head angled toward the back door, "Bryce is here."

"You're kidding me." I grabbed Zoey and pulled her to the wings of the stage, hidden from view in the audience.

"He's walking up the aisle," she said.

"We broke up less than twenty-four hours ago. What is he doing here?" I ran behind the stage and shut the door of the girls' dressing room.

"Ivy," Zoey said. "Bryce is right here. He wants to come in and talk to you."

"Shhhhh," Ethan hissed from on stage. "Shut up."

I was alone in the dressing room, everyone's coats and costumes strewn all around the tiny space. I sat down on a bookshelf ledge, pushing aside someone's book bag. All five of us girls used this dressing room. They boys had to use the men's room in the hall.

My phone buzzed and I looked down. It was Phoebe. She was on the stage with Ethan. "Let Bryce in. He wants to apologize. Come on, you know you love him." The director was going to get really mad if I let this become a huge interruption to practice. I got up and opened the door. Bryce stood, head hung low, and held out his hand. There was a black velvet box in it.

"What's that?" I asked, with no enthusiasm in my voice.

"It's for you. My apology. Can we talk for a minute?

"Bryce, I'm in the middle of play practice." Zoey gave me the thumbs down from behind Bryce's back. Ethan and Phoebe stopped saying their lines for a minute and Phoebe waved and then gave me the thumbs up. Ethan drew his finger across his throat, the universal gesture for "cut it." What was this, a group decision? It was not.

From onstage, Ms. Bucci, the drama coach said, "Come on, we have two more scenes before we're done. Ivy, you have ten minutes to work out whatever it is you've got going on personally." I turned and motioned for Bryce to enter the dressing room.

Once inside, I said, "What's up? You don't need to give me a present. We broke up."

Again my phone buzzed. Again, it was Phoebe, coaxing me to take him back.

I remained standing, facing Bryce, who continued to hold out the jewelry box.

"Open it," he said, tentatively. "It's my way to say I'm sorry. Really, really sorry."

Being so close to him again after only twenty-four hours apart, my heart automatically beat faster and I felt that familiar tug in my lower half. His smile was sincere. His eyes were clear and he stared into my eyes. I started to cry.

"Why were you so mean, Bryce? Why did you turn on me in such a flash? It was not OK."

"I don't know what happened. Honestly, I was high. I know you hate it and I know you want me to stop or that I'll get in trouble somehow, but that's not it. I don't want to upset you. I really like you, Ivy Green. I really do."

I felt my resolve melt a little bit. Bryce's dimples deepened. My stomach tipped over a bit. My body temperature rose. I began to sweat in my outfit. Suddenly I wished I had on a tank top under this thick chamois shirt.

"You look pretty." He touched my hair and let his fingers drift down to my cheek. "Come on, open this."

I took the little box from him and unwrapped it. Inside was a silver Lotus insignia on a thin ribbon. "I know you're spiritual."

"It's perfect, actually," I said. "Namaste."

"A peace offering." He leaned toward me. His breath was sweet, a hint of mint and a whiff of chocolate. He reached out and put his arms around me and we kissed, long and heavy. Then he pulled away and stared into my eyes again.

"Ivy, I'm sorry." He spoke clearly and with contrition in his voice. "I lost my temper. I said terrible things. I didn't mean it. Can we go back to where we were?"

"I'd like to think that we could," I said. Our arms touched and our wrists nudged one another. Tingles ran up and down my spine and my stomach lurched as it always did when I was around him. The dressing room walls seemed to close in on us. It was like we were alone in the universe.

"Bryce," I hesitated. I couldn't think what to say, but my body responded regardless.

"Ivy, give me another chance. I didn't mean to swear and call you a bitch."

"Oh, so you remember that?"

"Of course I do. I'm really, really sorry. I can't say it enough."

"OK, I forgive you." I caved. I could give anyone a second chance, couldn't I? "Namaste to you too."

"OK, so we're good?" He was smiling unabashedly now. "Let me put on the necklace for you." He reached behind my neck and gently attached the clasp. "Perfect."

I couldn't see, but I loved it and I was pretty sure I loved him again. I didn't know if I was doing the right thing by going back, but my body sure wanted his and my brain was willing to take the risk. We opened the door to the dressing room. Phoebe, Ethan, and Zoey were all walking off stage. They looked at us and Phoebe began clapping. Ethan just stared with accusation in his eyes. Zoey looked away. Clearly my friends thought I was making a bad decision.

Bryce glanced over at Phoebe and she was smiling at him. I gave her a thumbs up and a wide smile.

"We're better." I bit my lip and Bryce leaned in and kissed me.

"Hurrah," Phoebe said. "And now, we need you to finish play practice."

"Yeah, hurry up," Ethan intoned. "You're making us wait."

I didn't know what to do except kiss Bryce again and run onstage. Ms. Bucci smiled at me. I guess she was used to the vagaries of teenage romance.

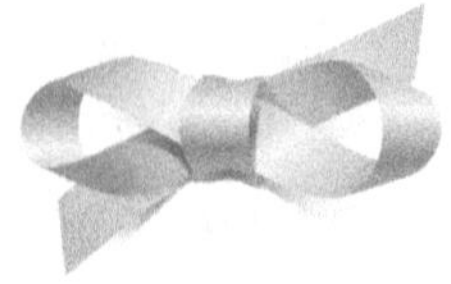

Chapter Twenty—Confronting the Enemy

"Hey, guys, wait up." I scrambled up the aisle, zipping up my jeans, in order to catch up to Zoey and Ethan, who were heading toward the back door of the auditorium. "I need a ride home."

Zoey stopped in the aisle and whirled around. "Why don't you ask your BFF Phoebe Li? She seems to have your best interests at heart."

"What do you mean? Don't be mad. I can't help it. I like him a lot."

Ethan touched my arm. "He's a dick, Ivy. You said so yourself. Why did you go back so easily? Don't you know, once a dick, always a dick?"

"Of course, you're mad because I got back together with Bryce." I put my hands on my hips. The elastic was loose and the pants slipped to my butt. My throat constricted and I sucked in my cheeks. I really couldn't deal with their judgment right now.

"We're not mad." We stood huddled in the aisle near the doorway out. Zoey spoke, presumably for the two of them. "We think you're making a big mistake. Big."

"Why? I like him. He likes me. He apologized and said he wasn't going to deal drugs or sell them to friends, however you want to put it. Why can't I give him a second chance?"

"You can do whatever you want," Ethan said. "But we think he's going to bring you down. He won't stop using, and you will somehow get sucked into his world."

"You know, I'm nearly eighteen years old. Don't you think I'm smart enough to know what I'm doing with my boyfriend?"

"No, I don't." Ethan took my hands, but I dropped them. "I've known you most of those eighteen years, and I don't like you when you're around him."

"You're rude," was all I could think to say. "What about you, Zoey? Are you on his side or mine?"

"I've known Bryce for almost as long as you and Ethan have been cousins. I have to be honest. I agree with Ethan. Bryce is all polished and fancy on the outside, but I don't like what's underneath. I don't think he's good for you, mainly because of his drug use. I've been through what you're going through with Carly. Nick relapsed four times before he OD'd. It's best to stay clear of people who are so heavily involved with drugs."

My head felt full of cotton balls. Their words were swimming around, the deep meaning of what they were saying not quite making sense. Were they dumping me? Was I being forced to make a choice? It seemed that way. Suddenly, I felt really angry. Who the heck were they to tell me how to feel and what to do? How dare they give me ultimatums?

"You know what?" I said, keeping my hands crossed in front of my chest, trying to remain as calm as possible. I didn't want to explode. "I need to think about what you're saying. Bryce has apologized over and over again. If that means you're going to blow me off, then I may have to accept that, although I think it would suck."

"Ivy, we're not going to stop being your friends," Zoey said. The other cast members were clearly avoiding us and using the side door to leave. We were the last ones in the auditorium except for Phoebe and Ms. Bucci, who were talking onstage. "We really just want you to know where we stand."

"We're making a point," Ethan said. "I love you too, you know that."

"I'm going to go," I said. "I think I'll ask Phoebe for a ride home. She already offered to take me to Bryce's and honestly, whether you like it or not, that's where I want to go right now."

"Have it your way," Ethan said. "Let's go, Zoey."

"Bye," Zoey said to me, as she walked away. "I'll text you later."

"I won't, at least not tonight," Ethan said.

"Thanks a lot, you're real good friends." I layered on the sarcasm, but questioned myself a little. Maybe they were right, and I just didn't want to hear it. I sat alone in the auditorium while I waited for Phoebe. This was so confusing. I had just met most of these people, including Bryce. Should I trust them or trust Ethan, who I've known my whole life? Or should I trust my gut? I felt drawn to Bryce's personality and I wasn't ready to dump him, but his nasty insult, Bitch, kept resounding in my head. There's really no excuse. Zoey and Ethan were correct, even if I wasn't ready to act on it.

"I'm so glad you got back with Bryce. You two are meant for each other," Phoebe said, pulling into the supermarket near the high school. "Want to come in with me a sec? I just want to get a couple of things before I go home."

I followed her into the supermarket, trailing behind as I texted Bryce and my mom. "Be right over," I wrote to Bryce. "Be home around midnight," I told my mom.

In a near-repeat performance of the last time we went to the supermarket together, Phoebe scooped up two Reese's cups, one box of Mallomars, and two bags of M&M's. "I just like variety when I binge," she explained, as she paid the girl at the register. To me she said, "We can eat what we want and toss the rest."

"How can you eat so late? Don't you feel sick when you go to sleep?" I asked, as we tore open the M&M's and each poured some directly down our throats.

"I like the sugar rush after a long day, but I can't do this all the time. I have auditions in the city. Come on, I'll take you to Bryce's. By the time we get to his house, I'll have finished eating all this candy. Would you take out the trash for me though? I can't have any evidence around. My mom will go wild."

"Wow, that's rough," I said. "Come to my house. My mother bakes all the time." Phoebe handed me a plastic bag full of empty wrappers. "Thanks for the ride. My other friends think I'm making a big mistake with Bryce."

"Ahh, he's great. They're just jealous."

"I don't think so," I said, stepping out of the car onto the Houstons' expansive driveway.

Bryce opened the front door. "Hi! Is Phoebe coming in or going?"

"Going," she chirped, and she drove off.

"Jonathan's home again?" I was shocked when I walked through the front door and Bryce told me. "I thought you told me that he was going to some kind of clinic."

"He never went," Bryce admitted. "He promised to stay clean and sober and take his meds, and my parents gave him one more chance. He's doing OK so far."

Bryce led me through the sleek foyer, past the living room, and into the family room, where Jonathan was slumped in a chair in front of the television. Here I thought we were going to have a romantic reunion, and instead I had to deal with his brother. I inhaled the clean-linen aroma of the scented plug-in Flora Houston used all over the house.

Bryce pulled me in close. I could smell the foresty cologne I loved. My heart beat a little faster and I smiled, in spite of Jonathan's presence.

"We gotta go," Jonathan demanded, slurring his words. Messy as always, Jonathan's white button-down shirt had a big red spot on the lower front of it that appeared to be salsa or ketchup.

"Ivy," Bryce spoke into my ear, his breath igniting a momentary thrill, but his words deflated any hope I had of a romantic reunion upstairs. "I have to drop Jonathan off somewhere and then we can be alone. Sorry, but it got complicated. Can you drive my car?"

"What? Why?" I stepped away from Bryce, whacking my knee on the thick glass coffee table. "What's going on? Why do I need to drive?"

"I need to be somewhere. We can't drive. We're wasted already." Jonathan got up and headed toward the front door. I stared at Bryce.

"What? You're wasted?" I looked at him, my face frozen in surprise. All the excitement drained from my body. I stepped away.

"I'm not wasted." Bryce tried to pull me into a hug but I pulled further back, grabbing my phone to text Carly or an Uber.

"I'm not high. We smoked a little, and I don't want to get busted with Jonathan in the car and . . ." He let his voice trail off. I headed toward the front door.

"Ivy, I know you don't like this, but it's not a big deal." Bryce followed me. I shook my head as I walked. This was exactly why we broke up.

"I'm an idiot. I'm just not into this, Bryce."

"Just listen to me. I just need to unload some stuff I got from Dauber. I'm dumping it precisely because I know you don't want it around. I'm doing this for you."

"You've got to be kidding. I don't believe you. I'm going home. Now." I tried to speak clearly and with resolve, even though I was shaking. It was one thing to get high once in a while, but it was quite another to make it part of your everyday existence. I couldn't do it. It just wasn't right. As much as I felt deeply connected and attracted to Bryce, I hated how drugs were so central to his life. "Honestly, Bryce, I feel a little scared."

"Ivy, please." He pulled my hand and pulled me toward him. He kissed me on the lips and for a second, I felt myself acquiescing.

"We're going to drop off Jonathan and then we'll come back here alone. I just have to unload some stuff. And I'm not gonna lie, I had to take one of the pills to make sure it was legit. That's why I need you to drive."

"What the—? What did you take? You're high and you took a pill? This is just too much for me, given what my sister just went through."

"Ivy, come on, don't be such a . . . so straight. Please, I'll be fine. I barely feel it, but I had to test. Like you tested the vape to see what it was like. No harm done there either."

"OK, that's not the same thing, and please stop reminding me about it. I wish I never did. I feel guilty enough about it. And what if your little pill, whatever it is, is bad? What am I supposed to do? Dial 911 like I was supposed to for Carly? News flash, my reaction time sucks in a crisis. I'm going home." I headed outside and texted Carly again. She sent back a thumbs up.

"You are such a stuck-up bitch, Ivy Green," Jonathan said, standing by Bryce's car. "Bryce could do much better."

"Jonathan, no love lost here, but I do hope you don't overdose," I said angrily. "I'm sorry I even came over tonight. This is never going to work." I reached around my neck and undid the necklace. "Take this back. Namaste yourself."

Bryce stood next to me. "Jonathan, give me a minute. Let me handle Ivy."

"Handle me?"

"Ivy, you are making this into something way bigger than it really is. I'll be done in half an hour. Can I come over then?"

"No. You can't. Zoey's brother died from an overdose. My sister almost did. I can't have it around me. I just can't."

"I'll stop. I will."

"If that's the case, get in the car with me when Carly comes and we can go get something to eat at my house. No weed, no mollies, no whatever."

Bryce stood there next to his car. Jonathan had backed off and was waiting by the garage. The air was brisk and I felt a cold wind blow through the air. Bryce looked me in the eye and then looked over at his brother. He looked at both of us several times over and then he said, "I have to protect Jonathan, Ivy. I have to sell these drugs and then I can help him the way you've helping Carly."

"But you're not helping him, you're enabling him. He needs to stop and you need to stop."

"You don't understand, Ivy. You think you know what to do because you went to a few family counseling sessions and because your sister just got out of rehab, but we've been dealing with Jonathan's drugs and behaviors since he was young. I need to stay with him tonight to make sure he's OK."

"Bryce, I know one thing is true for sure. Enabling a person who has a drug-abuse problem is only encouraging the problem, and it's a recipe for disaster. So, say what you want, you're wrong if you get or give him anything that will mess with his head. And yours too. You know, I really like you, but I won't be with anyone who buys and sells drugs. I just can't."

Just then, Carly pulled up in our beat-up Camry. "You coming?" I asked him. He shook his head. I got in and we headed home. I was afraid for him, but I couldn't help him, not now.

When we got home, Carly and I sat for a while on the brick wall alongside the driveway.

"Thanks again for coming to get me so quickly," I said. "I had to leave. They were about to sell some drugs."

"No problem."

"I don't want any part of that scene. They're going to get caught one of these days for sure," I said, noticing the parked cars along the street.

I crossed my legs on the cement wall and looked down at my shabby Converse high tops. My jeans were ripped at the knees, a look that was rapidly going or had gone out of style nearly as fast as it had come into style. Carly wore leggings and a striped button-down that was tight around her boobs and long and loose as it hit her thighs. It was annoying how great she always looked.

"So, you're done for good?" she asked.

"I really like him, Carly, but I can't deal with his brother."

"I get it. You know Oliver from Blue Hills?"

"Of course."

"He was in Blue Hills with me, but he's been in and out of rehab for three years."

"Oh my God, wow." I remembered how cute and sweet Oliver looked when I saw him at Blue Hills. "He doesn't look like someone who abuses opiates or drugs of any sort."

"Do I?" Carly threw up her hands. "Listen, most people start out just like me or Oliver, doing drugs at home, getting high, hanging with friends, and then it's a painkiller or two or three or twenty, and things spiral out of control before you even know what hit you."

"Sucks." I didn't know what else to say. We had talked about this multiple times.

"Yup, it does." She wrapped her arm around me and pulled me in toward her shoulder. "Trust me."

"I do," I said. We sat outside for another few minutes, looking up at the stars. I stared at the shiny black motorcycle parked on the street, the silver kickstand holding it up.

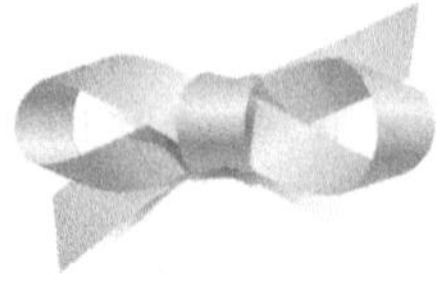

Chapter Twenty-One—Party

"You were right," I said to Carly, the night after she picked me up. We were on my bed, eating my mom's best raspberry jam dot cookies. Tears dripped onto the plate and the cookies tasted saltier than they should have.

"Ivy, don't cry. He's not worth it," Carly said, trying to cheer me up.

"It's not so much Bryce as it is Ethan and Zoey. I pissed them off too. I need to find a way to apologize to them. But I'm glad you're home. I have no one to go out with tonight."

"Me too. Would it be so terrible to stay in for a change?" She took the cookie plate and brought it over to my dresser. "I think we've both had enough of these." She sat back down on the edge of the bed. "Come on, we'll watch a movie together."

"I don't think so." I shook my head and stood up. "There's a party at this girl Annie's house and I want to go. I'm not going to sit home and cry myself to sleep. I don't think I did anything wrong. I thought I liked a boy and I stood up for myself to my friends. OK, so he turned out to be a bit of a jerk really, but that's no reason for them to hold it against me. We're supposed to stick by each other."

I started pulling out jeans from my drawers, trying on one pair then the next. The third pair fit the best and I began shoving the others back in my drawer. I opened other drawers to find a top to wear. I wanted to look good. I wanted to be cool. This would be my first real party at Marble Springs without a boyfriend.

"Here, wear this." Carly handed me a shirt that had been folded in a pile on my desk. "Red always looks great on you."

"OK, thanks." I pulled my hair into a ponytail and added some lip gloss, smacking my lips together. "Screw them, that's what I have to say."

But I couldn't stop thinking about Ethan and Zoey. I had a rapid-fire looping conversation in my head with them about how they treated me, what they said, why I was hurt. I felt more sad than mad. I didn't like being in a fight with my friends and I wanted to go to the party with them, but they weren't available to me tonight.

Reluctantly, I texted one of the cheerleaders and confirmed that they were all going to the party, and I fixed a time to meet them there.

"Bye girls," my mom yelled from downstairs. "I'm going out with Auntie Allie for dinner and maybe a movie. Be good."

We both called down, "Bye Mom."

"You're not going with them?" I asked Carly, who was on her phone.

"Obviously not. I guess I'm the one who's going to be alone tonight. It's just me and you, sweet little Kelly Green." She lightly touched the dog.

"Oh no, now I feel bad. I'll stay home with you."

"Absolutely not." Carly grinned at me. "You're going to be fine. Don't worry about me. Maybe I'll call an old friend or something. Do you want me to drive you?"

"Nah, if you don't need the Camry, I'll drive myself. I'm not going to be drinking at all."

I twirled around in front of the full-length mirror and then switched out my earring studs for rhinestone hoops. "Maybe I'll meet someone new tonight. There's an upside to going to a new school; I hardly know anyone yet."

"Or better yet, maybe I'll call Oliver," Carly said off-handedly, as though she said she was going to order in Chinese. "He asked to see me."

"I thought you had to stay away from him till you're both stable."

"Mmm, I think it's OK," she demurred.

"Are you sure? Carly, if he's not ready, you shouldn't be with him." I felt a little tightening in my belly, and not the good kind like I felt when Bryce made me excited; the bad kind, like something was not right.

"He's doing great. Don't worry about me, Ivy. I'm fine. Really. I'm strong and doing great. Get going already."

I drove the Camry over to one of the girls' houses where they were pre-gaming—drinking lots of beer and doing shots of tequila in the basement. The parents were upstairs watching a television show, completely oblivious. We carried Poland Spring water bottles, mine probably the only one with just water in it.

"Ivy's the designated driver," Kerri said. "Not one drop tonight, right?"

"Right," I said, taking a whiff of Kerri's water bottle. "Wow, that's strong. Do you even have anything mixed in with that?"

"A little lime seltzer. It's like lemonade. Hey, is Phoebe coming here first or meeting us over there?" she asked anyone who was listening. I had expected to see Phoebe here with all the cheerleaders.

"Not sure," Emma said. "She was gonna score some X for later and then meet us at Annie's. Ivy, you know anything about that?"

Emma stared at me. The rest of the girls were sitting on matching plaid sofas with the large-screen TV showing a Kardashians rerun set on some random island. I didn't know a thing, but I could guess.

"Bryce and I broke up. I don't want to talk about it." I took a sip of Emma's lemonade drink. It was good and I felt the burn of the liquor go down hard, but I was driving, so I didn't take any more than the sip. "Let's go."

We piled into the car, me driving, and headed across town to Annie's house, a large McMansion not too far from Bryce's street. Her little sister, the one I was supposed to babysit for, was sitting on the upstairs ledge overlooking the party. She was cute. I hoped we weren't corrupting her.

Annie had the glass sliders open from the kitchen to the back deck. Lots of boys and some girls were out there smoking, and I wandered outside. "Hey," I said to people I only mildly recognized from the halls. "Hey," they said back. It was very boring being the only sober person at the party. I drank seltzer and water and wandered from the deck to the kitchen and back to the basement where my new so-called friends were playing beer pong.

I spotted Ethan when I went outside to and sat by the firepit. "Hey, Ethan, what's up?" I had raised my voice but didn't get up.

He looked over. "Nothing."

"Are you going to stay mad at me forever?" The firepit was cozy. A couple of girls from the drama class were sitting with me. They didn't seem too wasted yet.

"Maybe," he said. He walked toward me.

"Is Zoey here?" I asked.

"Nah, she stayed home. Thought it might get a little rowdy tonight and she didn't want to be a part of it." His tone remained deadpan. He hadn't forgiven me yet.

"I wish I was with her," I said, looking down at the fire, avoiding Ethan's eyes. "Seriously, Bryce and I broke up for good. You got what you wanted. Can we move on now?"

"Ivy, I'm not mad at you, I'm mad for you. There's a difference. And yes, we can move on, but not because you broke up with Bryce. Because you realize people like him are douche bags." Ethan was not only a great cousin, but a good friend too, whether I liked it or not.

"Whatever, Ethan. He made me laugh and he was sweet and we had fun together, but I get it. He's toxic. We're done."

"Well, good for you. I'll talk to you later. I might need a ride home, actually."

"OK, sure," I said. "Just let me know."

After Ethan walked away, my mood immediately improved. I texted Zoey, "Hey, if you want company, just holler—or text." But she didn't write back. I guess she was going to be harder to win over than Ethan.

The girl sitting next to me passed over a vape pen. I looked at the little blue light and held it up to my nose. Couldn't smell a thing. I looked at it again. Just one puff of the vape is like nothing, I decided. Fuck it. I took a hit and inhaled off the end of the electric stick. I didn't feel any different, which was good since I had to drive everyone home. When it came back around a second time, I inhaled again. Last time, I rationalized.

Music blared from the basement and a different tune could be heard from the upper deck area, where the football players were hanging out. They weren't drinking because it was still football season and they would get kicked off the team. I wandered up there onto the deck, where the trees overhung onto the porch area. Two large white metal tables were surrounded by plastic chairs, mostly filled with my new classmates.

My head felt a bit fuzzy. My thoughts were coming in a bit slower than usual. I guess the vape did alter my mind a little bit. I looked for Ethan and saw him in the kitchen, gabbing away with some of his friends.

Some of the hot football guys started talking to me, asking about friends of mine from my old school. One person knew my old boyfriend. "He's going out with Meg Coogan now," this guy told me. I didn't care one bit.

The air outside was filled with the musky, sour odor of bodies mixed with the strong smell of fresh fall pine trees. It reminded me of Bryce and his house, specifically of the upstairs playroom where he and Jonathan used to get high out the window. I started to wonder what he was doing.

I began to think maybe I made a mistake, being so harsh and black and white. Here I was at the party, pretty high actually. That was really hypocritical. Ugh, this is why I hated to smoke. I didn't sit around talking about the meaning of life and superpowers. I panicked that everything I did or said was wrong, that I was out of place, that people were making fun of me, like those girls at the other table. It looked like they were laughing at me. Was I being paranoid because I was high? I couldn't tell. I wanted to be sober again.

I went into the kitchen and looked on the counter for some Diet Coke or a Keurig maker for coffee.

"Are you OK?" It was Ethan, by my side. "No judgment. I saw you with the vape pen."

"I'm fine. I just wanted to test it. I feel a little lightheaded, that's all. I think I'll call an Uber and leave the car here."

"I thought you were the designated driver?"

"Yeah, they're going to be mad at me. I agreed to drive everyone home."

"Leave me your keys and I'll drive. I'm sober. I'd drive you home too but I'm having fun. I don't want to leave yet. Why'd you get high?"

"I didn't really. Just took a puff or maybe two. I don't even feel it."

"Listen Ivy, do what you want, but don't drive. Take the Uber and I'll get your friends home. Don't be a hypocrite." He stared hard at me. I looked away, a bit ashamed. Thankfully he wasn't acting all high and mighty. Everyone smoked pot. It wasn't a big deal, I rationalized. Unless of course your sister was tucked away in bed recovering from her stint in rehab.

"I know," I reluctantly admitted. "I'll meet you back at my house later and by then, I should be OK to drive you home."

"You sure you're OK? I could leave now if you really need help."

"An Uber's easy. See you later." I tossed him my keys and he walked me to the street. I wasn't one hundred percent sure he believed me when I insisted I wasn't high, but I knew enough to stick to my story, even if I felt like a total lying jerk in the process.

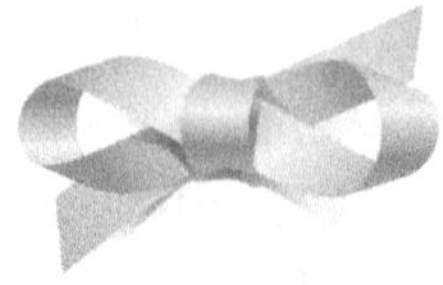

Chapter Twenty-Two—Truth

When I got to my house, all of the lights were on. That was weird. And actually, I realized, Bryce's car was parked in front of the house. That was confusing. Did he come over to apologize again and beg me to take him back? Well, maybe I would think about it. I wasn't innocent at all. I couldn't be so judgy all the time.

I smoothed out my hair and tucked in my shirt. I added more lip gloss and smacked my lips together, tasting the perfume of the gloss. I marched up the front steps, ready to listen to whatever Bryce had to say.

The pungent odor of weed completely overwhelmed me before I noticed the tall glass bong sitting on the coffee table with bags of chips laying open. Bryce and Phoebe were on the sofa with Carly and some skinny guy who looked vaguely familiar.

"What the hell?" I yelled, trying to keep my head together and my thoughts ordered. I knew what I was seeing, yet the facts seemed dubious. I must have still been a bit fuzzy. "Why are you all here? Who is that?"

"I'm Oliver." The skinny kid started to stand up.

"Ivy, don't be mad." Carly got up. Rolling papers dropped from her lap. "We're not doing any hard drugs. Bryce brought over some weed, that's all. Oliver, this is Ivy, my sister."

"Are you kidding me?" I stared at my sister, her face glowing, her smile intense, her eyes tiny black pinholes. "Oliver from Blue Hills? You're supposed to be sober. Bryce, did you get my sister high?"

Phoebe stood up and came over to me. "Ivy, it's not what it looks like. We just stopped by for a minute. Dauber will be here soon. And besides, you have no legs to stand on. I've got your number." She held out her phone.

"What are you talking about?" I grabbed her phone and looked at the screen. There was a picture of me, sitting around the firepit from earlier that night. In the Insta picture that she had saved, I was passing the vape pen to the person sitting next to me and I was smiling. I looked wasted. Fucking social media. I regretted even going out that night.

"Who sent you that?" I demanded. "What I do isn't your business. It's no one's business."

"Well, it's my business," Bryce said with a sneer. "You're so high and mighty all the time, but you smoke just like the rest of us."

"Bryce, you fucking asshole," I screamed. "Get out of my house. Get out of my life. You're a total dick."

"And you're a self-righteous prima donna," he said back. "Where do you get off judging me when you like a good toke just as much as the next person? There is no such thing as a double-standard. You should know that better than anyone."

Everyone was quiet except the two of us. We were breaking up all over again, only this time in public. Oliver took another hit off the bong while Bryce and I were fighting. My sister came over to stand next to me.

"Ivy, I get it. You party socially. You don't have to feel bad about that. It's nearly legal in this state. I'm the one with the problem, not you."

"I know. I don't feel bad. Well, maybe a little. I feel pissed off at Bryce for getting his asshole dealer friend involved with you. Why are you here?" I glared at Bryce.

"I'm here because your sister called me, that's why. You are such a little hypocrite. I can't believe I ever loved you."

"You didn't love me," I whispered.

"Yes, I did." Bryce looked at his feet. I fell silent. No one spoke for a moment. Finally, Phoebe spoke up.

"Let's go, Bryce. I'll text Dauber and tell him to meet us at your house. He's almost here."

"We weren't in love." My head whirred. My stomach pounced. How dare he play with my emotions like this? "We weren't."

"If you say so." Bryce winked at me. So inappropriate, I thought. This time, his charm and allure didn't tempt my resolve.

"Bryce, we're breaking up because you're a dealer. You came to my house to sell drugs to two people right out of rehab. What does that say about you as a person?"

"I called him, Ivy." Carly put her arm around me. I gently removed it but looked at her kindly.

"I know. He should have known better. It was completely insensitive to agree to sell to you, that's what upsets me. Is Oliver going to be all right?" I asked, directing my gaze to Carly.

"He'll be fine," Bryce said. "He's just smoking, same as you. Jonathan, let's go." He cocked his head toward the kitchen.

"Yeah, right, same as me. Exactly the same." I looked past him, into my mother's formerly immaculate kitchen, which was now strewn with plates of cookies and cake. Jonathan sat at the counter, shoving chocolate cake into his mouth, dripping crumbs onto the floor. Kelly Green was beneath him, happily licking up the mess.

"OK." I felt more in control. "Everyone needs to leave now."

"Ivy, I'm sorry. I didn't mean to upset you." Bryce tried to follow me, but I pushed him back with my arm.

"Don't come near me, just go."

Phoebe stepped back. "Lighten up. Don't blame him." Phoebe tried to talk to me, but I was holding the door open for them. "Your sister called him. She asked us to come over."

"I caved. I was wrong. I'm an idiot." Carly was crying earnestly now. "Oliver was so insistent. He convinced me it would be OK."

"Carly, it's never going to be OK. For you or for Oliver or anyone else who has problems struggling with drug abuse." I spoke as calmly as I could muster. "But why would you call Bryce?"

"For the obvious reason," she said. Bryce just stood there staring blankly at me. His eyes didn't blink. His dimple didn't deepen. He looked like a sad puppy.

"I said I was sorry," Bryce mumbled.

Oliver sat quietly on the sofa. He wasn't saying a word. In fact, he was puffing on the vape pen, over and over again. He was going to end up right back in rehab, but I'd be damned if I was going to let Carly go back. If I was ever high at all tonight, I was definitely not now.

"Phoebe, you're right, it is Carly's fault," I said in as authoritative voice as I could muster. "But you shouldn't have come over, any of you. And to bring him," I pointed to Jonathan. My face was red. I grabbed the door and waved it open and shut. "Just go home." My face was inches from Bryce's.

Jonathan ran right by me, a cupcake in his fist. What a pig. Ugh.

"I'll call you in the morning," Phoebe said. "Just don't blame us. We had nothing to do with this." She waved her phone at me again, the photo of me her temporary homescreen. I wondered again who sent her that photo.

"Hey," I said to Phoebe, an idea crossing my mind. "Are you and Dauber together? Is that why he's on his way over? You'd better stop him."

"I won't hold this against you, if that's what you're wondering." She held up that picture again. Dammit, who took it? "And you don't judge me for who I hang with."

"No judgment, Phoebes, but ewwww, you're more screwed up than I thought you were," I said.

"Ivy," Bryce said as he walked out the door. "I wouldn't have let Carly do any hard drugs. She's fine. She just took a puff or two off the vape, nothing you didn't do tonight."

My knees felt weak and my arms hung limply by my side. I looked at him. His shiny gold chain sparkled in the hall light and I inhaled his strong cologne. I couldn't believe I had nearly slept with him. He held no attraction for me anymore. He was just some cute guy who looked out for himself first. His hair fell in front of his eyes. I recognized the twinkle that had hooked me first, but now, his soulful eyes enraged me.

As everyone left, Ethan drove up and came into the house. "What's going on?" he asked, looking around at the mess in the house. "Who's that?" He pointed to Oliver, who had slumped down onto the arm of the sofa and looked to be asleep. "And why was Bryce here? Or should I ask, why was he leaving?"

"We had a little misunderstanding," Carly said, a half smile curling from her lips. "My bad."

"Ethan, did you see a post with my picture on it from the party?"

"Ugh, no," he sputtered, looking away.

"Look at me Ethan," I demanded. Carly was trying to get Oliver to lay down on the sofa and sleep. "What do you know about this?"

"Someone took a bunch of pictures while we were at the party, just random shots. Nothing personal."

"Ethan, there is a picture of me holding a vape pen. I'm applying to college, duh!"

"I don't know, Ivy. There were a bunch of pictures posted on the internet. Do you need help?"

"I don't need anyone's help." I felt clear-eyed and strong all of a sudden. I understood this picture for what it was. "Carly, are you feeling OK? Do you want my help getting Oliver home? I think he needs to call his parents."

"I'm so sorry, Ivy," she said. "I didn't mean to disappoint you. I hit a weak moment. I'm going to get more help. Don't let anyone call you a hypocrite. If you can control yourself and your behavior, power to you. I cannot. I got hooked on oxy way back, and now I can't even try one hit of one vape. I'm afraid, but I know how to get help."

"Thanks Carly. You'll be OK too. I'm here for you. Mom's here for you. Let's clean up and get these guys out of here."

Suddenly, the doorbell rang. I opened the heavy oak door. Dauber stood in the entrance, all six-feet-something of him. His sandy hair flopped to one side. Somehow he was tan and looked like he had just come from warm, sunny weather. He wore a leather jacket and flip-flops.

"What's up, dudes?" he said, big smile across his face.

"What's up?" I said, struggling to keep my voice low and calm. "You gotta go. Bryce and those guys left."

"Where'd they go? They owe me money."

"Hey, who's here?" Ethan stuck his head out from the kitchen where he was cleaning up empty chip bags and eating left-out cookies.

"No one, Ethan. You don't have to stay," Carly said. "I got us into this mess and I'll get us out. First off, Dauber, leave."

"Do you owe me any money?" he asked, looking over at the bong, still pointedly in the middle of the table.

"No. Please leave," I said. "Bryce and Phoebe went back to one of their houses. You can collect your money there."

"I'm going, I'm going." Dauber turned on his heels and collided right into my mother, who was coming in the door. She pushed him aside with her big brown handbag and walked over to Carly and me. We stood in the foyer side by side, creating a wall blocking the living room.

"Ivy Green, is this you?" She held out her phone, the same picture Phoebe had on her homescreen. "Have you learned nothing?"

"Mom, who sent that to you?"

"Never mind that. And who is this boy?" She took a whiff. "And what's that smell?"

"Mom, relax," Carly said. "We've got this." She pushed Dauber out the door and shut it. "Ethan, you'd better go. This could get ugly and fast." He left, grasping a handful of cookies and waving to me.

"OK, girls, how is he getting home and what's happened here?" Mom faced us and looked grim. Carly and I stood together, the wall of solidarity, and explained to her the events of the night, starting with my party and ending with Carly's get-together here at the apartment.

"So, I called Bryce and asked him if he could score for me," Carly said. "I know it was wrong, but Oliver was pressing me."

"And how did he get here and how is he getting home?" My mom walked over to the sofa and spread a throw banket over Oliver.

"Ah Mom, we're both not quite right yet, but Oliver is exceptionally vulnerable."

"My concern is you, Carly. If you're reaching out to buy drugs, I'd say you need some additional support." She looked at me. "And you too. Do you have a problem with drugs or alcohol?"

"I do not." I was able to stay calm and explain. "Someone passed the vape so I took a hit. Can I see your phone, Mom?" She handed over her phone and I looked at her messages.

"What? Ethan sent you the picture? Are you kidding me?"

"He was only looking out for you," she said.

"I'll deal with him later."

It took forty-five minutes and it was after midnight by the time the house was back in order.

Oliver remained asleep on the sofa. Mom made some tea and we sat around the kitchen table together, each of us apologetic in our own way.

"I wish I had better self-control," Carly said, tears forming. "I thought I could do this, but it's so hard."

"I'm sorry I let thoughts of Bryce take over my better judgment," I told Carly. "I should have known better than to get mixed up with him. I brought drugs right in front of your face."

"No, it's not your fault, Ivy," Carly said. "Drugs are everywhere. I need better tools to get through the tough times. You are not my babysitter, but you're a damn good friend and sister."

"Thanks, but I don't feel like it." I put down my teacup and stared hard at my mom. "I feel like I let you both down."

"I'm the one who should feel like I let you both down." My mother got up and went to the bookshelf. She pulled out a photo album and came back to the table, flipping through the pages.

"I knew the dangers of drug abuse all too well in this family."

"What do you mean?" I asked, trying to look at the photos she had turned to. They were pictures of her honeymoon with my dad in Israel.

"Drug abuse and alcoholism run in the family," my mom stated, her eyes downcast on a photo of her and my dad dancing under the stars at some outdoor cafe in Eilat, Israel. "Your dad."

"Huh? Dad? Why wouldn't we know this by now?"

My mom was all-out crying now, and I passed her the box of tissues. Carly looked bewildered but began turning the pages of the album. "Why are you showing us these pictures now?"

"Because it was on our honeymoon that I confronted Dad about his drinking and drug use. We went to college in the early '80s. There were lots of drugs, and in the beginning of college, the drinking age was eighteen."

"Really?" I said. "That was convenient. And dangerous."

"Exactly." My mom gained her composure and continued. "Your dad always drank more and smoked more and did more coke than anyone else, but he was funny and sweet and everyone took his outlandish behavior as part of his charm. But he always had a hangover and he always was looking for the next high. On our honeymoon, it was so easy to get drugs in Israel.

"We barely went to Jerusalem or Tel Aviv or any of the other typical cultural highlights. He only wanted to stay in Eilat, until he OD'd and landed in the hospital in Beersheba. He stayed there for the rest of the honeymoon. After that, he got help here and there but never managed to stay sober for very long. We hid it from you girls. I didn't want you to think he was less than perfect." My mom grimaced. Her eyes were shut.

"Is that why you got divorced?" I asked. "Why we never see him?"

"Yes. I was protecting you from the disappointment and sadness he brought into our home. He lost several jobs because of his drug habit, and he lost a lot of our money too."

"But Mom, I needed that information for my intake history. It would have helped tremendously in therapy."

"I know, honey. I'm sorry. I should have told you before. I thought that you could work through your own demons without dredging up those of your father. I didn't want you to think that because he failed, you might too."

"Mom!" Carly went to my mother and hugged her from behind. My mom got up and they embraced. "I am strong and I am smart. I'll get through this. It doesn't matter if Ivy smokes pot or dates a drug dealer—well OK, that matters to Ivy, but not to my health. Only I can help me. You should have told us about Dad, if only so we could have been there for you more."

"I was ashamed of my mistake with your father. I was embarrassed that my husband stayed out all night and came home high as a kite. He did coke with his secretaries and pretended he was at meetings. Meetings? In the middle of the night? I let it go on far too long. I thought you could tackle your own problems without having to process your dad's." They continued to hug. I felt a little left out of the lovefest so I got up and wrapped myself around the two of them.

"We all made mistakes, but we're a family and we'll get through this together."

"Yup, we just have to face the truth," Carly said. "One day at a time."

"Touché," my mom said, fist bumping the two of us with both hands.

"Right, Mom. Touché." Carly laughed. "Now back to therapy and outpatient group I go."

"Whatever you need, I'll be there to help," I said. "But only honesty from now on, OK Mom?"

"Yes, of course," she said. "I'm sorry."

"No more sorries." I pointed to the kitchen, "We'll cook and bake our way out of this. Together."

"You got it. Dinner, Dear will be our salvation and our income," my mom said.

"Yeah, but we have to do something about Ethan. What a snitch!"

"Honey, he's your cousin and one of the best friends you'll ever have."

"Except me," Carly said.

"Except me," I repeated back to her.

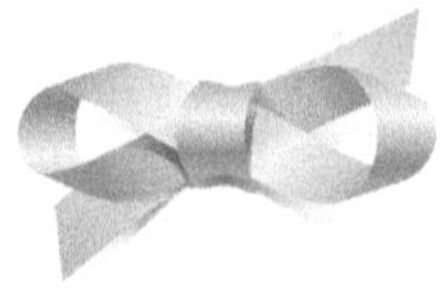

Chapter Twenty-Three—Cheers to Friends

When I woke up, I immediately texted Zoey. She didn't respond, so after fifteen minutes, I called her. And then I called her again. And then again after I showered, and then again at nine when I went downstairs for breakfast.

"She won't answer," I said to my mother, who was at the stove. "She's really mad. What can I do to make this up to her?" More than feeling bad about losing Bryce or even the fact that Carly relapsed a little because of Bryce because of me, my eyes burned from shame and sadness that I hurt Zoey. Disappointing Zoey was one hundred percent my fault.

"You could bring her breakfast in bed," my mom suggested. She was in the middle of cooking scrambled eggs and toast, which I assumed correctly were for Carly, who was still sleeping but I'm sure had to get up and go to a meeting this morning.

I thought about that idea and figured it couldn't hurt. I had to do something real and concrete to make up to Zoey and show her how much I cared. So, I texted her mother and told her I'd like to come over with breakfast. She said that would be great.

Mom helped me with the menu: ricotta pancakes, a bowl of fruit, and a chocolate cream-cheese brownie, "Because who doesn't like a little chocolate in the morning?" Mom said. And finally, she suggested I stop at the supermarket and pick up some flowers.

When I got to Zoey's, her parents were on their way out the door, together. They both were smiling for the first time since I met them.

"Zoey's in the den, dear," her mom said. "We're off to help my mom move into her assisted living facility. Wish me luck!" I had never seen Mrs. Marks so put together. She wore a lovely pair of cotton slacks and a cream silk top. Her hair was blown out and she wore lipstick. Wow, I hoped this was the beginning of her recovery from grief. Mr. Marks smiled at me. He always looked the same. Jeans and a button-down.

I brought my picnic basket full of goodies into the house. As promised, Zoey was sitting in the big leather rocker, sipping coffee.

"I come with a peace offering," I said. She gave me a wry smile and let me unpack the food. Her mom must have given her the heads up that I was coming. I laid out the pancakes, a small bottle of syrup, the fruit, the brownie, the wildflowers, which I had actually picked on the side of the road, and a glass of fresh-squeezed orange juice.

"Can we get past Bryce Houston?" I asked, sitting down opposite Zoey on the ottoman to her chair. She clicked off the news and took a big bite of the pancakes.

"If you keep bringing me breakfast we can," she said, smiling. "I'm sorry I was so tough on you. I know you liked him a lot."

"Sure, he was great," I said. "His charisma got under my skin and he was hard to resist, but I'm so sorry I let that blind me to what he was really about. He's all about himself and you're all about your friends and I should never have put him first. That was a bogus move." I took the fork and took a bite of the pancakes. "Mmm, I didn't do half bad, did I?"

"They're delicious," Zoey crossed her legs. She was wearing white-and-black polka-dot pajama pants and a matching top. I was fully dressed in jeans and a gray Taylor Swift T-shirt. "You didn't have to do this, you know. I would have forgiven you anyway."

"I know, but I'm grateful to you for so much, the least of which is being my friend on the first day of school when I really needed someone special to help me in a new place. You weren't just any old girl who agreed to talk to me; you were empathetic and kind and a good listener. And you understand what I'm going through with Carly. I don't want to jeopardize our relationship."

"We're OK," she said, pushing the tray to the side. "Your arrival in Marble Springs was a gift to me too. No one can understand what I'm going through, my grief about Nick, and what's happened in this family. But I couldn't sit back and watch you let Bryce steamroll you into trouble. He looks great on the outside, but he's bad news on the inside."

"I know," I agreed. "But I really liked him. He was really charming and sweet. It was hard to ignore all that cuteness." I smiled in spite of myself. "He's like one of those sneaky aliens on a TV show that peel off their skin and clothing and underneath is a bad person."

"Is he bad or just misguided?" Zoey asked.

"You're right, just misguided. His brother is messed up and I don't need to take that on too. I have to focus on Carly and my own family."

"Now will you consider taking on a larger role with SOAN? Maybe you and Carly can talk about your individual experiences, hers as the person taking the drugs and you as the family member left home to deal with the aftermath?"

"Sure, I owe you something."

"No, you don't owe me anything." Zoey reached across the chair to me on the ottoman and wrapped her arms around me. "You're a good person and a great friend. We're both so lucky we found each other senior year of high school. But I think working on the SOAN assembly in January will give us both a positive way to help others who might be dealing with drugs in their families. It's pervasive, Ivy. Lots of kids are suffering in silence."

"I'll do it." I pulled away from her and stood up. "How about taking a run along the reservoir? I want to reclaim that space as my own, without memories of Bryce ruining my experiences there."

"Deal. Do we have to run, though? These pancakes are going to be slopping around in my stomach for a few hours."

"Let's go back and get Kelly Green and we can walk. I just hope I don't run into Bryce."

Zoey stood up and picked up the tray of food I had laid out. "We can bring the fruit and the brownie for a snack. And you can't worry about him all the time. You have to concentrate on yourself for a change."

"Here's to me," I said, and laughed. "Actually, here's to us. Cheers to friends."

Chapter Twenty-Four—Understudy

"I cannot fit into this dress," I yelled from the bathroom.

"Well it's from four years ago, before you hit puberty. You had no curves," Carly called back. "Try wearing something that's actually your size. Here, how about this?" She threw me a pale-pink button-up dress with a collar and a cute floral pattern on the bottom.

"This actually looks like someone named Fran Larraby would wear it," I commented.

My mom stuck her head in the door. "Are you nervous, honey?"

"Mom, you blew out your hair. Why?" Carly made a face. "You look so, so . . ."

"So what? So pretty? So glamorous? So natural? What are you trying to say?" My mom came in and sat down on the bed.

"Mom, you do look nice," I said. "I love your jeans." They were mine.

I gathered up my purse and a lipstick from my dresser. The room was a disaster from all the clothes I had tried in an attempt to find the perfect costume for my part. I tried all kinds of combinations for rehearsals and thought I was going to go with that for the real play, but just today I got the bright idea to wear a dress and heels.

"Break a leg," Carly called after me.

"We'll all be cheering you on," my mom trilled. "Look for us in the second row."

At school, the stage crew and the cast were all running around backstage in a frantic tizzy. Zoey darted up to me, wearing the flowy dress that Phoebe had chosen for her role as Madame Zenobia. "Something's up. Ms. Bucci told me to put on Phoebe's costume."

"That's weird. What do you think is going on?" I asked.

"You are not going to believe this." Ethan sidled up beside us. "Phoebe is missing in action. She's not answering texts and no one has heard from her. She's not going to make it to the play tonight. Zoey is standing in for her and you are standing in for Zoey as Glenda, the buyer's wife." Ethan was so agitated, he was shouting.

"Whaaaa?" Zoey moaned. "Whatcha talking 'bout? That makes no sense. I can't be Madame Zenobia."

Ethan paced in front of us. "You're going to have to be, Ms. Bucci said. The show must go on."

"Where could she be?" I said.

"I hope she's OK," Zoey muttered.

I looked around for Ms. Bucci. She ran up to me from around the back of the stage.

"Ivy Green, you are now Glenda, the buyer's wife. Good thing you changed into a dress. It's a little frumpy for her. Maybe you can belt it."

"I don't understand. Why can't we reach Phoebe? Or her mom?" My voice was shrill as I struggled to put the pieces of this story together. "This doesn't make sense. She wouldn't miss opening night when she has the starring role. I'm sure she'll be here soon," I said, my head bobbing up and down in a yes motion.

"I told you, there are no stars. It's an ensemble cast," Ethan emphasized for the ninety-millionth time.

"Just explain what's happening," I said. "I have Phoebe's cell phone number. Let's just call her. Wherever or whatever, she'll be here soon. I'm sure of it."

Ms. Bucci spoke very slowly, enunciating each of her carefully chosen words. "She's not coming, Ivy. I spoke to her mother. Zoey will have to play her part and you will have to play Zoey's, speaking whatever lines you can remember from rehearsals and improvising the rest. It's the best we can figure out at this late time. We don't have room for discussion now. We have to do the best we can." Ms. Bucci looked like a daddy long legs with all its arms and legs moving at once. She was pacing in front of us as she spoke. She was clearly very upset and nervous.

"OK, I'll do whatever you say, but where is Phoebe? Is she OK? I asked.

"I don't know. I hope so. Her mother sounded frantic on the phone. I'm sure we will find out what's wrong before the night is through. In the meantime, the show must go on," Ms. Bucci said. "And, we're going to collect everyone's cell phones for the duration of the play. We don't want any backstage distractions during the performance. Please put your phone in this basket."

"That's different," Zoey said, but she put her phone in anyway. "I've never heard of anyone doing that."

"You'll get your phone back after the show," Ms. Bucci said.

I quickly checked my phone for any messages and looked at my social media accounts to see if anything was posted. Nothing. This was very weird. I handed it over.

The auditorium was packed. Throughout the performance, Zoey and I both remembered a lot of the lines we needed and made up the rest. The audience didn't know the difference and laughed their heads off. Zoey put on a weird, I guess it was supposed to be Eastern European accent, as the fortune teller Madame Zenobia, and she was terrific. Even better than Phoebe would have been.

Zoey's parents and little brother were in the audience, and I was so glad to see them laughing at the funny parts. They probably hadn't laughed much since Nick died. I felt so strongly about my friendship with Zoey. Our makeup breakfast was just as important as my breakup with Bryce.

I rubbed one arm with the other hand and felt a chill as goosebumps appeared on my arm. I walked onstage for my curtain call. The audience beamed and clapped and gave us a standing ovation. I loved bowing to so many smiling people. Carly clapped and hooted like a maniac. I was thrilled to see her acting like her old self. I looked for Bryce. I thought he would show up, even though we hadn't spoken in the week since I kicked him out of the house. And Phoebe? Where was she?

Right after the final curtain call, Ms. Bucci asked us to please come sit with her for a moment. She held the basket of cell phones in front of her chest. We sat on the floor of the stage. I thumbed my fingers on the ground, waiting for her to tell us where Phoebe was or make a speech about how well we did and give directions about tomorrow night's performance. I wanted to get outside already and celebrate with Carly and my mom and Ethan and Zoey. They were all coming back to our house for a cast party.

Ms. Bucci looked out at all of us, cast and crew, with a very serious frown. "Folks, first of all, you did fantastic tonight. It was a wonderful play and I thank each and every one of you for giving it your all. I especially want to acknowledge Zoey and Ivy for so quickly switching up parts and somehow, with no preparation other than a keen ear and attention during rehearsals, pulling off their new roles in the play. You were naturals. I look forward to seeing what you can tomorrow night, now that you've done it once already."

Ethan was rolling his eyes at Zoey and she was trying to catch my attention. We were all wondering what else she was going to say. From the wings, out came Mr. Marshall, the school principal.

"Ah hum," he announced. Mr. Marshall had a goatee and was bald and looked more like a pro-baseball player than a theater geek. "Everyone, you did a fantastic job tonight, and I echo what Ms. Taylor said about stepping up to the plate, playing unexpected roles at the last minute and putting on a terrific play. Thank you Ms. Bucci for all of your hard work and dedication to our cast and crew."

I crossed and uncrossed my legs. I was dying to look at my phone. Other people were moving around on the floor too and staring at the basket of phones. I hadn't been off my phone for this long in months.

Mr. Marshall continued. "So, sadly, I do have some very unfortunate news about Phoebe Li. We didn't want to upset you before the play, and we didn't have all the facts until just a few minutes ago."

"What happened?" someone yelled out. "Tell us already," someone else said.

Ms. Bucci picked up where Mr. Marshall stopped. "Folks, I'm sorry to say that Phoebe was in a car accident on her way here tonight. She will be OK, but she's in the hospital. Bryce Houston was in the front passenger seat. He is hurt badly, but Phoebe's sister said he will be OK too. The driver, a young man Phoebe was dating, is in critical condition."

"Oh my God, I can't believe this. I don't know what to do." I stood up and paced around in circles. At that moment, Ms. Bucci held out the basket of phones and everyone grabbed for their own. When I had mine in my hand and turned it on, I took one look and saw that it was exploding with texts from kids from school. Bryce hadn't sent a text, but there was one from Jonathan.

"Ivy, Bryce is OK. It's Dauber. He's dead."

"Dead? Oh my God. I thought he was in critical condition, not dead." My face was hot. My limbs felt weak and my heart was racing.

"No, he's gone." I wondered if Jonathan was crying.

"I know who died," I said to Zoey, who was hovering over my shoulders. "It was their friend, the guy they bought drugs from. I think Phoebe was dating him."

"That's awful," she said. "Thank goodness you weren't with them." At that moment, I saw Carly had made her way onstage and was standing next to me.

Carly held my hand. "Thank God."

Kids were talking all around us. The word drugs kept coming up. Coke and mollies and Adderall. I didn't know what they were talking about at first, then Zoey told me.

"It's all over social media," she said softly. We were sitting in the front row of the theater, the adrenaline from of the performance long gone now. "The police found street drugs in the car. They are going to be in big trouble."

"What about the kid who died?" Ethan asked. "Who is it?"

"It's the boy that was at my house last week," I said, tears streaming down my face. "Wow, I never thought anything like this could happen."

"You're kidding, right?" Zoey said. "After what happened to my brother, I'd believe anything could happen when drug abuse is part of the picture. It's a terminal epidemic." She was crying too.

Ms. Bucci and Mr. Marshall were circulating amongst all of the students and the parents in the room. Lots of people were crying and many of the adults were on their phones, trying to get information.

"Let's go," I said. "I have to get to the hospital." I texted Jonathan back. "Should I come now?"

"You're not going alone," my mom said.

"I'll drive her," Allie offered. "You stay back with Carly. This is way too close for comfort for her."

"No, I think Ivy should come home first," my mom said. "Honey, you have to stay away for a little bit. I know you want to get involved, but this is too big and too emotional right now. We're going home and you're coming with us." My mom was insistent. I didn't have any emotional strength to argue.

Then Jonathan texted back, "Not now. Too much going on. Dauber's dead. Drugs were in the glove compartment and in bags in the trunk. It's beyond." For the first time, I was grateful to Jonathan Houston. For once, he was acting responsibly to me. So sad that it took a death to get him to be nice.

I went home with everyone for the cast get-together. It was hardly the festive cast party we had anticipated, but my mom and Allie put out food and Zoey and Ethan had some other friends over to help eat it all.

Bryce didn't respond right away to my text. I wrote, "Do you want me to come to you? I don't know what to say except that I still care about you."

When he finally did write back he said, "I'm OK. Thanks for your concern. No need to come here."

I ate the cake and the cookies my mom put out. She even poured me some wine to calm me down. "Sorry, Carly, only for Ivy. Now that you know our family history, I think you understand. I'm so sorry I kept the truth from you two."

"Mom, I'm good. No more apologies," Carly said. "I'll have an iced green tea." She smiled and held up her empty glass. "Cheers to sobriety."

"Cheers to sisters, cheers to friends," I said.

"You got that right. Cheers to sisters," she repeated.

—THE END—

Author's Note

While this is purely a work of fiction, I was inspired to write a novel about the dangers and deaths associated with teens using hard drugs like oxycodone and heroin because of the pervasiveness of its abuse in suburban towns in the New York tri-state area and around the country. Many people think that people who abuse hard drugs live in cities or in less-advantaged towns, but drug abuse and rampant teen overdoses are sadly experienced in wealthy suburbs as well as more at-risk neighborhoods. High schools across America have lost too many teenagers to drug abuse. Below are some resources to reach out to if you or someone you care about needs help.

• • ⚜ • •

Substance Abuse and Mental Health Service Administration: SAMHSA's National Helpline – <u>1-800-662-HELP (4357)</u>.
PARTNERSHIP TO END Addiction: https://drugfree.org/article/get-one-on-one-help/
National Institute on Drug Abuse: https://teens.drugabuse.gov/

About the Author

Susan Gilbert received her MFA from Manhattanville College in Purchase, New York. She completed the Stony Brook University Children's Lit Fellows program in 2017 and a Masters in Social Work from Fordham University in 2010. A writer and social worker, Susan spends much of her time helping others discover the benefits of creativity, reading, and writing. A mother and grandmother, Susan spends her time in Westchester, New York and Eastern Long Island.

Read more at https://tellmeyourstoryworkshop.org/.

www.ingramcontent.com/pod-product-compliance
Lightning Source LLC
Chambersburg PA
CBHW071606030726
47593CB00001BA/337